# Temporary Address

Elaine Glimme

ISBN: 9798569262991

# Contents


Acknowledgements          pg.  *i*

Chapter  1                pg.  1

Chapter  2                pg.  8

Chapter  3                pg.  23

Chapter  4                pg.  27

Chapter  5                pg.  32

Chapter  6                pg.  37

Chapter  7                pg.  48

Chapter  8                pg.  54

Chapter  9                pg.  56

Chapter  10               pg.  60

Chapter  11               pg.  65

Chapter  12               pg.  68

Chapter  13               pg.  80

Chapter  14               pg.  91

Chapter  15               pg.  95

Chapter  16               pg.  102

Chapter  17               pg.  110

Chapter  18               pg.  115

Chapter  19      pg. 118

Chapter  20      pg. 123

Chapter  21      pg. 127

Chapter  22      pg. 131

Chapter  23      pg. 135

Chapter  24      pg. 139

Chapter  25      pg. 151

Chapter  26      pg. 155

Chapter  27      pg. 163

Chapter  28      pg. 171

Chapter  29      pg. 175

Chapter  30      pg. 179

Chapter  31      pg. 191

Chapter  32      pg. 195

Chapter  33      pg. 201

Chapter  34      pg. 207

Chapter  35      pg. 215

Chapter  36      pg. 227

Chapter  37      pg. 231

Chapter  38      pg. 243

Chapter  39      pg. 249

ACKNOWLEDGMENTS

Thank you to Mary Wandler and to iStock for the awesome cover photo.

Thank you to my friends and family who disagreed with the !@$%$ voices inside my head that said I was a silly old lady who hadn't a chance in %&*$$@ of being taken seriously.

Thanks to Tom and Kathy who proofed, to Eric who understood computers, To Selene, Lissa, Judy, Linda, Maxine, Muriel, Elaine, Mother Susan, Father Pat, Mary Anne, Christine, and Lynx who helped me find courage. To the Pinole Writers' Group, the Pinole Library Writers' Group, and to everyone else who showed me how to make it better.

# Chapter One

∞

The effects of the sedative were wearing off. At first the foggy sluggishness was too compelling, and Johanna basked in the languorous calm of prescription medication, not caring how disturbed, how unsettled, everything was. Then fear kicked in, startling her with that thudding sensation of waking from a nightmare. Only, this wasn't a nightmare. This was real.

The room was dark; no sounds floated down the halls. There was no way to tell time until some light made its way through the bars of the tiny window opposite her bed.

Weak and frightened, Johanna tried to sit up, then fell back down against a pillow. A restraint held her. Had she been kidnapped? She shivered from terror. Where was she? Why was she tied down? None of this made sense. Who did this? And Why?

Several hours passed. A watery beam of light crept into her room. Now, Johanna could make out shapes of objects around her—two closed doors and a couple of pieces of furniture. The room was small—bigger than a closet but not by much. And the air had a strong smell of disinfectant, the kind they use in hospitals and other institutions.

Johanna dozed and woke. She listened for sounds, but there were none—no one talking outside, no ticking clocks, no motors. She moved her foot along the bed, hearing the shushing sound it made rubbing against the sheet. So loud against the backdrop of quiet!

She peered out at the semi-darkness and tried to come up with a plan to escape from this. Except that she didn't even know what "this" was—didn't understand what was happening. She had no control over her body, and that was terrifying.

How did she get here? Weird images swirled and bounced in her head, but she could recall only flashes—small bits of memory without any context. She remembered bedsheets, white and smelling of soap. And wind. There had been wind. Perhaps a storm. Johanna was terrified of storms. Had always been terrified of storms. And that wind! Whistling, howling, and threatening to pull the sheets from her hands.

Why?

Why was she remembering sheets? Were they important, somehow?

Or was she losing her mind?

What else? She tried to pull more information out of the sticky goo that was her memory, but she couldn't think for more than a second or two before she lost her train of thought and was back, like Alice, in a medicated wonderland.

Dawn broke. Things happened. They let her use the bathroom. "They" were a hospital sort of "they"—two men in white jackets or smocks and how-are-you-feeling-today smiles—the kind of smiles you could cut out of a magazine.

They fed her some mashed orange stuff, which they shoved into her mouth with a spoon. The taste was similar to sweet potato, only it had a gritty feel to it and was so sweet that she gagged on the second mouthful. Johanna considered not eating, but that would have taken more effort than she could muster.

After the meal, Johanna hung limp while they washed her face, took her temperature, and gave her juice. They asked her what day it was, and who she was, and where she was. Johanna could only answer the second question. Then, they untied what seemed to be a vest which had held her attached to the bed with two plaited straps. And, finally, they left her alone.

With the restraint gone, Johanna dragged herself up off of the bed and stumbled around the room. Both doors were locked. The furniture consisted of a chair, a waist-high bureau, and a bed, all bolted to the floor. Johanna made two full circles around her room, touching, probing, looking for something to come loose. Then she plopped back down on the bed, tried to fight the sedative, and dozed, and woke, and dozed some more.

Hours later, with a sound like a cricket makes, the door creaked open, and Johanna stirred awake. "How are you feeling today, Miss Johanna?" The woman who spoke wore a nurse's uniform, and the words were startling after the quiet. She was young, barely old enough to have made it through nursing school, with black hair cut into a pageboy and light brown skin. "My name is Maria." Her voice was calm and soothing, with a hint of a Filipino accent.

"Uh," said Johanna.

"Come with me, please. You're going to see Dr. Nelson this morning." She put a hand under Johanna's arm to support her, and Johanna leaned against it. Maria's touch was gentle. And Maria was the first human who had told Johanna her name.

Still groggy, Johanna was able to walk with Maria holding onto her arm. Together, they made their way down a long hallway. To Johanna it seemed to go on and on forever. Finally, they reached an elevator, and Maria held up a plastic card to activate it. The elevator dropped a few floors, and then they walked through a maze of corridors that ultimately led to a cherry-wood door. Maria opened the door with her card, ushered Johanna inside, and sat her down on a folding chair.

"Is this Dr. Nelson… is this his office?" It was an effort to speak. Probably Maria didn't understand her because she just nodded and smiled. Johanna looked around, scuffing her feet against the floor as a child would do. In fact, Johanna felt very much like a child—a miniature person in an adult world—and very much out of control.

After a time, a large, brisk man in a white doctor's coat walked Johanna into an inner office and positioned her, like a throw pillow, onto a cream-colored, overstuffed couch. Standing in front of his walnut desk and towering over her, he seemed menacing.

"Good morning, Johanna, I'm Dr. Nelson," said the doctor-looking person. "How are you feeling today?"

"Okay." The words were thick, muffled, falling through her teeth like wilted lettuce. Her head nodded to the left, and her thick, black curls dangled matted, some pulled back into a snarled tail behind her neck. Greasy wisps drooped sadly down around her ears.

Dr. Nelson smiled with his teeth, a professional smile. While his lips turned up in greeting, his steel-gray eyes examined Johanna, alert for any information that her body language might give away.

"We'll be meeting like this every day for a while," he told her. "Please feel free to tell me anything that's on your mind." He stared into her eyes. "You're safe here. You can say anything, anything at all, and know it will not leave this room."

Johanna looked up into his eyes. He was so tall! With neatly-trimmed gray hair, and a neatly-trimmed gray mustache that hid a bit of his upper lip. Johanna felt like she was staring up at a stone monument. Words buzzed inside her head like mosquitoes. Don't be afraid; Nothing to fear. Who am I kidding, thought Johanna, I'm scared out of my mind. "Okay," she said out loud.

"So… my friend," the doctor continued, "Tell me your name." While he was talking, Dr. Nelson casually touched some buttons to start up a tape recorder and a video camcorder; then he pulled up a chair from behind his desk, and sat down, a notepad and pencil poised in his hands.

'I'm not your friend, thought Johanna. "Johanna Jacobson," she said.

"Good. Now tell me a little about yourself."

The words came slowly, with large gaps of silence between them. "I'm forty-three," She stopped. Talking seemed frightening somehow after the silence of her room.

"Please go on," said the doctor. "What are you thinking about right now?"

Bedsheets, thought Johanna, but she had presence enough not to say that.

"You're thinking about something. What is it?"

Signs! Johanna remembered signs. Messages. She'd written them on bedsheets. Somehow, they were important. But, why?

Johanna shrugged.

Dr. Nelson tried a different tack. "How are you feeling?" he asked.

"Tired. Confused. I don't know."

"You don't know what?"

"Why am I here?"

"Tell me about your job."

"I write a newspaper column. For the *Upstart Gazette*. It was hard for Johanna to talk, but she put together a few phrases. "Just silly stories and poems. To, you know, lighten the mood. Make my readers smile."

He let her ramble for a few minutes to give her a chance to feel comfortable, to drop her guard. Johanna talked about working for a newspaper, and about her editor, Ivan Buncheski. "He acts tough. And then he snarls and… and his face gets all red and twitchy… and he looks so funny… I just want to laugh."

Dr. Nelson laughed. Then he stared into Johanna's eyes. "Who told you that they torture prisoners at Guantanamo?" he asked, and his eyes searched Johanna for clues.

The word, Guantanamo, startled Johanna. "No one," she said.

"That's supposed to make your readers smile? You thought it up by yourself?" There was a sharpening in his voice.

"Yes."

"No one told you?"

"No."

"And yet you wrote, 'They're torturing prisoners in Guantanamo.' And you wrote it on a sign which you hung above a freeway! Just below the American flag. A symbol of our freedom. It's not true. No one's being tortured. Who told you that?"

The room was still for a second. Dr. Nelson waited and studied Johanna's face. What was she holding back? What insider was she protecting?

"Tell me about your other signs."

Johanna just stared, not saying anything.

"Johanna, tell me about the signs." His voice was sharper. It carried the idea of threat.

"What signs?" she asked.

Dr. Nelson looked down at his notes. "You wrote, 'The president's lying.' 'Anthrax didn't come from bin Laden.' 'There's no link between Saddam and bin Laden.' 'Make me a channel of your peace.'

Yes, the signs! She'd written them on the bedsheets. And she'd fastened them with wire. Someone had hung American flags over several freeway overpasses, and she'd hung her signs under the flags.

"You realize these signs are treasonous… don't you?" Dr. Nelson paused letting the word, "treasonous" sink in. "You are guilty of treason." Another pause. "And whoever fed you this, this garbage, should face a firing squad."

A needle stick! She remembered. After she'd hung the last sign, she remembered men in uniforms. About six of them, shouting at her like angry gorillas. And then a needle stick in her left thigh. And then nothing.

Johanna didn't say anything, and the doctor jotted down some notes. "Why did you hang them under the American flag? When your country is on the brink of another war?"

Johanna shrugged like a little girl. She was too woozy to actually explain what she believed. Be not afraid. Be not afraid. The words kept on buzzing, but she was very afraid, and her brain ached with the effort of thinking.

"Are you a member of Al-Qaeda?" he asked. "Is that what this is all about? Are you a Moslem?"

Johanna shook her head. "No, I'm Catholic."

"Then why did you write those signs? Why? Why would you betray your country and your God? You said you're a Christian. Do you fear hell?"

"Just hung some signs."

"Why… my friend?" Johanna shrugged again. Dr. Nelson watched her breathing and her eye movements. He looked for twitches, coughs, or grunts, any movement that might indicate discomfort, but there was nothing conclusive.

"No reason."

"There's always a reason."

Johanna sighed. She knew better than to tell the truth, but the words had to be said. Otherwise, she'd be denying the core of her being. She took a breath.

"Well?"

"God… told me to," she whispered.

Here Dr. Nelson wrote some more notes on his pad.

Shortly after his meeting with Johanna, Dr. Nelson received a phone call from a confidential number. So confidential, in fact, that Dr. Nelson only knew the caller as Simon.

"Well?" said the Simon. "Did you learn anything."

"It's got me puzzled, sir," Nelson answered. He figured that the person on the phone was probably a "sir." "She doesn't seem to be holding anything back."

"She's protecting someone, and it's someone with access to

highly classified information. You need to find out who that snitch is, and you need to find out now. This a matter of national security."

"She said that God told her about all of it."

"God doesn't work in the White House."

"No, sir."

"Well, find out God's first and last name, and do it soon. Do whatever you need to. Drugs, therapy sessions, whatever. You're supposed to be the best. Prove it."

# Chapter Two

Johanna had learned early in life, if you have a conversation with God, for Heaven's sake, keep it to yourself. Now it wasn't as if her mother didn't believe in God. She did. She took Johanna to church every Sunday. And at home she'd kneel before her statue of the Virgin, thumbing the pink rosary beads while praying Our Father and Hail Mary. But her prayers were nothing like Johanna's conversations with the Almighty.

Martha Jacobson, Johanna's mother, was a wispy, nervous sort of lady, very much concerned about how she appeared to others. "My baby's such a clever girl," she'd tell her friends in a falsetto voice. "And, oh my, what an imagination! She surprises me every day with something new." And Martha laughed. But she never elaborated about Johanna's imagination.

<<<<>>>>

The terrible twos had turned into the terrible threes, and Johanna had perfected arguing. Bedtime was always a struggle. One fine evening in June, she informed her mother matter-of-factly that she couldn't put on her pajamas. She folded her arms across her chest, and her dark eyes gleamed with determination.

Martha used the sternest voice she could muster, "Bedtime! Pajamas! Now!"

"I can't, Mommy. There's a frog in my pajamas. Right there." She pointed to the pink and yellow quilted bespread covering her big-girl bed.

"A frog?"

"A yellow green frog, and he's doing a handstand. Now he's turning cartwheels." She clapped her hands and jumped up and down excitedly yelling, "Yay, frog. Yay, frog." Her thick, brown hair bounced along with her.

"Johanna, quit dawdling and get ready for bed."

"But now he's flying to the moon with my pajamas on."

"Johanna…"

Johanna began to sing, "I see the frog, and the frog sees me. And the frog sees my daddy, who I like to see."

All this time, Johanna's father Stephen had been reading the paper and laughing at the two of them. Finally, he decided that Martha had had enough, and he jogged into Johanna's bedroom singing. "The frog needs to sleep and so do we." He grabbed Johanna up in his arms and slung her over his shoulder. "Frog, get out of those pajamas and give 'em to me."

"There's that frog," he yelled. "Get him. Get him." And he raced around the room with Johanna, still slung over his shoulder squealing.

"Got him," Stephen yelled. "You silly old frog. What are you doing in those pajamas? Take them off at once."

While Johanna giggled, Stephen pulled a pair of pajamas out of her dresser drawer. He handed them to her, and she began dressing for bed immediately.

My daddy is the strongest, and handsomest, and best daddy in the whole world, thought Johanna. Stephen's hair was curly-black, cut just a bit longer than Martha would have liked. His face had Roman features, and he stood six feet tall. As big as Superman, Johanna thought.

Martha just sighed. It was so unfair! Next to Stephen, she was a plain Jane, with dull gray eyes and a figure that was turning paunchy. Johanna was an angel for Stephen, but she gave Martha nothing but grief and frog stories.

Around her friends, Martha put up a brave front, but, in truth, she was embarrassed and terribly worried about her daughter. Why did Johanna have to be that way? Okay, maybe some kids held imaginary conversations with their dolls and stuffed animals, But Johanna even talked to plants. What child does that?

Once, Johanna was holding a lively discussion with all the

flowers in the garden. Nervously, Martha curled a lock of gray-black hair around her finger. "Stop petting the roses," she told Johanna, her voice louder and sharper than she had intended.

"It's only pretend. Don't worry, Mommy," Johanna said. And Martha was comforted. But then Johanna told her Teddy, "Don't worry. The roses are my friends. They won't prick me." And then she told the roses. "Shh. You have to be quiet now. Mommy's worried because we're talking too loud." And Martha started twirling her hair around her finger all over again.

Pascagoula in the sixties was a quiet city in Mississippi, and Martha had carved out a comfortable niche for herself there. She had a circle of acquaintances, and she'd figured out the rules of conduct required of its members. There were expectations, and people kept them. Martha kept them. You didn't raise your voice at the supermarket. You brought a casserole when a friend was sick. You didn't wear stripes with plaid, and you never wore white shoes after Labor Day.

And you knew which topics to discuss and which ones to avoid. If a young girl were to go live with her aunt in Utah for a year, you didn't ask about her. If there was shouting at a neighbor's house, you pretended not to hear it. The system worked. People got along. Friendships were not jeopardized. No one was made to feel uncomfortable.

But Martha worried that Johanna was different from the other children. Even before she began her strange conversations with God, she invented activities (Were they games?) with unseen friends. And Johanna would ask odd questions. "Mommy, If I poke the air, can I, maybe, touch God's belly button?" And Johanna would pull at Martha's skirt. "What if cats are smarter than people? Maybe they talk meow. Maybe Whiskers isn't a cat at all." Whiskers, their marmalade cat, looked up at the mention of his name. "Maybe Whiskers should sit at the table instead of eating out of the cat dish." And Martha had no answers. An alpha female, Martha was comfortable steering and guiding her family by tight reins, but Johanna's fantasies were beyond Martha's limited imagination, beyond her control.

Stephen was no help either. If anything, he encouraged Johanna in her fantasies. It was all well and good to spend time with your children, but the activities Stephen would pick! "My butt's all soapy, Daddy," Johanna squealed as she left "bumpus prints" —modern art done in soapsuds on the bathtub walls.

And instead of putting out Bug-geta, they trapped the snails under flower pots and held snail races in the back yard, then released the snails in a vacant lot down the street.

Worst of all were their pirate adventures in a cardboard-box boat, because their boat usually sailed on the front lawn within plain sight of the neighbors.

One night after bath time, Martha told Stephen. "You've got to stop encouraging her with this silliness. She doesn't know the difference between fantasy and reality. I'm not saying she's crazy, but … I worry about her mental state. I'm not about to have the only child in Pascagoula visiting a psychiatrist."

Yes, Martha was jealous, jealous of Stephen's easy way with his daughter, of the unseen bond between the two of them. But she was also genuinely worried about Johanna. "Stop encouraging her craziness before it's too late," she said. "In a year and a half, she'll have to fit in with the other kids at school. That's all I'm saying."

"What's a mental state? Daddy? Is it like Mississippi?" Apparently, Johanna had been listening at the door. "Am I crazy? Why am I crazy, Daddy?"

Martha turned her head in horror. I'm a terrible mother, she thought.

Stephen picked Johanna up in a strong swoop. Martha had washed Johanna's hair, and it still smelled of soap. "It means you're getting too big for bumpus prints. You'll have to make hand, finger, and elbow prints from now on. And as for crazy, Puppy Face, I'm crazy about you."

<<<<>>>>

Another night, as Martha listened from the other room, Stephen began reading Johanna a bedtime story.

"The town of Hamelin sat nestled amid snow-capped Alps. Twilight shimmered through the leaves of the trees, and the world shifted from blue, green, and yellow to gray, and white, and then to darker gray. Cupboard doors popped open, and a scratching "shut-shut" sound was heard throughout the village as thousands of rats came out to search for ham, cabbage, cheese, or any kinds of crumbs their benefactors, the humans, left unattended."

Ugh, thought Martha. She couldn't help hearing the story. Rats! I wish he'd find something else to read to her. Martha remembered a time when a mouse had run across the kitchen floor. She had screamed and climbed up onto the table, while Stephen had just stood by laughing at her. Well, eventually he had chased the mouse away, and taken her out to dinner. And he'd set traps. But he hadn't understood.

Stephen continued reading. "More and more rats joined the nocturnal parties until some of the kitchens in the village looked like wriggling carpets of dark gray. Tails and whiskers twitched to and fro."

"Rats are cute, Daddy,"

"Yes, Puppy Face, they are."

"Could we get a rat sometime?"

Stephen chuckled imagining Martha's reaction to a pet rat. "Well, maybe some time."

Meanwhile in the other room, Martha drummed her fingers against the wall. Why couldn't Stephen just tell the child, "No"! He was the one who got to read the stories and tell the jokes. Martha was the one who washed the dishes, cleaned the toilet, and scolded, and punished. And she would be the one telling Johanna that, no, they weren't getting a rat. Stephen's answers were always frivolous.

Martha was the one who had to teach reality to Johanna. Those conversations had a way of ending in an exasperating litany of Johanna's questions: "But why?" "How come?" "But why not?" Usually both mother and daughter would be whining before the conversations were over.

Stephen's reading broke in on her thoughts. "The villagers were panicked. 'We have to get rid of the rats,' they said."

"But why, Daddy? Didn't they like the rats?"

"Because there were too many of them. One or two rats are cute. Thousands of rats are a big mess. Just think of all the rat poop!"

Johanna and Stephen laughed. "Maybe they could wear diapers," Johanna suggested.

Stephen read on. "The pied piper was dressed in a shirt of forest green, and a matching green hat sat jauntily on his head. And when he played his flute, it was as if fairies were laughing."

Mesmerized, Johanna was now in another world. She saw herself dressed like a forest elf, with a small wooden flute in her hands. In her imagination, she put the flute to her lips. Eyes closed, her lips quivered, and she wiggled her fingers over imaginary holes.

I'll save the rats, she thought, snuggling against her daddy's chest as he read on. Me and Daddy.

Taller than a mountain, stronger than a lion, that's my daddy, she thought. And the handsomest daddy of all the daddies on earth. To Johanna, he was a god.

"… And all the children followed the pied piper out of the village and into the woods. The end."

I'll save the children, too, thought Johanna. Daddy and me, together, we'll save them all.

For two weeks after that, Johanna had nightmares. She considered a world where there were so many rats that they looked like a wriggling carpet. What would it be like if that happened with children? What if there were too many children? During the day, Martha heard the same thing over and over: "But, Mommy, what if there were too many people, and we were all squished together until we got squished off of the world?"

"That's not going to happen, Johanna. Now go and play with your Teddy."

"But, Mommy, in the story there were too many rats. What if there were too many people?"

"That's just a story, Johanna."

"But what if there were too many people in real life?"

"God won't let that happen, Johanna. Now go play with Teddy."

"But how, Mommy, how will God not let that happen?"

"I don't know. But He'll take care of it. Now please go play." My child is three years old, and she's already a hippie freak, thought Martha. Had she somehow heard about Zero Population Growth? Of all the books in the world, Stephen had to read her *The Pied Piper of Hamelin*!

<<<<>>>>

Trouble really began when Johanna was three weeks shy of turning four. Stephen had to fly to London on business. Before reading Johanna's bedtime story, Stephen told Johanna about the trip. "I'll be gone four days. Can you hold up four fingers for me? That's right. Good girl!"

Outside, an early storm made whistling, howling sounds, and Johanna jumped, startled, as a branch snapped off a maple tree, hitting the house with a "thunk".

"Each night, when you and Mommy say prayers, make a mark on this calendar. After the fourth mark, I'll be on my way home." Then Stephen brought out four envelopes. "And each night, before you say your prayers, open up one of these envelopes and see if there's a surprise inside."

"But what if Mommy forgets my bedtime hug? Or what if she messes up with my bedtime story? Maybe you should stay here with us instead."

"Mommy will do just fine. In fact, she can give you an extra hug at bedtime—one from her and one from me. But I'll need you to be extra good while I'm gone. Can you promise?"

"No."

"No? Why not?"

"I can't promise to be good because something could happen on accident. But I'll try." She squeezed him. "I'll try this hard."

"That's my girl!"

<<<<>>>>

So Johanna tried to be good. She tried her very best. Really, she did. It was just that Daddy was away, and Johanna was nervous, and Mommy didn't seem to understand.

"But, Mommy, what if Daddy needs a sandwich or something?"

"Hush, dear. He'll just go to a restaurant and order one."

"But what if they make a peanut butter and orange marmalade sandwich?" Johanna wrinkled her face—the "prune look," Daddy called it. "Mrs. Wyatt made one for me once and it was very yucky."

"Your daddy's a grown man. He can eat a peanut butter sandwich with orange marmalade." Martha's voice was mechanical.

"But what if he wants to watch TV?"

"They have TV's in the hotel rooms. He can watch all the TV he wants."

"But do they get Mr. Rogers? That's important."

"They get Mr. Rogers." Martha rubbed her forehead. Something about the questions made Martha's head hurt. *I love you, but you're driving me to distraction,* thought Martha. *Aren't children supposed to be seen and not heard?*

"I don't think Daddy should have gone away without us. Do worms have teeth?"

"What?"

"Do worms have teeth? They don't have arms or legs. Do they

have teeth?"

"I don't know." Martha shook her head. She felt more nervous, more brittle, than usual without Stephen, and Johanna's worrying wasn't helping. Stop asking so many questions, she thought. One more word, just one more, and I'm going to lose my mind. Please, Lord, please make her stop. Why can't she stop asking questions!

"If Daddy were here, he'd look it up in the fat books."

If only Stephen were here! But he wasn't, and Martha had to deal with Johanna by herself. "Johanna, I don't have time for all this nonsense. Go talk to your Teddy."

"He's sleeping."

Well, go talk to God then. He's always awake." The words were out before Martha was aware of them. She couldn't believe that she'd actually said them. Martha was pious, properly pious. What did she think she was doing telling Johanna to ask God about worm teeth! For one guilty minute, Martha considered taking it back, telling Johanna that she should be more reverent, more serious about her prayers. But then Johanna would ask, "But why did you say that Mommy?" And Martha would answer, "Don't be disrespectful, young lady." And Johanna would say, "But why…" No, best to leave it alone.

"Okay, Mommy." And as Johanna left the room to consult the Almighty about worms' teeth, a blissful quiet replaced the whining voice.

Relief! No more difficult conversations for a while. Answering Johanna's questions was like juggling knives. Martha never knew what was coming next. And, although she wouldn't admit it, Martha was anxious about Stephen as well. She'd say three, no five, Hail Mary's next Sunday in church, just in case.

Johanna climbed up on her bed and sat cross-legged with her teddy bear resting in her lap. "God, Mommy's tired. Can I talk to you for a while? If you're not too busy. See, I'm kind of worried about Daddy. I don't really care about the worm teeth, but Mommy was starting to get upset, so I figured I'd better not talk about Daddy anymore."

The last calendar mark had been drawn. The last envelope was opened. It contained a Hershey's kiss. (We should have opened it before brushing teeth, thought Martha.) There was also a note from

Daddy: "I'm flying home tonight, Puppy Face. Not like a bird, but in a big airplane. Sleep tight. I'll be home when you wake up in the morning. I love you, Daddy."

Outside, the wind was crying. Big blobs of rain fell at a slant, and an occasional rumbling of thunder sounded in the distance. Martha shivered. She'd witnessed three hurricanes during her life, and, while this storm was nowhere near hurricane force, it still set her on edge.

Johanna ate her chocolate. Martha dropped the wrapper into the trash container. She read a bedtime story, and Johanna knelt for prayers.

"Now I lay me down to sleep.
I pray the Lord my soul to keep.
If I should die before I wake,
I pray the Lord my soul to take.
God bless Mommy and Daddy..." Johanna stopped and stared at the wall. Waves of sadness and longing washed over her and tears started to roll down her cheeks. "I miss Daddy," she said.

In the midst of the sadness, two arms reached out to her. "I'll always be with you," a voice seemed to say. She didn't actually see two arms, and it wasn't really a voice that she heard—more like a feeling, a feeling of stillness and peace. Like all was right with the world.

Martha put a tentative arm around her daughter's shoulder. "What's wrong?" she asked. But her high, sharp voice and her tense muscles betrayed her. Martha was also afraid of the storm.

Johanna didn't answer. She was too confused to match words to her feelings. She just knelt and cried in silence, and felt sadness, and peace, and strength, and sorrow all at the same time.

"What is it? Are you hurting? Tell me. Johanna? Johanna, please say something." But Martha was hopelessly the outsider, frustrated and powerless to understand or give comfort. Her voice kept betraying her; it hinted of her own fears.

Through the tears, Johanna was smiling now—a funny half smile. Martha didn't like this at all. "Daddy will be home tomorrow," said Martha.

"But what if... he..."

Martha's voice tightened still more. "Stop this fussing and dawdling, and finish your prayers. God bless Grandma and Grandpa,

Mommy and Daddy, and Whiskers, and make Johanna a good girl. Amen." Martha recited the words with a robot's voice.

"But God… has… lots of time." Johanna's tongue stumbled over the words like feet trudging over large boulders.

"Maybe God does, sweetheart, but I don't." Martha kissed her daughter and hugged her tightly. Thank goodness Stephen would be home in a few hours.

Johanna snuggled down under the covers and started crying again. For a long time, she sniffled and sobbed, and the comforter rose and fell with her sobbing. After the tears, she put both arms around Teddy, clinging to him as if he were a life preserver. "Please, God …" She wasn't sure what she was asking Him for. "Please, God…" Somewhere in between the gulps and sobs, Johanna fell asleep.

*In her dreams, she was falling down a dark shaft calling, "Daddy." And, as she fell, two arms cradled her, slowing down the fall. She landed in a parking lot. Now she was looking for something. What was it? A white puppy with a brown face. She had lost a puppy. "Where are you?" She ran faster and faster. She tried to whistle, but couldn't.*

*There was a hole in the ground, a cold, dark hole, about the size of a rain puddle, but deeper and with jagged outcroppings of fang-like rocks. Probably the puppy had fallen down into it. She bent over and tried to see into the darkness, but couldn't. The hole was too dark. She put her hand inside and reached down, feeling around for the puppy. Nothing. There was a second hole. And another. The ground was covered with holes. Ugly, scary, nasty holes. Too many holes. She'd never be able to look into all of them. But she had to try. She had to try.*

That night, while Martha tidied up and prepared herself for bed, she could hear sounds coming from Johanna's room—whimpers, and squeaks, and the sounds of a small child thrashing. When Martha came up for a peek, she found Johanna's blanket on the floor and her top sheet twisted into a fat ribbon around Johanna's chest and legs. A nightmare, thought Martha. Johanna didn't wake up, and Martha didn't wake her either. Thank goodness Stephen would be home before long. She covered Johanna with the blanket, kissed her gently, and went to bed.

The next morning Johanna woke remembering what day it was. She remembered the bad dream and the bad feelings of the night before. But Daddy was coming home today. That would make everything all right. Daddy had promised, and he'd never break a promise to Johanna. Daddies never break their promises. She jumped on her bed because there was too much happiness inside for Johanna to just sit still. Daddy was coming home. Maybe he was home already. Probably he was home already. Johanna scampered down from the bed and started calling, impatient to see him after four very long days. "Daddy, Daddy, Daddy!" she called. "Where's my daddy, my daddy, my daddy?" She ran off to her parents' bedroom. "Daddy." Her voice was loud, but no one answered. "Are you in the bathroom, Daddy?" She knocked tentatively. You had to be polite and patient if someone was in the bathroom. She listened for sounds—the shower, the toilet flushing—but there was nothing. The room was quiet. "Where's my daddy?" she called, running down the stairs. Daddy wouldn't go to work without hugging her.

Martha was in the kitchen. Ashen-faced, she clutched the phone tightly against her cheek, sometimes stroking it as if it were alive. Her breath was jagged, coming in fits and starts, as if she were fighting to get her words out between gasps.

Johanna stared for a minute. She put two thumbs into her mouth and sucked noisily. Then she put her arms around Martha's knees, but Martha didn't acknowledge her, preoccupied with the voice on the phone. "Over the Atlantic Ocean… slim probability of survival… I'm so sorry." Martha heard the words, but she didn't really believe them.

Johanna let out a scream. "Where's my daddy? Where's my daddy? Where's my daddy?" She chanted the words over and over like a mantra, and the words took on a power of their own.

Like an automaton, Martha finished the call. She cradled the receiver, rocking back and forth. Now that the bond between them was broken, Martha understood how well she and Stephen had fit together. She was the keel; he was the sail; and, together, they had navigated their personal ocean. Dating, marriage, parenting, they had completed each other, each gifted with qualities that the other lacked. Why hadn't she seen it until now? When it was too late to tell Stephen that she understood his uniqueness! Too late to thank him! If only he were here to comfort her now—to see her through this stretch of turbulence. But looking for comfort, she found only a terrified little girl, and, in a haze of shock, she finally set the phone down.

Johanna's temper tantrum was filling the kitchen. She hit the table leg with her fist; That hurt, so she threw the butter dish across the room instead. And she shrieked till her throat was too sore to shriek any more. The words came out crackling like wrinkled paper. "He promised. Daddy promised. Where's my daddy?"

How do you explain death to a child? Martha stared at her daughter. She tried to put an arm around her, but Johanna fended off all overtures of comfort. Can she understand what death means, Martha wondered. She's not even four years old yet. Martha tried. "Johanna, I have to tell you something—something very sad. Do you know what it means when someone dies?"

Johanna remembered the prayer. She remembered the arms and the feeling. The screams subsided to whimpers as Martha talked about Stephen being with God in Heaven. Johanna watched Martha in silence, half-hearing the words and understanding even less.

Now listen to me, God. You give me my daddy back. In her mind, while Martha spoke to her, Johanna gave God a stern lecture. Right now, God! You're a meany. Give me back my daddy right now. You shouldn't have done it, God. You shouldn't have taken my daddy, even to be in Heaven. You just shouldn't have done it. Daddy shouldn't have let you. He should have stayed with me. He never should have gone away.

I must be saying the right thing, thought Martha as the shouting and sobbing died down. Johanna stared silently while Martha filled the air with the words she thought would comfort her daughter. Johanna said nothing. Finally, Martha asked, "Would you like to play with Teddy now?"

Johanna gave a half nod and walked to her bedroom to deal with her grief as best she could.

<<<<>>>>

At Stephen's funeral, Johanna stared at the floor and held onto Teddy so tightly that she all but crushed him. After that, she hardly spoke. Mostly, she stared into space and sucked on her two thumbs.

On the ninth night after Stephen's death, Johanna looked out her window at the stars. The window was open just a crack, and the air was almost still—and crisp with the chill that follows a hard rain.

"You shouldn't have taken him, God. He needs me. He needs to read me stories and to tuck me in at night. He needs to call me Puppy Face, and to make me peanut butter and jelly sandwiches the right way. Mommy never puts enough jelly in the sandwich. He needs me to hug his neck and to tell him how much I love him. He talks to me like I'm a grown up. He understands. No one else ever understands."

The leaves outside rustled gently in the wind. Johanna pushed and tugged at the window until it opened all the way and put her face out into the cool moonlit night. A breeze whispering by her cheek reminded her of her father's hand, the way he used to stroke her face. Like a living presence, it kissed her aching spirit. "I understand," it seemed to say, "and I'll always be with you."

"Is that You, God? Are you really talking to me? And will you always be there? Daddy said he'd always be there, but then you took him to Heaven, and I love him so much, and he's gone."

That night, Johanna brushed her teeth without being told, put on her jammies, and tucked herself into bed. When Martha came into Johanna's room to start the bedtime ritual, she was pleased to find her daughter already asleep.

After that, Johanna dreamed about her daddy—a different dream every night. One night, she dreamed about him roaming the earth on a giant pumpkin, looking for her.

Another night, her daddy was fighting tigers, many tigers. And the tigers turned to butter, just like in the book *Little Black Sambo*.

The night of her birthday, she dreamed that her father was soaring through the clouds and swooping over mountaintops. "You're going too fast. Look out! You're going to crash!" But it was too late. He crashed into the side of a mountain, and a whiskery old man grabbed him by his collar and pulled him up into the clouds. Johanna woke up with a jolt. She cried and couldn't go back to sleep that night.

She dreamed of mice and rats, and of her father dressed like the Pied Piper of Hamelin. The villagers were screaming, "We have to get rid of the rats!" They chased the rats and the mice, and they chased her daddy, and the villagers made them all fall into a hole—the rats, and the mice, and her daddy.

For forty nights, she dreamed fantastic stories about her daddy. Sometimes she was with him sailing on a pirate ship in a stormy ocean with waves as high as houses crashing around them.

Sometimes they'd be running through fire trying to save rats. And sometimes her daddy was alone, fighting a hairy giant, and Johanna was trying to save him, but couldn't get out of her bed.

On the fortieth night, she saw her father's image shimmering like wispy currents of hot air on a July afternoon. His eyes shone with love and his face was peaceful. "Puppy Face, I'll always be with you, but only in your heart. You're in God's hands now. You'll be fine. You are loved." And her father's image shimmered more. "You are loved. You are loved." The image gradually faded as Johanna woke to a pale morning sun lighting her room through the bedroom window.

After that, whenever Johanna was sad, or happy, or lonely, or had found a pretty leaf in the yard, or didn't understand something, she talked to God. And sometimes Johanna would hear God's voice answering her. Or maybe it was her conscience, or her imagination, or a hallucination, or something. Martha could never tell, and Johanna didn't know enough to care.

Johanna liked to sit and rock back and forth. She'd take out the middle cushion of the living room sofa and sit in the empty space, her arms resting across the cushions on either side. She was the queen, and the couch was her throne, and she'd sit there smiling and rocking back and forth.

"What are you doing, dearest?" Martha always tried to keep her voice casual and steady, but she was terrified because her daughter was so different.

"Nothing, Mommy, just talking to God."

At first Martha kept it light. "Why don't you play outside, sweetheart? God has to take care of the Chinese missionaries for a while." Maybe Johanna would outgrow it. After all she was only four years old. Lots of children had imaginary playmates. Why couldn't one of them be God? But this all seemed so sacrilegious! Was it a sacrilege? Maybe she could ask a priest from a different parish, someone who didn't know her and Johanna. But then she'd have to explain about Johanna and tell him… No, she'd just wait. Surely Johanna would outgrow this in time. Martha worried. But then Martha worried about a lot of things. It was what she did best.

# Chapter Three

The following year Johanna started kindergarten, and Martha couldn't have strangers finding out that her child held conversations with God. "Stop all this talking-to-God nonsense right now, or everyone at school will think you're crazy. What's the matter with you, anyway?" Martha's voice was angry. She knew she was being unreasonably hard on Johanna, but how do you explain conformity to a four-year-old? You can't tell your own daughter how embarrassing it is when someone catches her talking to herself. Martha had to be hard on Johanna, very stern. Otherwise, who knows what the child would say in school! "You say your prayers at night, and you say grace at meals, and, on Sunday in church, you pray. And that's all. Do you understand me? Look at me when I'm talking to you."

"Yes, Mommy." Johanna already knew she was different from other children.

<<<<>>>>

Johanna was one of the youngest children in her class and one of the smallest. Her eyes gleamed jet black—with gypsy coloring. Her dark brown hair hung thick and curly, framing her face like cocker spaniel ears. And when Johanna's mind went off to other worlds, her eyes glazed over and her mouth took on a Mona Lisa smile, like she knew secrets that no one else did.

Johanna's favorite place in the recess yard was a small patch of earth nestled in the far corner behind a playhouse. They'd planted carrots there earlier in the year. Each child had been given a handful of seeds and a paper cup with clean soil. They'd poked their fingers into the earth to make depressions and then carefully laid their prizes, the tiny seeds, into the soft soil. Every other day they'd poured a little water into the cups, and Johanna thrilled at the smell of the wet earth, a comforting, you're-coming-home sort of smell. A few days later, like magic, the seeds began to sprout, small green babies with delicate leaves reaching upward. Johanna was like that—a baby—just like the sprouts. Later, they'd transferred the sprouts to the tiny garden— really only a plot of dirt about three feet by five feet sheltered behind the playhouse. Johanna liked to go over to the garden and talk to her baby plants. She'd pet the feathery greens on the carrots that grew from her seeds, and sometimes she'd sing them a song or two.

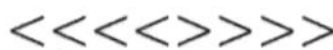

One morning, when the recess bell rang, Johanna ran to the vegetable garden and touched her carrot greens. "Are you ticklish?" she asked the carrots. "Are you cold? Do you want my jacket?" It was the middle of October. A gentle breeze brushed by Johanna's face with the first hint of autumn's chill. Pearly dewdrops were still clinging to the tiny plants. She started to take her jacket off, but the breeze was cold, so she thought better of it. Instead, she sat down, closed her eyes, and began telling her carrots a story.

"Hey, kid, how come you're smiling like that and talking to yourself?" Alex Lidecker was a full head taller than Johanna and husky. A spray of freckles peppered his nose.

The voice startled Johanna. She knew she wasn't supposed to talk to carrots. "I was pretending that I was telling God a story," she said. She knew enough to use the word, "pretending," because she wasn't supposed to be talking to God either.

"That's stupid. You can't talk to God."

"You can if you know how."

"God's not even real."

Johanna was floored. No one had ever, ever, suggested such a thing. Her mommy and Sunday school teachers talked about God all the time, and they weren't stupid. "How do you know that?" she asked.

"Well, do you see him? Do you hear him? Do you smell him?"

"Well maybe I do." Johanna knew better. Really, she did. But the words exploded out of her mouth anyway.

"Well, maybe God farted and that's what you smell." Alex thought that was hilarious. He jumped around Johanna pointing his butt at her. "My brother's fifteen, and he says that there's no God, and that anyone who's got any sense knows that."

"Well, maybe your brother's a poo-poo head," she said. There wasn't time to think of a better answer. There wasn't time to think at all.

"You take that back."

"And maybe you're a poo-poo head too." There! That showed him.

"You take that back, kid," he said. He grabbed Johanna's thick hair and yanked hard. "You take that back. You take it back."

Johanna started crying.

"You take it back, or I'll make you eat dirt. Take it back."

Johanna kept crying.

That's when Alex knocked her to the ground in the carrot patch. Sitting on her stomach on top of the baby plants, he pulled up a fist full of carrot sprouts and dirt. Johanna squeezed her lips together and tried to keep her mouth closed, but Alex was able to stuff a giant hand-full of dirt and greens into her mouth anyway. She felt his breath on her face. She tasted the dirt, and gagged, and felt his hand pushing more dirt against her teeth. Like a cornered, wild animal, she snarled and snapped. She bit Alex's finger and held her teeth locked onto the finger for as long as she could; then she spit the mess up all over him. He jumped off of her. Johanna came up enraged, swinging and punching. Green leaves and dirt dribbled down the sides of her mouth and down her chin. And that's when the yard monitor noticed the two of them—Johanna screaming and slapping her hands at Alex, and Alex backing up, fending off her blows.

"She just went all crazy all of a sudden," Alex explained in a surprised, whining voice. "And I didn't know what to do. She was eating dirt. And I told her not to, and she hit me and she bit me." He showed the yard monitor his finger which was bleeding a bit.

Johanna didn't say anything. She just stood there with dirt and greens dribbling down here chin.

"Hi, God." Johanna had finished brushing her teeth, and she was rinsing the soap from her face as she spoke. "Did you know that I bit Alex Lidecker during recess and had to go to the principal's office? Oh yeah, you know everything. Well, it wasn't fair. Alex is a poo-poo head, and someone needed to punch him, and slap him, and make him eat dirt. Well, it's true, even if it's not nice. He deserves to get into big trouble for something he didn't do. Then we'd be even—well, almost even." She stopped her tirade to wipe her face with a soft, pink towel.

"And it better be a whole lot of trouble. He was the one who started it. And the teacher was on his side. He lied, and he didn't get in trouble for lying. Besides, I'm pretty tough. I could have beaten him up if that stupid teacher hadn't of come along."

But then Martha's words came flooding into her head. "… she's crazy." "I worry about her mental state." "She'll have to fit in with the other kids at school."

And Johanna sighed, defeated. "I'm different, God. That's why no one likes me." She carefully folded her towel over the towel rack. "But I don't care what anyone says—you're God, and you don't fart."

<<<<>>>>

So Martha was called in for a parent-teacher conference to discuss Johanna's problems, and that was the last time that Johanna was caught talking to God. "I'm trying to remember the words to a song." "I'm memorizing a poem." "I'm just kind of tired." Johanna had plenty of acceptable excuses for her ways.

Martha almost relaxed. I knew she'd outgrow it eventually, she thought                              to                              herself.

# Chapter Four

∞

In spring when Johanna was six years old, everyone in her class had roller skates and Johanna wanted them too. The winter rains had come and gone, and the air smelled of apple blossoms and newly-cut grass. Sometimes on Saturdays, Martha would take Johanna down to the park. "Children need plenty of fresh air," she'd say. There in the park, while Johanna was swinging on one of the swings, she could see the other children gliding around on their skates. The parents had gotten permission from the park's groundskeepers, and they'd cordoned off a large circle of smooth asphalt into a roller-skating rink. That was the place where everyone went to skate.

It wasn't even that Johanna wanted to skate all that much. Mostly she wanted to be like the other children. They twirled, they giggled, they told each other jokes, and then they laughed some more. Johanna, swinging by herself, wanted to be one of them. She figured that if she only had roller skates, then, magically, she'd know how to talk to the other kids—what to say, how to laugh, how to be like them.

Martha had some misgivings about the skating. "You're too young. You'll fall down and break something, and we'll have to go to the hospital."

But along with her fears about scratched knees and broken bones, she was keenly aware that all of the other children were playing in the skating rink, while her daughter sat alone on a swing singing to herself. Maybe, if Johanna had skates, she wouldn't be so odd.

So, in her Easter basket, along with jellybeans, marshmallow peeps, and a chocolate Easter bunny, Johanna found a pair of brand-new roller skates nestled in the bottom of the basket, half hidden by the Easter grass.

"Mommy, Mommy, Mommy! Look what the Easter bunny brought me. Can I try them out now?"

As Johanna hugged her with a six-year-old's unabashed excitement, Martha felt all warm inside. These moments were so rare, such a gift! Martha wished that Johanna could know to thank her for the skates, but, even with the Easter bunny taking credit for the skates, it was a happy moment.

Johanna wiggled through Easter Sunday service. At home she raced to change into some old jeans and then to try out the skates. In front of their house, Martha used a small metal key to fit the skates to Johanna's sneakers. Then she helped Johanna to stand up, and watched with pride as her daughter took her first steps on the skates.

Skating was even better than Johanna had thought it would be. With her arms outstretched like wings, she held her balance, correcting with the bobble in her knees and the wobble in her ankles. Her waist bent back and forth. Johanna thrilled to the shushing sound of wheels on the sidewalk, and she felt the vibrations coming up through her feet—a rumbling, rushing feeling that stayed with her even after she'd taken the skates off.

Johanna skated just about every day after school and on weekends, usually in front of her house. But sometimes on Saturdays after Martha had finished her chores, she would pack an Agatha Christie novel for herself and drive Johanna down to the park. Feeling very grown up, Johanna would glide into the rink with the other kids.

Spring became summer, and along with summer came summer vacation and plenty of free time for skating. Johanna got quite good at it. She learned how to skate backwards, and how to glide on one leg, and make tight circles and figure eights. Mostly, she liked to skate fast—so fast that the air she passed blew cool and strong into her face.

But all too quickly Labor Day came around—the last hoorah before school started up again. It was a glorious, balmy day—seventy-five degrees outside. Johanna managed to pester Martha into taking her skating in the park.

Johanna strapped on her skates and entered the rink, one of the shortest children there. She swirled into a glide for twenty feet, then twirled around in a perfect circle.

Meanwhile, more and more kids were showing up, like Johanna, wanting to end the summer vacation with an afternoon of skating. The rink had never been so packed. Elbows, backs, and legs—they were everywhere. On one side of the rink, older kids, teenagers, were playing crack the whip, laughing, and talking. Someone had brought a portable radio and they sang along and stomped in rhythm to the music. One of the boys had been eating raw onions; Each time he passed Johanna, she could smell his breath.

She wished that some of the children would go home, especially the ones playing crack the whip. They were a lot larger than she was, and they didn't always watch where they were going. Then, the boy with the onions skated into her backside, and she fell onto the ground. She looked and found herself surrounded by legs and skates. Suddenly the skating wasn't fun anymore. Johanna felt like she couldn't breathe. Children were everywhere, zipping beside her, in front of her, behind her. Johanna sat up. The music was overpowering, a disorienting, crashing percussion along with a vibrating thrum of base.

Hurting and fearful, she looked around for her mother, but only whirling, skating children and the tops of trees were visible from where she sat. Bodies bumped and jostled her as she got herself up and began edging her way to the side. She wouldn't cry. She was too big for tears now. She'd just make her way out of the rink and take off her skates. She could tell her mother that she had a headache and wanted to go home.

Then someone's foot hit her skate and she fell to the ground again. The rough cement scratched her knees and skinned the palms of her hands.

She wasn't going to cry.

No one noticed.

No one offered a hand.

They were just a twirling mass of people. Johanna skated to the rope that surrounded the skating circle. She looked for Martha along the benches where the parents sat waiting while their children skated.

"I'm done, Mommy. Can we go home now?" It was best not to get Mommy upset.

"Are you all right, sweetheart?" Martha asked. She had been reading, and she had seen Johanna tumble but hadn't realized how badly the falls had affected her. And Johanna had told Martha over and over that she was a big girl, and that she could skate in the rink with the other kids.

Martha clucked, and fretted some, and wanted to take a look at Johanna's knees.

"I'm okay, Mommy," Johanna said. She didn't cry. "And I'm ready to go home now."

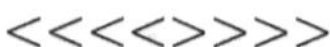

Johanna knew, climbing into her bed that night, that she would dream. In the night when she couldn't hold back the tears or stop the freight train of her fright, that's when the scary stuff always came back.

*In her dream, Johanna found herself wandering alone inside of an old house, her footsteps muffled on a rotten wooden floor. But in the living room, a boy in a mouse costume was playing Christmas carols on a large piano, while a crowd of children gathered around him. Johanna stood with them but had to hum and sing, "la, la, la," because she didn't know the words. She picked up a flute and put it to her mouth. It echoed the melody, with runs and trills like water rushing over stones. Another spirit, another soul was born in the pulsing rhythm of the piano chords, the children's voices, and the warbling of the flute.*

*And as they sang and played, the children's bodies swayed, trance-like, in a stylized dance, each body so fragile, so perfect, a piece of art created by the Supreme Artist. Still more children came. The flute laughed in syncopation.*

In her sleep Johanna rolled over, eyes twitching, her mouth making blowing motions.

*Still more children came. "We need more room; we're getting squished!" they shouted, and they looked to Johanna to save them. She picked up the flute, but it was full of dirt. "More room! We'll be squished!" Bodies were everywhere, and the music became garish, discordant. Hate, anger, floated in the air like ash after a fire, replacing the spirit of the dance. Johanna felt it. She wanted to scream, to hit— anything to get more room for herself. Still more children came.*

*Johanna wasn't sure who swung the first punch. Now it was hard to breathe.*

*"Remember this lesson, Johanna; remember it well." A voice like God's boomed inside of her head—low, rumbling, all-powerful. And the words crackled like fire—sharp, like the blow of a hammer. God was not comforting or loving now. He evoked fear—demanded obedience. This was the God who had drowned Pharaoh's army in the Red Sea, who had told Jonah to preach at Nineveh. Now he*

*commanded Johanna to... to do what?"*

She woke with a start, and her eyes felt sore as if rubbed by sand. "What lesson, God? Don't forget, I'm only six years old." She made her prune face, remembering the claustrophobic sensations of the skating park and of her dream. And she had no idea what to do about them.

<<<<>>>>

That evening as they did the dishes—Martha washing and Johanna drying—Johanna decided that it was the right time of day to ask Mommy something important. "Could children really be squished off the world? I mean, what if there were so many people that they couldn't all fit?"

But all Martha said was "don't be ridiculous," and passed her the salad bowl to dry.

# Chapter Five

∞

Martha never did get comfortable with Johanna's non-conformist view of the world, and Johanna never did outgrow it. When it came time to apply to colleges, Johanna's first choice was the University of California, the Berkeley campus, home of the free speech movement, Mario Savio, and the Black Panthers. UC Berkeley offered Johanna a full-ride scholarship.

"But, honey, Berkeley is so far away." Martha clucked, fussed, and sputtered. Johanna was such an ingénue. How could she ever manage so far from home, without Martha taking care of things? What if Johanna came back a hippie!

Still, the more Johanna read about the University of California, the more she wanted—no—the more she knew she had to go there. "Mom, I don't know if I can explain it." She left the God-told-me part out. "Pascagoula is a great place for you, but I never fit in. I do believe that our world is overpopulated, and I want to do something about it. And I can't do it here. You think Berkeley is full of dirty hippie radicals, and you're partly right, but it's also full of people who care about problems that Pascagoula ignores. And I want to be a part of that."

"It's quiet now, but, sweetheart, the riots, the sex. For Heaven's sakes, they used teargas! Teargas! How many colleges anywhere have had to use teargas to control their students? Why don't you enroll in the University of Leopoldville, or, or, or Hoboken clown college and completely destroy your mother's will to live."

Don't worry. I won't take drugs. And I won't get arrested or get teargassed. Promise. But Berkeley's where I have to go, Mother.

There's no place else for me."

Martha didn't relinquish control easily. She forbade Johanna, tried to distract her, tried to interest her in other colleges. But it was like trying to hold back a waterfall with your hands. Eventually, Martha gave in.

At least she won't be the craziest one on campus, thought Martha.

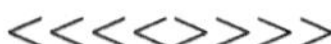

Fall semester, two weeks before classes were scheduled to start, Johanna got her first experience of Berkeley. She drove a baby blue and white comet four-door with her window rolled down. A warming sun, a gentle breeze, and a cloudless sky welcomed her to California. She smiled at the sight of rolling, straw-colored hills with scrubby oaks rippling down the sides—so different from the flat marshes and slate green pines of Mississippi.

Johanna pulled into the parking lot of Malcolm Hall, her new home and the beginning of the next part of her life. The room assigned to her was 316. A twenty-something woman in bell-bottom jeans and a vintage-lace blouse pressed a key into her hand. Johanna smiled and was acutely aware of her own cotton shirtwaist dress with matching green flats and purse. "Third floor. Take a left off the elevator," the woman told Johanna.

But the elevator was stuck on hold on the fourth floor, so Johanna had to trudge with her suitcases up three flights of stairs to her dorm room. Johanna was breathless—partly from excitement and partly from shoving suitcases up three flights of stairs. She swallowed, fit the key into the lock, and walked in.

A willowy stick of a girl was hanging clothes in one of the closets. She wore an orange and yellow tie-died dress that hung about her in a large circle reminding Johanna of a tent. A thick curtain of straw-blond hair all but hid her face. "Are you my roommate?" the girl asked.

"I… Yes. I'm Johanna."

"Temple McGregor."

"What… an unusual name."

"My parents were Zen Buddhists at the time I was born. On a commune in Montana. So I got the name Temple."

"You lived in a commune?"

"For eleven years of my life—four years in Montana, three in New Mexico, and four in seven different communes in California, mostly in the Santa Cruz Mountains." Then we moved to Berkeley and protested the war."

"Did you ever get arrested?"

"My parents did, and I had to stay with a neighbor while a friend posted their bail. What about you?" Maybe Temple was bragging, or maybe she was apologizing. Johanna wasn't sure.

"I lived in Pascagoula, Mississippi all my life. It's just a small city with petroleum, hot summers, and a bunch of chemical plants. And I never got arrested, and I never protested anything, at least not out loud."

"It's overrated," said Temple.

They had orientation one week before classes started. Johanna found out where the buildings were and learned about the history of the college. Temple showed her the student bookstore, and Johanna found out that even the used books were expensive.

But the important things she learned on her own.

She found Everett and Jones and learned that the South wasn't the only place with good barbeque.

The Pacific Ocean was gray and moody, and the powerful crashing of breakers against rock spoke of daring adventure. And it stirred her soul.

On a day hike behind the college, Johanna found Strawberry Canyon. It wound around the back of the campus, through the hills, and wandered up to the Lawrence Hall of Science and the Lawrence Berkeley Lab. She rambled alongside Strawberry Creek and whistled at the birds while sunshine warmed her skin.

In a secluded part of the canyon, a copse of oak trees stood in a small circle. Inside the circle, the air was cooler, and the green branches rose majestically above Johanna about twenty feet into the air, coming together in a dappled-green and sky-blue ceiling. Like a cathedral, Johanna thought, only better. She belonged here, where the sky and oaks met, and the breeze carried the scent of pine trees and dry grass. "If I were you, God, this is where I'd live," she whispered. No, Johanna hadn't outgrown talking to God. And she'd just found a perfect place to do it.

<<<<>>>>

Berkeley in the late seventies was an angry place, an opinionated place, a gathering of Nobel laureates. Science reigned above God. Religion was tolerated but ridiculed. With the discovery of quarks and neutrinos and with DNA codes being cracked weekly, it seemed as if God was an obsolete concept, a charm for the superstitious. But He'd be dissected and studied and explained before too long, along the amino acid sequence for insulin. Johanna didn't talk much about God. Her chemistry teacher was an atheist and laughed at the silly believers. He reminded Johanna of Alex Lidecker, and, just like years ago, she got the urge to punch him out.

"So, will science replace you someday?" she asked God. "Do we know so much that we don't need you anymore? Are there no miracles? Or maybe everything's a miracle, and science is just how we describe what you do and how you do it?" Johanna thought about the days before grocery stores and electric light bulbs. Surely faith came easier to those who had to fill the dark corners of a winter's cabin with prayers instead of extra wattage, to those who prayed for rain to save their crops, and died if the rains didn't come.

<<<<>>>>

Temple sat crossed-legged on her bed smoking a cigarette. "My sister used to believe that Jesus was resurrected to save us. She held on to that till her senior year in high school. Is that not weird?"

Johanna laughed in agreement, and felt like she'd betrayed her best friend.

"What? You don't believe in God, do you?" Temple asked. It was almost a challenge.

Johanna snorted. She shook her head in vehement denial. And then she said quietly, "Yes, I do." She had tried to be cool and had failed. After that, everyone knew that Johanna was different, even by Berkeley standards. Everyone knew it, but especially Johanna knew it.

But it wasn't just her faith that made Johanna so different. Johanna had a dark secret, something so embarrassing that she would have truly considered suicide if anyone had guessed it. Johanna was a virgin! As far as Johanna could tell, no one on the entire Berkeley campus was still a virgin. Probably no one beyond puberty in the entire world was still a virgin, except Johanna.

Johanna noticed another disturbing thing. Most of the women

35

were in some stage of relationships. They were going steady, or breaking up, or getting engaged, or starting to date, but the quest for men was very strong in their lives. Johanna didn't even know how to begin to play that game. What were the rules? Boys just naturally seemed to avoid her, but if she did actually find herself in a conversation with a boy, she usually managed to stutter herself into the most awkward, embarrassing, unpleasant exchange. Even the nicest of boys would find a reason to leave after a few minutes. Her life as a loner simply hadn't equipped her with any social skills. And Johanna wondered, what if some guy ever paid attention to her, or—dare to dream—what if he liked her? Would she go all the way?

As Johanna saw it, most of Berkeley's young people had wrestled with that question in high school, if they wrestled with it at all. The sexual revolution had come and gone. Virgins were as rare as clams in dormitory chowder. You'd have a better chance of finding oil in the ground than a virgin on campus. I'm weird about so many things, Johanna thought, but being a virgin is the weirdest of them all.

# Chapter Six

∞

Psychology 1A was Johanna's favorite class. It promised the elusive formula for how to fit in and make people like you.

Darren Connors, the psych teacher, spent most of the semester discussing the segment on marriage and family. "Living the Open Marriage" was the textbook for this segment, and it was written by Darren Connors. They talked about communication, respect, and freedom. Neither partner in the marriage should feel confined, hemmed in. If the relationship was wrong for half of the partnership, then it was wrong, period.

"So, is anyone in this class still a virgin?" Darren asked. (He had told his class to call him Darren.) General giggling followed. Darren had a way of making class interesting. Johanna looked around to see if anyone was raising a hand, but of course no one was, and Johanna, for certain, wasn't going to volunteer such information. She wondered if somewhere in the room anyone else was looking around scared to admit to being the only virgin. Probably not.

They discussed open communication about sex, being free to examine their bodies and their feelings, being free to communicate their desires, free to explore the possibilities of the oldest and finest of pleasures. According to Darren, sex was the most important aspect of marriage, and, although he didn't exactly come out and say it, he implied that sex was the act that validated a person. A healthy sex life was the mark of a psychologically healthy being. It felt so, well, so liberating to say words like orgasm, and clitoris, and penis in the middle of a room full of strangers. Imagine Martha's reaction if she could see what her daughter was doing now!

Darren was a fascinating, charismatic lecturer. It didn't hurt that he was six three and had a boyishly charming and slightly crooked grin. He'd look out at his adoring students, and yes, at least the women in his class adored him. With hazel eyes full of mischief, he'd give a wink and a funny smirk any time he alluded to sex. When the room got hot, he'd take of his jacket, and Johanna couldn't help but notice the well-defined muscles that showed through his shirt. She found herself running to class, trying to be there early enough to get a front row lecture seat.

"We've talked about the shackles and restraints of traditional marriages," said Darren rustling his papers, "and the resentment and damage they can foster, but so far we haven't addressed the most confining of the marriage myths: Thou shalt always have a monogamous relationship." Here, while the rest of the class giggled knowingly, Johanna did a double take.

"It's normal for humans to lust after more than one partner. We men, and, by men, I mean humans, we want to be challenged. We want to win. We need the excitement of the chase. Learning about a new partner in this most intimate way is the single greatest wonder in the world, and yet so many married people go on year after year bitter, depressed, unsatisfied, clinging to a relationship with the passion sucked dry."

Johanna suddenly felt like a little girl. But you're not supposed … Thou shalt not… Adultery. She shuddered at the thought of the word. Was she one of those primitive unenlightened boors who plodded through life with outmoded rules—with a lifestyle that no longer worked in the modern world?

"Instead of a midterm, I want you to write a paper, at least 5000, words describing your ideal marriage. Include all the issues we've been studying—communication, responsibility, partnership, sex. Make it personal. Include those wants and needs that matter most to you." And with that, class was over.

"You see, Darren has this way about him." Johanna was hiking along Strawberry Canyon, and she'd never broken her habit of talking to God. "He'll kind of shrug and half-smile, and it doesn't matter what he says—he could be selling nuclear bombs to Quakers—you just can't argue with the body language."

The wind sighed.

She sat down under the oak branches and pulled out a Steno Pad from her book bag. "I don't want to sleep with anyone but my husband." She wrote it and scratched it out.

"Anyway, God, even if I wanted to argue with Darren's logic, which I don't, I wouldn't know how to say it without sounding like a Sunday school teacher. Or a pathetic virgin."

Johanna wrote about communication, compromise, friends, and careers. She wrote about everything except sex. Then she sucked on her pen, fiddled with her hair, and watched the hawks circling above her. Finally, she wrote: "I'll be so hot and horny he'll never want to even look at anyone else. So there!"

Back at the dorm, she typed the paper up on the portable Underwood that her mother had given her the day that Johanna had left for college. It was well after two in the morning when she put the crisp, finished sheets into a folder and refused to think any more about them.

When the papers came back, Johanna expected a D- on hers since she'd dared to disagree with her professor. After the rest of the class had left, she stuffed it in between her books refusing to look at the grade. No, better to get it over with. She peeked at the top, right-hand corner. "A+ Provocative and insightful. See me after class, Darren."

Johanna quivered. This was new territory. Provocative and insightful. Heady stuff! She walked up to the podium where Darren was surrounded by a half-dozen other students.

After the others had left the room, he turned to Johanna. "I was intrigued by a couple of the points you made," he said, "and I'd like to discuss them with you further." He casually checked a black appointment book lying next to his lecture notes. "Damn it, I'm going to be tied up for most of the afternoon, but, say, could you meet me for dinner?"

Johanna was numb. Finally, she nodded.

"Great! Meet me here, about five-thirty, and I'll figure out some place where we can grab a bite."

Standing outside of the psych classroom, Johanna could hardly believe it—she'd soon be having dinner with Darren Connors, easily the most popular professor on campus. And when Darren drove up in a dark green MG convertible and ushered her into the passenger seat, she had the sensation of floating.

"When I read your work, I sense a passionate nature," said Darren pulling away from the curb. "A sensitive soul, but also a courageous woman, a woman lusting after adventure, a woman who takes risks." He drove on with his left hand on the steering wheel, and his right hand casually resting on Johanna's knee. "I have a keen mind for spotting my students' gifts. I'm never wrong."

The ride to dinner took about an hour. Johanna never noticed the time going by.

They parked in front of a restaurant resembling a Swiss Chalet nestled against the shoreline hills. Inside, candles burned, and the walls were cheery with vibrant folk art—children playing in the snow, a team of oxen pulling a plow, a family sitting around a wooden table. All the vignettes were framed by generous loops of vines, hearts, and flowers. A huge picture window looked out over the Pacific Ocean, with waves endlessly pounding over the rocks in mesmerizing, frothy perfection.

"One glass of wine for each of us," Darren told the waiter, slipping him a twenty-dollar bill. "Chateauneuf-du-pape." The waiter eyed Johanna, then pocketed the bill and nodded. Darren looked deep into Johanna's eyes and smiled.

Johanna couldn't remember what she ate that evening, but she remembered Darren's cologne, a sweet, heady odor, like incense. She could remember the way he smiled into her face, the way his eyes crinkled at the corners when she told him about her father and how they used to read stories, and the way her father looked at her, his gaze penetrating, as if he could reach into her soul.

Being with Daren was like stepping beyond the normal world, like existing outside of time and space. As if the universe and eternity had stopped in honor of the two of them. His attention was the banquet after the famine.

Walking out to the car, Johanna marveled that these sorts of feelings really existed. Dr. Zhivago and Lara, Heathcliff and Cathy— she'd read the stories, seen the movies but she'd never understood until this night.

He parked the car at an outcropping of rock, one of those spots that seemed made for lovers. The moon was almost full. The stars were brilliant, and, far below, the ocean crashed on the rocks.

Darren cupped Johanna's face in his hands and looked into her eyes thoughtfully. Then he kissed her, oh so gently at first, then harder, and more passionately. So this was what it was all about! Wilder than the ocean below them, a rushing excitement suddenly came alive within her. The feeling was more than anything else on earth. No wonder people sold their souls for this!

He reached into her blouse and touched her breast. I can't resist this, she thought. No one could resist this. It's just too wonderful to say "no" to.

Now he was reaching down her back, and touching her panties. She was drowning in a sea of rapture, and she didn't care, didn't want this to end—ever.

The windows had steamed over with their heavy breathing. Johanna was now completely naked, body and soul, as Darren kept finding new ways to stroke Johanna. His tongue brushed her neck and her ear, and then he kissed her stomach. It tickled her, and momentarily she surfaced out of the overwhelming waves of her feelings. This was it, she thought. Sex. Tomorrow she wouldn't be the odd one anymore. Curious, she watched Darren, a master at this game. Next, he should be putting on a condom. Johanna wondered what a condom looked like. He was going to use a condom, wasn't he? How do you ask a guy to put on a condom?

Johanna tried to sound casual. "What kind of condom do you use?" she asked. Her voice was squeaking with passion and embarrassment.

"I don't use condoms," said Darren with a disapproving tone in his voice. "They're too restrictive."

His words jolted her brain back to life. Omigosh, pregnant—I could get pregnant, she thought. The sea of passion turned into a splash of cold water. "Oh, wait, I just remembered… I forgot my birth control." She stammered.

He drove her home, and neither one of them said a word.

The following day, she went back to her grove of trees. "Would it really be so wrong?  It's not like he's married or anything. There's no ring. I looked. And he's never mentioned a wife in his class, and, if she existed, he'd have said something about her by now. It's that kind of a class—very frank and honest. Darren says if a relationship's not honest, it's nothing. So, he couldn't be married. Maybe that's why he says those things about marriages being sucked dry of passion. Maybe if he were married, he'd know better. Anyway, please understand, God. Please forgive me but I can't stop thinking about Darren and the way I felt when he touched me." Johanna shivered and hugged herself, savoring the memory of Darren's fingers on her body. Feeling dissatisfied, she walked back out into the bright sunlight.

For the next few days, Johanna slept terribly, remembering the sensations and Darren's impatience. Each morning, she bolted her prayers like a cup of coffee.

Four days later, Johanna made an appointment with Doctor Berman at the student health center. Johanna could barely lie still as he examined her. Finally, the ordeal was over, and Johanna was trying to get her clothes on as quickly and modestly as she could.

"You're fine, just fine," he said. With his left hand he gestured absent-mindedly towards the door, not understanding, or choosing not to understand, why she had come to his office.

"Wait." She all but shouted the words from the doorway of his office. An awkward silence followed. "Wait. I… need birth control." There she said it, and with those words, she proved her love for Darren. Dr. Berman was old, maybe in his sixties. His eyebrows were shaggy and his hair was balding, and Johanna had told him that she needed birth control. It was the single most embarrassing experience of her life.

Dr Berman looked up and stared. Johanna blushed. "Birth control! What do you want it for?" he asked.

"I… please."

He shook his head in disapproval but reached for a pad and wrote out the prescription.

Darren had finished lecturing, and the class was filing out of his room except for four girls milling around his desk with questions about the day's lesson. Johanna hung back, wishing they'd hurry up and get on to their next class. Finally, she and Darren were the only ones left. How was she going to tell him she'd gotten birth control?

She should have practiced her speech.

"I, uh, I found some of your points interesting and, and, um, I was wondering if we could discuss them, maybe sometime tonight." And she smiled with what she thought was a provocative, sexy grin. None of those other girls would do this, she thought.

Darren stared at her for a minute. "Come by my office about six thirty," he said.

<<<<>>>>

The psych. building was all but deserted as Johanna knocked on Professor Connors's door that evening. His office was small and crammed with books and papers. A black and white photograph of Carl Jung hung on the back wall, and he had an assortment of personal odds and ends—a troll doll, some photos, a "World's Sexiest Man" plaque, and a half-filled brandy decanter with two matching snifters lined up along the back of his desk. From a closet, Darren pulled out a pale green futon mattress, patterned by a random spray of bamboo leaves. Unfolded, it spanned the width of a double bed. He locked the door, settled Johanna down on the mattress, and he stroked her and kissed her till Johanna's breathing came in gasps and starts. Then he stopped, backed off, and looked at her. "You're not going to change your mind—tease me and leave me—are you?"

Johanna shook her head.

He stroked her belly thoughtfully. "You're sure?"

"Yes."

He teased her neck with his tongue, his left hand feeling her racing heart all the while. "Maybe we shouldn't." he said.

"Please." Johanna begged.

Darren lay down beside her and began the lesson that he taught best of all.

<<<<>>>>

Well, thought Johanna, I'm not a virgin any more. Alone in her dorm room, she stared at her naked body in the mirror. Horns hadn't grown out of her head. No warts were sprouting on her face. Nothing had changed. She was the same person she'd always been, except that she was outrageously happy, happier than she'd ever been in her whole entire life. She examined her feelings, probed her insides. Nothing felt different. No miraculous transformation. No sudden insights. No pain of eternal damnation. She just felt normal, very happy and very normal. I guess I can't pet unicorns anymore, she thought.

She ran a hand over her cheek, her breasts, and her belly. She remembered Darren's fingers caressing her body and was jolted by the memory.

Johanna and Darren dated when they could, but they had to be somewhat circumspect. Even in Berkeley in the seventies, it was frowned upon for a teacher and his student to be an item. They dated throughout the rest of Johanna's first semester at Berkeley, and by May, Johanna knew that Darren was the man she was destined to marry.

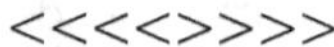

It was one of the last psychology classes of the year, and Johanna's mind kept wandering to memories of a previous evening with Darren. As he lectured about Piaget's theories of cognitive learning, Johanna struggled to get everything important written down in her notebook and tried not to daydream about being married to Darren Connors, psychology professor. She'd probably have to give fancy faculty parties. And she'd do all the cooking herself—much better than hiring a caterer. No, Johanna, pay attention. How would it look if she didn't get an A in her future husband's class!

The squeaking sound of a door opening startled Johanna. She looked up as a woman walked into the room. High heels clink-check-clinked as she walked up to Darren's podium. She was maybe thirty and smartly dressed in a maroon suit and a cream-colored blouse. On the right lapel, a pin of a family crest accented the ensemble. Her blond hair was expensively coifed into a sleek bob, and she walked across the floor with a confident stride. She looked up at Darren and kissed him as if he belonged to her. "Sorry to interrupt your class, Luv," She muttered with a quick wave towards the class, "but I couldn't risk missing you. You got the date wrong. We're meeting Professor Conrad and his wife tonight—not next week. Six thirty, their address is taped to the fridge. I'll have to meet you there; I'll be rushing around the rest of the day, and won't have time to come home before then."

"Six thirty. Address taped to fridge. Got it." Darren smiled at her in that incredibly sexy way. "You're a true champ." And he gave her what looked like a special hug and kiss, and scooted her toward the door with a playful spank on the bottom.

Johanna looked for a wedding ring on the woman's finger, but she was too far away to tell.

"Who was that lady?" she asked Darren after the class was over.

"That was no lady. That was my wife," he answered with a Groucho Marks accent, flicking imaginary ashes off of an imaginary cigar.

"Oh."

"You did know that I was married, didn't you? After all, what have we talked about all semester? Marriage and the family."

"Oh, sure." Johanna coughed, stalling, trying to find something not stupid to say. "Um, it's just that…" Could it be that, in spite of everything she'd experienced, Johanna was still just a little girl. She had to leave before she broke down and said something really crazy. "I have to go to the bathroom."

She walked/trotted out of the room through the doorway, then ran past the bathroom, bumped into a few students who happened to be in her way, then ran to the grove of trees.

Adultery, adultery, her brain squeaked and shouted. She just wasn't this modern, this sophisticated. Johanna was still trying to wash away the guilt pangs of sex with any man and now he turned out to be married!

"But I didn't know, God. Honest, I didn't know. So I guess I should stop sleeping with him?" She asked the question, knew the answer, and pretended she hadn't thought of it. Not sleep with Darren. Not sleep with Darren? Just thinking about him brought back intense feelings of pleasure.

His touch was a part of who she was. As Darren's mistress, Johanna was exciting, vibrant, confident, important. She was a woman. She understood the world. But without him—without him she was just a boring little girl who couldn't admit to being the only virgin in a psychology lecture room. It was as if a cardboard box had just lowered itself around her.

<<<<>>>>

She met Darren in his office at the very end of his scheduled office hours. "I can't see you anymore," she said. "Maybe there's nothing wrong with an open marriage, but I just can't do it."

"You can't?"

There was a silence and Johanna felt herself blushing. "I guess I'm just not ready…" It sounded like a better way to say no.

"You're only eighteen. That's still quite immature," he said. The word, immature, stung. "Of course, I understand."

"We can still be friends, can't we?" Johanna asked, her voice squeaking like a six-year-old's. Was that the corniest line in existence! Just be friends.

"So, in spite of Jung, Freud, and seventy years of psychological research, interactions between men and women still remain as they were in the dark ages." Darren snorted a tiny laugh and shook his head, but he smiled. Surely Johanna was only imagining that he was being condescending.

"Just friends, huh? Did you learn nothing in my class? Well, come here and give an old friend a hug."

His arm bent around her waist and he leaned his head against her shoulders. Oh, so gently, he kissed her cheek, then her ear, then her neck. Johanna wanted to back away. No, she didn't. She hung on tightly. His hand reached up brushing her breast. She tingled and the pleasure took over. Right now, she thought to herself. Stop it right now and walk or run out of the room before you get in any deeper. Stop while you still have a shred of will power. But she didn't. She just stood there, unable to move. Electricity, chemistry, whatever it was, she couldn't resist it. Darren closed and locked the door to his office. She kissed his mouth as he began fumbling with the buttons of her blouse.

The lovemaking was as sweet as ever.

While memories of Darren's caresses raced around in her head, Johanna trudged up to her special place. Nothing stirred. Crickets chirped a monotonous mantra, "Crick-crack, crick-crack, crick-crack." The green hills had turned a straw color, and, from all of spring's blossoms, only a few scraggly flowers remained.

"I couldn't help it," Johanna whispered. As she sat down quietly, composing herself, two mosquitoes flew about her, eyeing their prospective lunch.

She waited for magic to touch her heart, for the sensation that God's presence was all around her.

The sun was high overhead, and the warm air was making Johanna drowsy. She began to daydream, imagining herself on her wedding day—after he'd divorced the other wife, whoever she was. She imagined Darren in a tuxedo, handsome, charming, and hers. Her husband!

One of the mosquitoes buzzed her ear and she squirmed in reaction. She tried to turn her attention back to God, but there just wasn't anything to say.

And Johanna was suddenly struck by the absurdity of it all. Here she was sitting on a tree stump talking to herself about doing something that all of Berkeley was doing without any regrets. Look around you, Johanna. Do you see fire and brimstone, or pillars of salt, or anyone struck down by lightning bolts?

She fidgeted some more, and finally admitted to herself that she was very bored.

I guess I've finally grown up, she thought to herself chuckling at the mystical significance she'd assigned to the trees. They were trees, living wood, beautiful, stately. But they were just trees—no more, no less—just trees. And the copse was a charming place to while away a few hours. And now that Johanna realized it, she wouldn't obsess about coming back.

In an old pine by the creek, a mocking bird staked out his territory, climbing the air currents then swooping down into the top of the tree, over and over again. Johanna watched, then got bored and walked back to her dorm, grateful that her room had air conditioning.

That summer was the summer of Darren. They spent long afternoons reading poetry and feeling each other's bodies. Johanna had          finally          outgrown          God.

# Chapter Seven

∞

As the fall quarter started, Johanna checked her schedule of classes. Then she checked Darren's, and it looked as if they both had a break after sixth period. She'd hustle into his classroom and surprise him.

She got there just as Darren's class had finished and most of the students were filing out of the room, with the exception of a girl who looked scarcely old enough to be a freshman. A little wisp of a girl, she had thick hair the color of flames framing her pale face. And she stared up at Darren with cat-green eyes fixed on his. Johanna understood the look. "Great insight," said Darren. "I'd like to discuss some of the comments you made. This afternoon's no good. I'm tied up in meetings. But would you consider having dinner with me?"

A bundle of thoughts hit Johanna at once, and her pain was physical, an ache deep inside, that knocked her feelings about like wheat in a hail storm. Don't panic, thought Johanna. Maybe he really does have meetings. Maybe the girl had some good insights. Maybe his interest in her was purely professional. And maybe the Easter Bunny and Santa Claus ruled the earth? No, Johanna was looking at this semester's dessert. This girl embodied the excitement that Darren talked about in his lectures. Johanna, on the other hand, was leftovers. She was melted ice cream, sticky, lukewarm, boring. Johanna skulked out of the classroom and down the hallway.

But maybe not.

"But maybe not!" Johanna all but shouted the words right in the middle of the hall. Maybe I'm just being paranoid, she thought. Darren was big on honesty, and he hadn't said anything to Johanna about breaking up. Probably she should talk to Darren and see what was going on in his head. Maybe there was some logical explanation that Johanna hadn't thought of.

Besides, even if the worst was happening, even if Darren was dating the red head, she should talk to him. She should try to win him back. His love was worth it. Resolutely she turned back towards his classroom.

It seemed forever before the red-headed girl left for her next class and Johanna was alone with Darren. "Hi, Darren." She smiled up at him, her voice edgy, self-conscious. "We're reading *Romeo and Juliet* in English Lit., and, hey, who could understand Romeo better than you? Right? So, could we grab a cup of coffee or something and talk?"

Darren thought for a minute. "I, uh, have a student coming in for a consult in a few minutes." He frowned. "But, hey, I know what you can do. My student teacher, Sheila! She's a real Shakespeare buff. She'll be able to help you with *Romeo and Juliet*. Just give me a minute." He tore off a corner from a sheet of notebook paper and jotted down some numbers on it. "Here's her phone number. Just tell her I said she should give you a hand." As Darren talked, he walked towards the door, and Johanna had no choice but to follow. Darren locked the door behind him, then gave Johanna a friendly squeeze around her shoulders and strode purposefully towards his convertible.

Defeated, unwanted, Johanna dragged through the rest of her classes, with time melting as in a Salvador Dali painting, and the walk back to her dorm room seemed to go on forever. Turning the knob to her door, Johanna felt about eighty years old.

"What's wrong," Temple asked.

The standard answer. "Nothing." And she flopped on her bed, dazed.

"It doesn't look like nothing."

"I'm fine."

"Do you want to talk about it." Temple sat down beside her.

"No," Johanna sniffed. "Just leave me alone." She turned toward  the wall, hiding her face.

"Okay," said Temple. "Have it your way. But it looks like a classic case of dumped by a bastard."

"I hate men," Johanna gulped. "I hate all men. I'm never having anything to do with any of them ever again!"

Mostly Johanna cried, and Temple listened. In between oh, so much sniffling and sighing, Johanna managed to tell her story.

Temple handed her a tissue. She put a hand on Johanna's shoulder and nodded. "Classic case of dumped by a bastard. Look on the bright side. At least you're not pregnant."

Johanna shrieked, and Temple left her alone.

<<<<>>>>

By the next morning, depression had replaced shock, and Johanna couldn't muster the strength to get out of bed until about two. She was still in pajamas when Temple got back at four.

"Did you go to any of your classes?" Temple asked.

Johanna shook her head. She had climbed back into her bed and was lying there with a text book across her lap. "Anytime I… love someone they leave. I'm… I'm unlovable." She wiped away tears with the back of her hand. "Look at me. I'm a mess. This is just pitiful."

"Have you eaten anything at all?"

Johanna didn't answer.

"Look, I know what it's like. I've been dumped. It sucks. and then you get over it."

Again, no answer.

Temple left the room and came back with a sandwich and coffee in a Styrofoam cup. "Eat this. You'll feel better," she said. Johanna sniffed the sandwich and put it back untouched.

Temple shrugged, then opened a text book and flopped on her bed to study.

<<<<>>>>

The next day Johanna cut all her classes. The following day, she made it to English Lit. The day after, Intro to Biology. Most of the time, Johanna sulked and stared at the wall or pretended to read. By the following week, Temple had had it with Johanna's moping.

It was a Friday evening, and the dorms were empty. It was time to party. "Get dressed. We're going out," Temple ordered. "It's time to join the rest of the world."

"Tomorrow," Johanna whispered.

"No. Today. Any more of this… whatever, and you'll flunk all your classes. Now move."

"Maybe tomorrow."

"Maybe right now. There's a movie I want to see, and you're coming with me. It starts in an hour."

"I'm not…"

"I don't care what you are. Get dressed. We're going out."

Johanna got dressed, but her face clearly expressed that she was only doing it to please Temple.

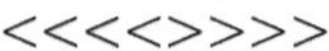

The movie was *Network*.

Johanna left the theater yelling, "Mad as hell." She raised a fist into the air.

Temple tried to shush her. "You're being weird."

Johanna kept yelling. "I don't care. I won't take it. Not ever, ever again." Now both her fists were raised.

Other students watched Johanna and snickered. "You tell 'em, sister!" "Right on!"

"Please hush," Temple begged.

Johanna let out one final "Shit." Then she began laughing. The laughter became hysterical; it took over her whole body, and she couldn't stop.

Temple dropped back a few feet behind her, and shook her head, rolling her eyes and pretending she didn't know Johanna.

Finally, the laughter subsided. "I'm giving up on men and taking up journalism," said Johanna. "If people can do that with the news, someone's got to get in there and tell the truth."

"It's just a movie. You do know that."

"Maybe. But it's what I was meant to do. Tell the truth. Men suck. But the power of the press is forever."

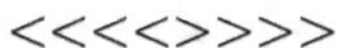

The next morning Johanna woke up at seven and started the day with a bowl of oatmeal, a donut, and a cup of coffee. Next, a quick jog in Strawberry Canyon, followed by a shower.

"You're back," said Temple.

"I'm back. But men are still scum, and I'm never letting another one of them break my heart." With that, she put on a sweater and walked out of the dorm room.

Johanna spent the afternoon in Strawberry Canyon. The grass had turned from green to straw-colored, and great swaths of scrub oak, mesquite, and coast live oak trees created dark green patches along the folds of the hills. She breathed in the spicey scent of bay laurel, and the lingering, musky scent of a skunk somewhere nearby. Johanna loved it all. She made her way through a tangle of willows down to Strawberry Creek, and found a large rock where she could sit and dangle her feet in the water. Frogs croaked. Crickets chirped. Johanna sat still and listened, absorbing the healing calmness of the hills and meadows that were Strawberry Canyon. Somewhere up in the trees, a scrub jay whistled. A squirrel chattered. The sun was warm on her face and shoulders.

While Johanna sat, and watched, and listened, the shadows grew long. A doe and two fawns appeared several hundred yards upstream. They drank and were gone.

Johanna stood up with a sigh and she left too. She left the canyon, walking briskly down to the city of Berkeley with its streets full of laughing students, coffee shops, and bookstores.

As she walked, the sky turned crimson. Johanna walked quickly because the autumn air was turning chilly, and because she had one errand left to do. She'd made an appointment with Fr. Joseph O'Brian at the Newman Hall Holy Spirit Parish, the church that served Berkeley's Catholic student body.

Through the open door to the Newman center, Johanna could see candles, a crucifix, and a plaque of the virgin mother with her son; and the sight of these brought back childhood memories of masses and mysterious Latin chants and hymns. The odor of incense lingered in the air, a comforting scent.

"Welcome. Please come in. I'm Father Joseph." He wore faded jeans and a black shirt with a clerical collar. "What can I do for you?"

"Please." That's as far as Johanna got.

"What is it?"

She fidgeted as she searched for the right words. He waited in silence. She had to say something because the quiet was unbearable. At the very least, she owed the man an explanation. "I need..." "It was..." "There was..."

"Just say it," he said. "Just say it. You can tell me anything."

For a second Johanna looked up into his eyes. "I committed

adultery," she said, then blurted out the whole story of Darren, his beliefs about open marriage, and his wife. "But I didn't know he was married. And then, when I found out, I tried to break it off, but I couldn't."

With her knees, her teeth and her heart shaking, she entered the confessional. "Forgive me, Father, for I have sinned. It's been about a year since my last confession," she said. "And I committed adultery," she whispered.

There! The words were spoken.

Father Joseph completed the ritual, Johanna breathed out a healing sigh, and Father Joseph added, "God has healed you. You were broken. Now you are whole. Go now, my child and sin no more."

No problem there, thought Johanna. I'm giving up men forever. She stayed for the evening service, then headed out into the night. It was about ten by the time she made it back to the dorm.

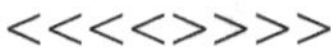

"You were out on a date tonight!" Temple observed. "It didn't take much time for your broken heart to heal, I see."

"No, I just got back from church."

"At this time of night?"

"Vespers. It's an evening service."

"Your cheeks are flushed. Your eyes are shining. That could only mean one thing. You're in love—head over heels in love. Church, my grandmother's eyeball! You're in love."

"Yes, I suppose I am," said Johanna. In love with God, but Temple wouldn't understand.

# Chapter Eight

∞

Johanna couldn't take Professor Marlow's journalism class as a sophomore, so she audited it. She sat in the back of the lecture hall, a pen in her pocket, a notebook in one hand, and a Danish pastry in the other.

"How many of you saw the movie *Network?*" Professor Marlowe asked his class. On the overhead screen, an excerpt from the movie *Network* appeared. Howard Beale shouted his famous "mad as hell" speech, and slammed his fist on the table, and the whole nation, pumped up and furious, opened their windows and shouted their frustration into the night.

"Now that's showmanship," said Christopher Marlowe. His bushy, reddish hair, beard, and eyebrows reminded Johanna of a leprechaun, and, when he moved, he jumped and danced more than he walked. "Reporters have to report the news, but they have to make it interesting, or no one will read it."

A photo of a fire appeared on the screen, with the caption, "Blazing Inferno Destroys Forty acres." Then a second photo appeared with a firefighter standing in front of that same fire, holding a beagle puppy in his arms. The headline for this photo read, "Heroic Firefighter Rescues Beloved Pet from Blazing Inferno."

Professor Marlow jabbed at the screen with a pointer. "Which headline sells the most papers?" He looked around the room. "You look surprised. Tell me this, how many of you show up for an eight o'clock class on a Monday morning, when you know the lecture is going to be boring?" The class chuckled. He nodded with satisfaction. Then he went on.

"Here's neat trick," he said. "Reporters use it all the time." He frowned. Then he smiled. Then he told the class, "Everyone, smile. Big happy smiles, all of you. Just keep smiling." He'd been standing behind a desk, and now he walked in front of it. "Look around you, everyone, see all those happy smiling faces. Makes you feel good, doesn't it?"

He paused. "Now, everyone, just relax. Relax your faces. Completely relaxed." Again, he paused. "Now, take a look around you. See the difference. You all look untrustworthy, some on you look scary, downright criminal."

He rubbed his nose and did a funny hop which made him look even more like a leprechaun. "When I'm teaching, I try to smile a lot. Here's why." And he let his face relax. The leprechaun turned into a troll.

Newspapers use this. They get an unsmiling picture of someone they want to discredit, and they run it. Who are you going to believe, a person with a winning smile, or someone who looks like a gangster? And that, folks, is the power of the press. This is huge! A photo can win or lose an election."

Many hands shot up, and a girl with a pony tail asked the question everyone was thinking. "But can they really do that? Aren't there laws against lying on the news?"

"Where's the lie? That's just a photo. Besides, the Fairness Doctrine was repealed in 1987."

# Chapter Nine

∞

Looking for work was hard. Johanna's resume really didn't have much to recommend her. She'd graduated from Berkeley with honors, done some volunteer work, and she'd held a few part-time jobs during her last two years, but they weren't very interesting jobs. A lot of her friends from Berkeley knew someone who knew someone who worked for personnel, but Johanna didn't have any connections like that.

Doggedly, she filled out applications and refined her resume, but the paperwork only got Johanna to the hardest part of the search—the interview. When she met with prospective employers, her face and neck blushed bright red, and she stuttered every time she talked about her few accomplishments. "We'll notify you within a week," they'd say, and Johanna was happier when they didn't notify her because she didn't want to know that she'd been rejected again.

The *Upstart Gazette* interview was different. Maybe all the earlier interviews had prepared her for this one, but somehow Johanna felt as if she'd come home, that she belonged at the *Gazette*.

"So you have no experience and you think you should be a journalist." The *Upstart*'s editor Ivan Buncheski didn't have great social skills. Peering over his glasses, he screwed his mouth into a scowl. A bulldog without hair, Johanna thought. She should have been intimidated. From behind his desk, he bent forward, leaning with his knuckles on his desk.

"I just graduated from UC. I know I have to start at the bottom. And you need me. The feature columns you're running are... could be improved." She had almost said "pathetic" but caught herself at the last minute. "I can write what you need. It'll be fresh, and relevant. And it'll be interesting, I promise you. I brought you some samples." From a briefcase, she produced four typed articles.

"What happens when the fifth one is due? And the sixth and seventh? Anyone can write four good articles."

"You think they're good?" Johanna interrupted.

"Hmm." Ivan scowled. "It took you, what, three months to write these? Or did someone write them for you? No, eh? What happens when you get stale?"

"Times change. Things happen. And there are always more topics to write about. The day I get stale, I'll resign and get a paper route."

He said nothing. Johanna grinned.

"What's so funny?" It was more a bark than a question.

"You like me. I can tell."

Ivan growled. "Anyone ever tell you that you got a lot of nerve?"

Johanna shrugged.

"What kind of column are you planning to write?"

"I'd call it 'Earth Songs.' And I'd take up issues—political, social, environmental, whatever needs to be told. But I'd write about them in fairy tales, or poems, or limericks or whatever. I'd make them interesting." She grinned. "I'm usually shy. I should be squirming right now. But all this feels right. Somehow, this newspaper feels like comfy pajamas, and you feel like my older brother."

"I'm not your brother," he muttered and brought out a pad and a pen. "So you like controversy?" And he laughed and rubbed his hands together. "Here. Write about overpopulation. A brand-new article. Make it fresh. You have a half an hour. After that, I go home."

She took the pad and pen. And fidgeted. A half hour later, she was still writing.

"Time's up," he said. Johanna kept on writing. "I said, time's up. Hand it over."

Johanna scratched out some lines and a couple of commas before he snatched the paper from her. "Christ, are you always this ornery? And your handwriting could use help."

Life is a teacher and you'd better pay attention because she doesn't pull punches.

I learned about overpopulation at the tender age of three when my father read "The Pied Piper of Hamelin," the story of a population of rats gone horribly out of control. And I wondered if that could happen with people. When I asked Mom if too many people could squish each other off of the world, (my exact words. Remember, I was only three.) she said that God would take care of the problem.

I think He will—but not by waving a magic wand. He expects us to use our brains, to sort it out ourselves.

In college when I heard about the world's population spinning out of control, it seemed like someone was finally saying what I'd known since I was three. So, here's my two cents worth:

## Farmer McGregor's Lament

Coyotes, foxes, mischief-prone—
Leave my chicken coop alone.
Slimy salmon gasp away.
Your water's mine for corn and hay.

I'll use my guns; I'll use my fists,
And eat environmentalists.
I'm not a bad guy, just, you see,
I have to feed my family.

So when someone hands you a brochure for Zero Population Growth, read what it says. Somewhere a coyote and an angry guy in denim overalls will thank you for it.

By the way, here's the coyote's answer:

I'd rather eat wild voles and mouses,
And stay away from humans' houses,

*But there's no space for me to roam;*
*You built a golf course on my home.*

He folded the paper and passed it back to her. "It's not a column; it's a goddamn poem."

"And a good one. Overpopulation's been done to death. The poem works and you know it." And she stared into his face daring him to disagree.

"Lot of nerve, that's what I know. Clean it up for Monday and the job's yours, one column per week. And we'll put you to work researching for the other reporters and mopping the toilets."

"Thank you." She jumped up wanting to hug Ivan, but stopped herself.

"I'm not kidding about the toilets. Okay, I'm kidding about the toilets, but you will have to do research."

Johanna shrugged, ran around the desk, and hugged Ivan. "I love research," she said.

# Chapter Ten

∞

With her column finished ahead of schedule, Johanna had time to daydream. She picked up her pen and tablet and began doodling, waiting for an idea to explode out of the ether. Computers were fine for editing, but Johanna still loved the feeling of pen on paper.

She drew squiggles and boxes. She drew a dog and a horse that looked nothing like a dog and horse, and she decorated the margins of her paper with hearts and stars. "God, I love my life, and I love my job." She still talked to God as if He were her best friend. It was a habit too ingrained to break. "I love my job. I really do. But it's as though I'm meant to dream and watch from outside. And being a reporter is the best job in the world, researching the stories, reporting on other's lives, but I'm always the observer."

She doodled a couple of question marks and turned them into eyes. Then, she drew a face around the eyes. "Just for once, I'd like to be the one making the headlines, catching a burglar, saving the world, and falling in love. Especially falling in love. Like in the movies, with the heart-stopping rush." She drew a cow that looked nothing like a cow.

"But will I ever get someone of my own? Someone real? Someone who can talk back to me? In the movies, the girl always gets the guy in the end. But in real life?" She drew a little man and gave him a pair of wings and a bow and arrow. "I know I said I was done with men. Maybe I was a bit too hasty."

In fact, Johanna didn't have much time for love, or, for that matter, for daydreaming. A newspaper was a rushing, bustling, shouting sort of business. As the smell of ink solvent wafted up from today's afternoon edition, the deadline for tomorrow's morning columns was only a few hours away. Johanna seldom wrote front-page articles. Along with "Earth Songs" she produced mostly background "filler" articles that added depth to the headliners, and she supported the front-page reporters with research. Home was either the library or the Internet connection at the office. Her apartment was a place to sleep, shower, and change clothes, and, occasionally, a place to fix something to eat.

Johanna never knew what to expect when Ivan entered her office. "I wrangled a plum opportunity for you, Johanna," he said. "A workshop. Are you interested?"

"Of course. What's it on? Not that it matters. I'll take it, whatever it is."

"WMD—weapons of mass destruction. The FBI's offering it for firefighters and police. They put it together after the sarin incident in the Tokyo subway."

<<<<>>>>

The WMD class was held at Berkeley's main police station, in an imitation-wood paneled conference room. A stocky character in a crisp white shirt, khaki pants and spit-shined shoes walked up to the front of the room. "I'm Gary Brown, your instructor." His hair was buzz cut short, and he stood as if at attention. "I've worked with the FBI for going on twenty-three years now, and you are about to hear the latest information on terrorist activities around the world. The odds of any of you having to deal with a WMD incident are extremely unlikely, but, if it does happen, we want you prepared."

With that, Gary turned on a projector, and a definition appeared on the screen. "Terrorism is the use of terror and violence to intimidate and subjugate, especially as a political weapon or policy."

Gary poked at the screen with a pointer. "Always remember— the goal of the terrorist is terror, not destruction, not loss of life, but terror. Killing is only a means to an end. It bears repeating. The goal of the terrorist is to evoke an emotional response, to frighten. Because frightened people are people that the terrorist can control."

Johanna pulled out a writing tablet and took notes as Gary went on. "Historically, the FBI focused on the radical left—the Symbionese Liberation Front, the Students for a Democratic Society, and so on. Today, the battle grounds for their causes have shifted from the streets to the political arena, and their issues—Civil Rights, Vietnam—have either gone away or become law."

"Here are the groups we're focusing on today." Gary clicked a button on a remote control. One by one the names of terrorist groups flashed on the screen.

"The Army of God. An ultra-conservative right-wing Christian group, they want to spread Christianity by means of force.

"Osama bin Laden is probably the most watched figure in the world today. A Moslem extremist, he believes that Western materialism and education are a threat to the spiritual life, and wants to replace democracy throughout the world with conservative Islamic totalitarianism. After the United States bombed Libya, he called for a Jihad, a holy war, against the United States. In the U.S. most of his activities are limited to fund-raising. Ironically, it was the United States that trained him back when Afghanistan was fighting the Soviet Union."

Garry nodded and showed the next slide "The Christian Militia. They plan to roll out their tanks and take over when New Year's Eve Y2K rolls around and all the computers freeze.

"The Ku Klux Klan and the Arian Brotherhood—both white supremacist groups. The Arian Brotherhood is a serious threat inside our prisons."

Johanna wrote it all down, and underlined and highlighted about half the words on her pages. Why couldn't she get assignments like this to write about? "This is Johanna Jacobson reporting live from…" Of course, she wouldn't be reporting live unless she were on television. Oh well! She kept on writing and wondering how she could squeeze WMDs into her environmental column.

Meanwhile, Gary talked on. "Our terrorists have many weapons to choose from. You're familiar with rifles and bombs, but today we'll be talking about more exotic weapons.

The words, "Chlorine gas," appeared on a yellow-green slide, as Gary continued. "Germany tried to use chlorine as a weapon in World War I, but it was hard to control. If the wind shifted, they wiped out their own people. Still, many Allied soldiers came home from the war with their lungs burned by chlorine. Saddam Hussein had better luck using it to kill the Kurds."

"Biological agents—anthrax, smallpox, bubonic plague." Gary pointed to the screen. "They're hard to handle without killing yourself first. Where do you think you'd go to get, say, a cup of smallpox?" he asked. Hands shot up.

"Universities."

"Private labs. Pharmaceutical companies."

"The United States military."

Gary nodded. "The U. S. Armed Forces has the biggest stashes of weapons of mass destruction in the world. And you better believe their security is stringent."

He presented the next slide. "Nuclear weapons. Please, don't call them nucular weapons. They're even harder to obtain and handle than biological weapons. Radioactive waste can also be used to make dirty bombs; they're conventional bombs but contaminated with radioactive material. Radioactivity takes a long time to decompose, so these bombs are the gift that keeps on giving… and giving."

He stretched. "And on that note, let's take a break."

Lunch for the class—consisting of sandwiches, cookies, chips and sodas—was catered courtesy of the FBI. Johanna sat with a group of firefighters who tried to outdo each other telling their stories.

A lanky firefighter named Kent began the tall tales. "The captain ordered me to stay out of the building, but I knew the family, and I knew Lucky was still inside."

"Who was Lucky?" asked Victoria, the only woman in the class besides Johanna. "The family dog?"

"Family racoon. They'd raised him from a pup. Cub? Baby? Anyway, he was their pet. Anyway, I—you know—selective deafness. I couldn't make out what the captain was yelling, and, just as I got inside, a chunk of burning roof fell maybe a foot away from me."

"A foot away?"

"It seemed like a foot away. Anyway, I found Lucky hidden under what was left of the kitchen sink, and I grabbed him by the scruff of the neck, and turned to high-tail it out the front door. But that's when a bunch of canned vegetable started exploding all around me, and the damn racoon panicked."

"Were you injured?"

"Hell yes! The racoon got hold of my other arm and bit the holy crap out of it. Then, a can of something bashed me in the back of my neck."

Johanna had nothing to contribute to the conversation, so she listened, worked on her sandwich, and took it all in.

After they'd finished lunch, Garry had a desk-top exercise for the group. "Pretend you're a terrorist. Your assignment is to kill the dictator and take over the palace. How would you do it? Work in groups of five."

Johanna's group considered the chemical, biological, and nuclear agents. "You know what, screw it," said the cop sitting next to her. "The easiest way to kill the dictator is to throw a bomb through his window." It's not as sexy as anthrax, but it's something a terrorist knows how to use."

"Time's up," said Gary. "What did you come up with?"

"Bomb."

"Molotov cocktail."

"Pipe bomb."

"High-velocity lead," one of the cops offered.

"That's cop talk for bullets," Kent said to Johanna.

"Good choices," said Gary. "Tried and true methods. Terrorists know how to handle rifles and bombs. These weapons have been around for a long time. They work. If you're trying to overthrow a country, you have enough to worry about without developing new technology in the bargain. But don't discount what you learned today. Your lives could depend on it."

Fascinating, Johanna thought when the class was over. But it had nothing to do with her day-to-day work. So she stashed her notes in the back of her closet, and she stashed the information in a back corner of her mind.

# Chapter Eleven

∞

Four-year-old Alex Lidecker was struggling to lift the toilet plunger. His footed pajamas had blue teddy bears printed on them and a flap at his bottom. A billowing cape—really a faded red pillowcase—was tucked into the back of his pajamas at the neck. Alex was Superman on a super-secret crime-fighting mission. Waving the toilet plunger as a weapon, he shouted into the air. "Get into the bathroom and think about what you did." The plunger drooped as he spoke, but Alex had captured arch-villain, Toiletman.

"Just what do you think you're doing, runt?" Victor was fifteen. Stocky to begin with, he'd spent many hours lifting weights until he'd developed a body to be proud of.

"I'm putting all the bad guys into the bathroom, and then I'm going to kill them."

"How can you tell who the bad guys are?" Victor was aiming playful slaps at his little brother, at his face, his bottom, his tummy.

"Because I'm Superman and I have Superman eyes." Like most four-year-olds of the 1960's, Alex worshipped Superman, the champion of justice.

"You mean these?" Victor pushed his hand into Alex's face shoving him backwards.

Alex sputtered and kicked. "You're a bad guy, and you have to go into the bathroom." And he waved his drooping plunger at Victor, poking him in the knee with it, while he swung his other fist about trying to make contact with the arch enemy, his brother.

Victor grabbed for the plunger and pulled it out of Alex's hand with one swift twist. Next, he reached around, picked Alex up by the back of Alex's pajamas, and carried the squirming superhero into the bathroom. There, he raised the seat of the toilet and held Alex over it. "You're going for a swim," Victor said.

Alex screamed.

"I'm going to stuff you in the toilet, and you're going to swim until you drown, and I'll flush you."

"NO."

"And you'll swim with the turds."

"Daddy! Help, Daddy. I don't… want to… swim with turds." But his father was upstairs napping in his den, and the bathroom was downstairs. Mr. Lidecker never heard Alex's screaming.

Victor turned Alex upside down, and, as Alex wriggled and protested, Victor held him over the bowl. "You're going for a super swim."

"NO!"
Victor laughed then lowered Alex's head inside the bowl until Alex's hair touched the water. "You're not a superhero because superheroes don't get stuffed into toilets." He held Alex there for a minute.

"And superheroes always win."

Alex began crying.

"And superheroes never cry. Victor dunked Alex's head up and down in the water submersing his face past his nose. "One, two, three, four," he counted as he dunked. The he reached for a towel, and wiped off Alex's face. Mopping up the evidence, as it were.

When he finally let Alex go, Alex ran straight to his father's den whining and crying. "Daddy, Victor said I wasn't a superhero, and he put… my head…" Alex couldn't finish the sentence, couldn't admit that someone had stuffed Superman's head in a toilet and made him cry.

"Victor, get up here!" Mr. Lidecker roared.

"What, Dad?"

"What did you do to Alex?"

"Nothing. I've been working on my homework all morning. And listening to the radio."

"Now what's this all about, Alexander?"

"He said…" Now Alex was whimpering between words. "I wasn't a superhero and…" his voice was very small—almost a whisper. He was fighting hard to keep from crying. "And he put my head into the toilet and…" Alex swallowed. He wasn't going to cry in front of his father. "And he said I was going to swim with turds." And then he burst into tears.

Mr. Lidecker turned away. While Alex sobbed, Mr. Lidecker reached around to his bookshelf and pulled down Volume A of Compton's Encyclopedia, then searched for the entry about Alexander the Great. "Stop crying this minute. Son, I want you to look at this," he said, pushing the encyclopedia in front of Alex. "Alexander the Great. You were named after him. Take a good look, son, a good look. Do you hear me?"

Alex peeked at the pages. The Great Alexander stood, arms folded, surveying a field of dead bodies. Blood poured out of the bodies from their wounds in great blotchy spatters, and their eyes rolled upwards fixed into stares of agony. Alex wanted to run away and throw up. Instead he looked up at his father.

"No, don't look at me. Take a good look, son. Let this be a lesson," he said. "If you get into a fight, make sure you come out on top."

Alex hid his face in his father's shirt, and his father pushed him back a bit. "You were named after the Great Alexander. Be a man if you can," he said

# Chapter Twelve

## ∞

On a chilly October morning, seven children stood out by the swings in the recess yard, telling ghost stories, their eyes wide and serious. They were debating the existence of Dracula.

Jo-Jo Vargas stuck his hands into his pockets and announced, "There is not any such thing as a vampire."

"Is so," argued Alex Lidecker. His brother had just finished reading *Dracula*, and he'd tried to scare Alex by telling him all about it.

"Is not," said Jo-Jo.

"Is so," Alex answered.

"Well, there's this book in my sister's room," said a smallish ten-year-old named Althea. "One day I sneaked in there and looked, and it had spells and incantations and stuff, and there was one spell for bringing vampires to life. I saw it."

"You're just making that up," said Jo-Jo. "You just think you're so smart."

"Am not." Althea was indignant.

"You are so." Jo-Jo did a don't-be-ridiculous sniffle.

"You know that old house at the end of Pine Street?" Alex looked around to see if any grown-ups were nearby, listening. Everyone knew the old house. The game was to run up to the steps, toss a rock at the door, or, if you were really brave, at one of the windows, and then run away down the street as fast as you could. "Well, it's haunted." Alex said it as a matter of fact, the same way he'd say that his sandwich had tuna fish.

"He's just making that up. Alex, you're full of it."

"There could be a vampire there," said Althea. "It's the kind of house that a vampire would like to live in."

"You mean the kind of house he'd like to haunt," said Alex. He tried to make his voice sound scary.

"You guys are such corndogs!" Jo-Jo picked at a scab on his elbow. "There's nothing there but some junky furniture and a whole bunch of dust."

"Here's what we'll do." Alex's eyes got big. "Althea, you get that book and we'll go down to that old house and we'll bring the vampire to life. Then we'll take his picture."

"I don't think you can take a picture of a vampire," said Carl Brown, one of the older boys of the group.

"That's looking in a mirror," said Alex. "You can't see a vampire in a mirror. They didn't have cameras back in the vampire days."

"Well, I'll bet you can't take his picture either."

"Never mind that," said Jo-Jo. "If there really is a vampire and you bring it back to life, what are you going to do with it afterwards? I don't want no vampires running around my neighborhood!"

"You think you're so smart, Jo-Jo." Alex spat on the ground. "There's probably spells to make it go away. Right, Althea?"

Althea nodded. At least she thought there were banishing spells in that book.

Now Alex was waving his arms around, excited to be planning this adventure. "On Halloween night after trick-or-treating, we'll go up to the old house. You get the book. I'll sneak into my parents' bedroom and take my dad's camera. And we'll get a picture of the vampire."

"But that's stealing," said Jo-Jo.

"Not if I bring it right back," said Alex.

"You're gonna need money for film and developing."

"We can shake down some nerds for their lunch money."

"You're going to get a licking if you do that again."

"We'll just make sure that the nerds don't tell on us." Alex made a fist with his right hand.

"My dad's a cop," said Carl, "and if I did anything like that, I'd be stuck in my room until hell froze over. I ain't going."

Suddenly, with all the talk about stealing money, and lickings and punishment, the idea of stalking a vampire lost its appeal.

"I'm out," said Carl.

"Me too," said Jo-Jo.

"I'll go," said Althea. "I'm not scared."

"What about the rest of you? I double-dog dare you." Alex used his best argument, the double-dog dare.

"I ain't messing around with no vampire," said Jo-jo. The other kids kicked at the dirt with their sneakers and looked away.

"You're all a bunch of chickens," Alex yelled at the rest of the kids.

Then, the bell rang for class, and everyone scurried back inside. Alex could hardly contain his excitement. How many kids ever got the chance to see a real vampire!

After sunset on Halloween night, thousands of pirates, ghosts, pumpkins, and fairy princesses begged their parents to hurry up with dinner so that they could start trick-or-treating. The rising moon was three quarters full. But this year, Althea couldn't wait for trick or treating to be over, and, as soon as she'd half-filled her bag with candy, she exchanged her ballerina costume for jeans, a shirt, and a jacket— more practical attire for summoning vampires.

Pretending to be a grown up, Althea tiptoed up the splintering stairs of the house on Pine Street. She tried not to make creaking sounds, but it didn't work. The wood was old, and the stairs sounded like cackling poltergeists, especially with the wind rustling behind her through tree branches. The Victorian had once been the pride of the city. Now it was junk. Althea gulped and breathed a few deep breaths. "Okay, here goes nothing." She tossed her pigtails back over her shoulders and peeked through the window. It was hard to see. She wiped dirt and soot off the glass with a denim shirtsleeve, then again peered inside. By the light of a candle, she could see Alex, all but drowning in an oversized pair of Osh Koshes. She could just make out his ash-blond hair and freckles. Like Althea, he'd taken off his Halloween costume—a rubber mask and sheet—in preparation for the night's adventure.

Althea tugged on an old-fashioned bell-pull next to the front door. Three tugs, three reverberating bongs. Alex had gotten into the old house by climbing inside through a broken window, but Althea was scared of the jagged glass.

Alex turned, startled by sound in the stillness, then pulled open the front door.

"It's in the bag," Althea whispered and pointed to a brown-paper shopping-bag with a dusty, leather-bound book poking out of the top. "Just like I promised. And on page 166 there's a spell to banish demons, so we're all set."

Scrunched over like co-conspirators, they slunk into a dimly lit living room. Alex held back a sneeze; the room was dusty and smelled of earth and rotten cheese. All the furniture was covered with sheets except for one couch of cotton roses worn away to threadbare, and that's where Althea set down the sack. A puff of dust rose up from the fat pillows, and Alex sneezed and wrinkled up his nose.

"I brought a flashlight too," said Althea. From out of the bag, she pulled *Chesterville's Complete Book of Spells*. They looked at each other silently, held their breath, and then both gulped in unison, awed by the title.

Are you sure... he... he's here?" Althea asked out loud. She was suddenly unsure about the safety of the venture. After all, vampires were supposed to be evil. "Daddy would kill me if he found out what we were doing."

Alex looked around quickly. He put his finger to his lips, the universal sign of for-God's-sake-shut-up. "I'll get the rest of the stuff," he whispered.

Althea sat on the very edge of the couch, moaning and talking to herself. "We're going to die. He's going to kill us in some creepy way. He's going to stuff us into a wall and cement us up till we starve. He's going to roast us over the fireplace like spareribs. Or maybe, maybe it'll be even worse. Maybe he'll torture us with needles, then suck out our blood like in the Dracula story or something, and we'll have to haunt this spooky old house with... him... forever." Her eyes got wider and wider as she imagined more and more ways to die.

Alex pretended not to listen. He was anxious to get on with the vampire plan, and Althea was just being a stupid girl. "Okay, I got everything," he said. In the heavy stillness, Alex's whisper sounded like firecrackers. Althea jumped. Alex dumped a cardboard box onto the couch next to Althea's book. "Charcoal, five candles, matches, a needle to prick us for blood, all kinds of magic potions—Drano, Windex, some rat poison, Clorox, and I don't know what's in these three bottles. I got us a caldron, too. It's really just a plastic mixing bowl, but I painted it black so it looks like a caldron."

"I'm not pricking my finger with that thing. It looks germy."

"We'll hold it in the flame of a candle." Alex's freckles danced with excitement. He was determined to call up a vampire, and nothing was going to stand in his way. Althea was such a sissy, but what else could you expect from a girl!

"Can't we just read the incantation?"

"No, we have to do this the right way." Alex jabbed the needle into Althea's finger before she knew what he was doing, and let the blood drip into the caldron. Then he pricked his own finger and added a drop of his blood to the bowl.

"You didn't sterilize it. You said you would. I want to go home." Althea started to cry.

She thought of her mother and father living without her. Althea was such a brave child. That's what they'd say if they knew what she and Alex were up to. I never really understood. If only I'd told her how wonderful, how special, she was while... while she was still... still alive.

"Stop acting like a sissy. We have work to do," said Alex. He thought of slapping her like they did in the war movies, (Thanks, I needed that.) but he figured that she'd just cry harder if he did.

"I'm not a sissy," said Althea. She dried her eyes and examined the cauldron critically, to prove to Alex that she was really brave and not scared of vampires.

They arranged the candles in a circle around a stained Persian rug, and Alex put the plastic caldron in the center of the candles. Next, he dumped the various potions into the caldron until it was filled to the brim.

With two bleeding fingers, Alex lit the candles, then picked up the book of spells. Solemnly, he turned the pages till he got to page fifty-three, "Spells to call up the un-dead."

"Omina, omina, omina barbarosa," he chanted, and he made his voice as low and manly as he could. They held their breath as the magic evolved.

The children exchanged knowing looks. The spell was working. They could feel a presence in the air. A thick, greasy, gray cloud rose from the caldron, proof that the spell was working. Alex continued to recite: Omina leatra. Omina, omina, omina leatra."

A howling sound came from somewhere outside as the wind

picked up more strength, a forerunner to a hard storm. Smoke hung suspended inside the circle of candles.

"Hear that?" said Alex. "That's no ordinary wind. We did it. That's a demon, or vampire, or something. We did it! And that smoke!" Alex lowered the pitch of his voice. "That's, that's not normal smoke."

"Now put him back, quickly," Althea squeaked, chewing on her pigtails in a nervous snit. The wind's howling seemed to come through the walls and it rattled the windows like a banshee, making her nervous. Small branches were breaking off of trees accompanied by sharp, cracking sounds.

A large branch hit the side of the house with a thunk that made the walls shake. Alex jumped and Althea screamed. Forgetting all about the camera, Alex flipped through the book to page one hundred sixty-six. The instructions looked complicated. Alex frowned.

"Hurry up!" Althea whispered.

"Spells to Banish the Undead: Vampires, Ghoulies and Other Beasties of the Unseemly Court," Alex read the directions out loud, "Three spells shalt thou utter, each human present having spat upon his right palm; each human present having counted five score prior to each utterance."

"That means we have to spit in our hand and count to one hundred," said Althea.

"Shut up. I know that," said Alex.

"Well, hurry up." Althea wrinkled up her nose, stared at her right palm for a second, then spit into it. "Oh, yuck, this is really gross!"

They counted to one hundred. Meanwhile, the liquid in the caldron was bubbling and making spooky, gurgling sounds.

"Abradax barbarosa, abradax barbarosa, abradax barbarosa" said Alex.

Alex and Althea spat again and counted. Then Alex recited the words, "Morituri, moritatum, morituri, moritatum, morituri." The plastic caldron melted, spilling its contents onto the carpet.

"This is worse than chopping onions," Althea complained, coughing, and choking and crying as more smoke filled the room.

"There's a big, old, oily, smudged spot," he said, "I can't read the last spell." He moved the book next to one of the candles trying to get a bit more light. But he was more frightened than he would admit. Suddenly the adventure had lost its appeal. His hand shook and he knocked the candle over. The rug began to smolder. Now Alex and Althea were coughing so badly it was hard to breathe.

The rug caught fire at the edges. The howling, crashing sounds outside lulled. Then, as if on cue, they started up again, louder, and more sinister than before. Meanwhile, tiny flames shot up from the carpet. Althea ran to the kitchen sink, spitting and counting as she ran. It was an old-fashioned type of sink with a pump handle. She pulled on the handle, as hard as she could, over and over until finally brown, smelly water dripped from the spout. Still pumping with her right hand, she held her cupped left hand under the trickle to catch the precious water and ran back into the living room to pour it over the growing flames.

Alex moved the book around under the flickering candlelight, trying to make out the words on the oil-stained page.

"Don't stop now." said Althea. "There's only one spell left. You have to keep going." She covered her eyes with her shirt and coughed and ran to the kitchen for more water.

But the heat and smoke were too much for the kids. Now, crackling out of control, fire spread to the couch and some of the sheets. Flames the size of roasted turkeys played on the rug and furniture.

Alex ran out of the house followed by Althea who snatched up *Chesterville's Book of Spells* on her way out the door. "We can't leave a vampire running loose in the neighborhood," she yelled.

They huddled outside the house amid the stumps of rose trees, trying to shelter themselves from the wind. Lit up by the flames from inside, the night sky looked bright as daylight. Althea opened the book, and Alex snatched it out of her hands. "Here, let me finish." After spitting on the stained page and rubbing at the black goop, he managed to read, "condemnari condemnomen, condemnari condemnomen, condemnari."

The howling sounds kept up. "It's over," pronounced Alex. "The vampire is exercising."

"Huh?"

"It means he's gone."

"I think you mean exorcised." Althea was a stickler for details.

"Who cares? We're in a shitload of trouble," said Alex.

The children looked around. Flames crackled. Heat played warm then hot on their cheeks. In the distance, fire engines, drawing ever closer, sounded their sirens.

"If Daddy ever finds out about this, I'm toast," said Althea.

"I'm out of here," Alex yelled, and the two raced home on panicky feet.

As Alex approached his house, he saw a cop car parked in front of his house and figured that the cops were going to tell on him, and he was probably going to get whipped. The living room window was open just a crack with the curtains blowing like ghosts in front of the lighted room. Two men in police uniforms were standing next to the doorway. Alex tiptoed up to the window and listened.

"... A girl and a boy. From the firefighters' description, it sounds like the boy is Alex." One of the officers, Kevin McNamara, was an old friend of the family. He used to baby sit for Alex before joining the force, and he and Alex had played cops and robbers not too long ago, hiding behind the picket fences and elm trees, and shooting at each other with plastic rifles. But now Kevin was a real policeman. He'd come over to the house just two weeks before, and Alex had been fascinated by his true-life stories about catching bad guys. Alex had decided then and there that he wanted to be a cop when he grew up. He'd catch the meanest, worst, bad guys and throw them in jail, and then his dad would be proud of him.

"Well, Alex has been trick-or-treating all evening," said Mr. Lidecker. "He should be coming home soon. You're welcome to wait for him, but I'm telling you, this isn't the sort of thing Alex would be mixed up in. Still, if it turns out that Alex was involved, he'll get what's coming to him. You can count on it."

Get what's coming to him! Eyes wide, Alex couldn't believe his ears. This was no way to treat a hero who had just saved the whole world from a vampire or something. Sometimes grown-ups just don't understand anything.

Get what's coming to him? What did that mean? If the police were at his house, did that mean someone broke the law? Maybe there was a law about setting a house on fire, although technically, Alex hadn't started the fire. The candle did, and Alex had even tried to put it out. Or maybe that was Althea.

And all at once, a new terror hit Alex. If the police were here and asking for him, did that meant Alex was going to go to jail?

Jail! The word made him shiver. They'd send him to jail where a bunch of hairy guys with tattooed arms would beat him up every day and he'd have to eat stale bread and water. That was what his brother had said, and he knew because he'd been to jail. Now Alex was really scared. He was going to jail for sure, and that was AFTER his father got through with him. Alex shuddered.

"I'm very disappointed in you, Alex." That's what his father would say, and he'd give Alex the look. Then, they'd go down into the basement, and Alex would probably get a whipping. He'd been spanked many times before, but he'd never been whipped. His dad kept a buggy whip in the basement, and he'd threatened Alex with it the time Alex got caught shaking down nerds at school for their lunch money. Probably, starting a fire was worse than stealing lunch money.

The night was chilly, but Alex was shaking and sweating as if with a fever. Quietly, he picked up his trick-or-treating costume and *Chesterville's Complete Book of Spells,* and sneaked back into the shadows and down the street. He would have to run away from home. Too bad he hadn't thought to bring money or food or warm clothes with him, but how was he supposed to know that this would happen?

Alex ran to the woods at the edge of town and crouched down beside a half-dead oak tree next to Puddin' Creek to think. After his eyes adjusted to the dim light, he thumbed through *Chesterville's* looking for some spell that might get him out of trouble. Everything looked complicated, and everything required stuff like strange animal parts. After about a half an hour, Alex grew cold and scared—scared of the night sounds, of being alone, of not having his parents to take care of him. So he wasn't going to run away. He'd have to go home and face his father somehow, but how could he? There had to be some way out of this mess. He was desperate. He needed a plan, an alibi, an excuse. There had to be a way out of this mess.

Suddenly, Alex got the feeling that he wasn't alone. He looked behind him, peered through the tall grass, behind the oak tree, but, try as he might, he couldn't see anything. There was no shadow, no movement other than the wind blowing through the brush, yet Alex was positive that someone was with him. Ignoring the disturbing sensation, he thumbed through *Chesterville's Complete Book of Spells.*

Page three hundred forty-two caught Alex's attention. Lying Spells. He pulled the book closer. The script was old and hard to read in the dim light.

"Remordia—The Craft to Convince." Alex bit his lip and read farther. "The power to dupe, deceive, and mislead the multitude or the single listener. This spell bestows upon its master the power to invent reality and truth. No matter how preposterous the tale, the conjuror **will** be believed. The gift is yours for a price." And here the page was smudged, and, try as he might, Alex couldn't wipe the page clean, nor could he read through the stain. Only one word was legible at the bottom of the page. "Remordia."

"Remordia." Alex said it out loud. "Remordia, Remordia." The words rang out into the darkness like bullets. "Remordia. Remordia." Immediately he felt that something was different, as though his body were shrouded by a sense of foreboding and despair. A hopeless bog of dark fear all but consumed him, and he shook more from the strangeness than from the night chill. But almost immediately, the fear shriveled like plastic in a flame. There followed elation, wild and terrible. His clothing seemed to twitch with energy. The sensation was as if a vampire, or something akin to it, was halfway inside Alex's shirt. "Is that you, vampire? I'm not afraid of you. I'm a soldier. I'm not afraid of you. Remordia. Remordia, Remordia, Remordia." As he shouted the words, gone was the sense of dread, the feeling of impending doom. With a start he realized that he wasn't afraid of anything—of the strange buzzing in his head, or the tingling in his fingers, or the darkness and chill of the night, or his father, or getting into trouble with the police. Instead, Alex felt purposeful, confident. "Remordia," he shouted and laughed. "Remordia. He laughed louder. "Remordia."

The craft to convince! Holy smoke! So, no matter what he said he'd been doing, his father would believe him! It was as if a fog had lifted. Alex saw clearly what he had to do. He dressed himself back into the ghost mask and sheet and ran down to the creek and splashed in the water to wash off any smell of smoke. Next, he hid the Osh Koshes and shirt at Jo-Jo Vargas's house behind a shrub in the front yard. Then, blue and shivering, he ran home. Smarter than the rest of them, he thought, smiling through chattering teeth.

The police cars were still there when Alex limped through the front door. Looking wet and miserable, he held back the tears like a brave little man. "It was Jo-Jo Vargas and Althea Vennable." His teeth chattered as he spoke. "They jumped me from behind, and took my clothes, and threw me into the creek. I had a hard time scrambling up the bank in the dark, and I think I twisted my foot or something." Alex leaned against the wall, taking the weight off his left foot.

"You walked all that way with a sprained ankle!" His mother rushed to Alex's side and sat him down on the living room couch."

"Let me see that ankle, son." Alex's father carefully took off Alex's shoe and examined the foot. Alex took in a sharp breath. "Does that hurt, Son?"

"Just a little."

"It doesn't look swollen or anything. Just give it some rest, and we'll see if it's still sore in the morning. That's my brave soldier. I'm very proud of you, Alex." He turned to the police officers. "It's as I told you. Alex wouldn't be mixed up with anything like what you were describing."

"We'd still like to hear from the boy as to his whereabouts this evening between the hours of eight and ten o'clock." Kevin's partner was very official and very stern.

Mr. Lidecker looked at his son. "Now Alex, I want an honest answer from you and I want it now. This is a very serious matter. Tell me exactly what you were doing this evening."

For a flash of a second Alex considered telling his Dad exactly what had happened—the spells, the candles, the fire, the screeching, Althea's sister's book. He especially wanted to tell his father about the book. But the moment and impulse to confide passed very quickly. He looked his father square in the eye, searching the worried face for a clue. "I would never lie to you, Dad." He stood up and squared his shoulders. Like a young cadet standing at attention before his sergeant. "I was trick-or-treating with Althea, but then she and Jo-Jo took my clothes and threw me into Puddin' Creek, and I spent the rest of the evening climbing out of the creek and walking home."

"Did Althea and Jo-Jo say anything about where they were going?" asked one of the officers.

"They said something about the old house on Pine Street," said Alex.

Alex's father watched out the window as the police officers got into their squad car and drove off. "Stupid-ass cops!" he muttered, then turned to Alex. "We showed 'em, tonight. We showed those dumb asses a thing or two. I'm proud of you, son." It was the only time in his life that Alex had ever heard his father say those words.

# Chapter Thirteen

∞

Over the years, Alex practiced and refined his craft. His father was fascinated by the military, and Alex found that he could use that. He'd square his shoulders as if he were standing at attention, his blue eyes looking up in concentration. It made him appear determined, powerful. And the spray of freckles remained splashed across his nose, giving him the air of innocence.

At the end of Alex's junior year in high school, his father called him into his den to discuss college. The den was Mr. Lidecker's sanctuary. Maps. Charts, and paintings depicting famous military battles decorated all four walls. Alex entered the room sat down in a chair opposite his father.

"It's time to talk about your future, son." Mr. Lidecker paused and sucked on the tip of his pipe. You'll be applying to the universities next year. I've given it some thought, and I believe Yale would be an excellent choice."

"Yes, sir."

"Your grades are certainly respectable, and I know some people there. A word or two from your old man certainly won't hurt your chances."

"No, sir."

"So it's settled then."

"Yes, sir, I think I can learn a lot at Yale."

Mr. Lidecker sucked on his pipe, then looked up at the ceiling as if envisioning Alex's prosperous future. "Contacts, boy, it's all about contacts. At Yale you'll meet the families that run the nation. Make the right impressions on the right people, and you can do whatever you want with your life. You can do anything, and I do mean anything."

Alex smiled. The advice was true in ways his father couldn't imagine. "Yes, sir," he said.

<<<<<>>>>

Of course, Alex had visited Yale several times before his orientation as a freshman, but he was still awed by the sight of the campus and the promise that this would be his home for the next several years. Stone walls surrounded the campus like battlements around a medieval city. Tradition seemed steeped inside these very walls. Lofty was the best description of Yale, thought Alex, the pinnacle of the United States and of the world, both geographically, and socially.

Alex felt like he was coming into his own. Even as a freshman, he was sure of himself. He walked around the campus probing, examining, and evaluating what of the campus he wanted to claim as his possession.

<<<<<>>>>

Vivian Owens sat next to him in History IA and he decided early on that, before the year was over, she would belong to him. Chestnut hair, done in a sophisticated bob, a slim figure, shown off by remarkable clothing, Vivian was the ultimate girlfriend. Her wardrobe cried of good taste. She was someone who'd look good on his arm. "Good breeding will always tell," as Alex's father used to say.

Not only did Vivian exude taste and class, but she was also knockdown gorgeous. A girl who would look great on his arm, and a girl his father would approve of, Vivian was someone that Alex needed to cultivate. Not only that, but Vivian was also smart. More to the point, she was smart in history, and Alex was struggling with his history class. So he decided to make his move.

"You're Vivian." Alex was appealing, and he knew it. His blue eyes shone with boyish innocence, and freckles danced across the bridge of his nose. "There's a place a couple of blocks from here where they serve really good coffee. Can I invite you out for something to drink and conversation with a promising law student, namely me." He said it as a sentence, not a question, and, after the history lecture was over, they walked out of the classroom arm in arm.

Alex had picked out a homey, cozy café that resembled a lavishly furnished living room. As Vivian sank back into the fluffy pillows sipping a steaming cappuccino, Alex looked up into her eyes and cocked his head. "You really are a beautiful woman." He tapped his chin with his finger and blinked at Vivian.

She smiled, and looked down. "Do you always say that to your coffee partners?"

"Only the beautiful ones."

Vivian giggled. "Only the beautiful ones?"

Alex put a friendly hand on her arm. "And only the ones who are women."

"So you do have lots of beautiful female coffee partners!"

Their conversation was like a dance or, maybe more like a chess match, first one moved; then the other.

"I guess I should tell you," Vivian tossed her head coquettishly. She took a slow sip of her cappuccino, putting off telling him the all-important "it" for just a little longer. Finally, she looked up, and, with a dramatic sigh, she said, "I'm seeing someone. We dated our junior and senior years in high school. We wanted to get married after graduation, but decided to wait out my four years of college. His name is Richard."

"So where is this Richard right now?" Alex smiled and looked into Vivian's eyes. He searched for clues as to what she was thinking, but the clues weren't forthcoming.

"He's in Maine—Bar Harbor, Maine, running his father's business. He has a fleet of fishing boats, and, in the summer, he charters fishing expeditions to tourists. See, Richard loves the ocean. He's spent most of his life on boats, and I guess it's just become a part of who he is."

Did she hesitate? Did she expect more from this Richard? Like maybe a college diploma? And she was probably lonely here at Yale while Richard played sailor up north in Bar Harbor. Alex pondered. What to say next. It should be something subtle, maybe just a tad derisive.

"So…" Alex pinched his nose with his fingers. "Do you like fish?" They both laughed. "Well, do you?"

"Actually, after living in Maine all my life, I'm rather tired of the taste, although a good lobster is still one of the best ways to my heart."

"Then maybe it's time to try something new." Alex, ever so gently, took her hand in his.

"Maybe," she said. "Maybe. But can we be friends, at least for now, at least until I think all of this through."

"Friends." Alex took a sip of coffee. It gave him a few seconds to think, to plot. "Just friends, huh? Well, my frat house is having a kegger next Saturday. Is there anything in the friendship rules about you and me going to a party together—just as friends, I mean." Again, Alex said this as a statement and not as a question.

He was truly charming, and Vivian was feeling quite bored. Maine was a long way off, and Richard wasn't going to be able to get down to Yale more often than once a month. He probably wouldn't come down at all during tourist season.

"So what's it going to be," Alex asked smiling, "an evening of chemistry and history books, or a night out with a charming, fascinating… friend?"

She giggled. "Oh, sure, why not? I'd love to." She tore off a sheet of notepad paper and wrote her address and phone number on it.

<<<<>>>>

After he'd left Vivian, Alex considered his options. Waiting for her to decide to dump Richard was too uncertain and time-consuming. He needed faster results, and the word came into his mind unbidden. "Remordia." He said the word out loud, and immediately a plan formed in his head.

Back at the frat house he searched out the Weasel. Jeremy Scoggins got the name Weasel because of his ability to weasel out of trouble and to weasel into unlikely opportunities.

"Can you get me Spanish fly?" he asked the Weasel. "I needed it for next Saturday night."

"I'll get you something like it. It'll make her really groggy, and she probably won't remember anything. But it'll cost you." With a prominent nose and slicked-back black hair, the Weasel actually looked a bit like a weasel. He had long fingers, and, when he was talking business, he'd flex them and crack his knuckles. "I'm going to need the answers to Cavendish's last Tuesday's math test, along with a $230 procurement fee."

"How will last Tuesday's math test help anybody?"

"Bernard had the 'flu' last Tuesday, and he'll be making up the test next week."

"What if Cavendish gives Bernard a different test?"

"Cavendish is retiring after this year. He's not about to go to the trouble."

Alex went to bed that night wondering how he was going to get his hands on the math test, (maybe by bullying Cavendish's teaching assistant) and how he was going to get his hands on Vivian.

*In his dream, Alex found himself in an elementary school classroom sitting in a fourth-grade desk and being interviewed by a man with a three-foot pointer.*

*"It's time to develop your craft, now." The man twitched, weasel-like, as he spoke.*

*"I thought I was doing just fine. So thank you, but no thank you."*

*"You're doing fine as far as it goes, but you're only thinking in terms of the small picture. I have great plans for you, Alex, great plans." Like one of Scrooge's ghosts, the weasel-man took hold of Alex's foot and pulled until Alex was standing alone in a desert. Sand swirled in dust devils borne on the hot, dry air. Alex had the sensation of helplessness, like the feeling of being a very young child and being very lost.*

*"Are you hungry?" A disembodied, weasel-voice seemed to ask.*

*In his dream, Alex nodded.*

*"Will you pay my price?"*

*Hunger jabbed at his insides. Then the aroma of warm yeast caressed him, while a line of waiters filed by, each carrying a loaf of bread on a plain silver tray. The bread took on a fascination, a power like an opiate, far more than any bread he'd ever seen in his life.*

*"Will you do what it takes to get this bread? Will you pay its price?"*

*The Weasel-like man probed into Alex's chest, poking between his ribs with clawed fingers and removed, not Alex's heart, but a wedge of Swiss cheese. Weasel-like man took a bite. "Not bad," he said. "But not that great either. Sharp, with a bitter aftertaste. A little aging, some instruction by the proper master." Here Weasel-man laughed, threw the chunk into the air, and caught it in his needle-like teeth. As Weasel-man bore down, Alex felt the tiniest of twinges.*

*"Will you pay?"*

*But Alex shook his head. "No," he stammered, shivering and sweating at the same time.*

*Then Vivian walked in and sat before Alex, not naked, but wearing filmy, translucent clothing like silk scarves, with just a hint of cleavage showing above the bodice. Alex couldn't quite see her curves through the cloth, so he tried to picture them. (Her breasts—slim or ample? Probably ample.) He imagined her skin, soft, curved, with a faint scent of lavender. And, as he reached his hand forward to touch her, she pulled away.*

*Alex gazed longingly at Vivian, then slowly nodded. "I'll pay." The words gagged him, sticking like plaster in his throat. And as he reached his hand forward to claim his prize, he sensed a twinge, almost as if tiny teeth were nibbling at something inside of him.*

*Vivian, the waiters, the bread, the scarves, they all blurred, and the scene ran as paint on a canvas sprayed with turpentine.*

He stirred in his sleep, screaming "yes" over and over until he woke his roommate Mathew.

"Knock it off," said Mathew, throwing a rolled-up pair of socks at Alex's face. "That must have been some dream. How hot was she?"

Alex smiled, still half asleep. "There's no way I could begin to describe it."

Saturday night, Alex and Vivian walked into the fraternity house living room together, and it was obvious to Alex that every guy in the house was eyeing his girl. Vivian was beautiful, and not only was she kick-in-the-teeth gorgeous, but she was dressed up for something much more promising than "just friends." Her jeans were cut low on her hips to show a sliver of smooth, creamy belly, and above the jeans, a tightly fitting, royal-blue blouse exposed just a hint of cleavage. And when she turned or stooped, her breasts jiggled ever so slightly. The look was classy and teasing at the same time. It was all Alex could do to keep from reaching out and touching her breasts right then and there. But he had to be cool. Rude and crude wouldn't work where Vivian was concerned. "What's your pleasure, beer or punch?" he asked her.

"Punch, I think." She smiled up at him. All Alex could think about was her cleavage. He walked over to the punch bowl, set on a folding table in the far corner of the living room. With shaking hands, he doctored up the cup of punch he'd hastily poured and got a beer for himself—beer instead of punch, just to make sure that he didn't accidentally drink from the wrong cup.

For a few moments, he watched Vivian from across the room, chatting easily with three of his fraternity brothers. She was seated on a brown, leather sofa, and the young men stood around her. Vivian was so beautiful! Alex's feelings were wild, thundering animals stampeding across his heart. She was beautiful, sexy, and yet so innocent and trusting. He remembered the warmth on his shoulder when she'd rested her head there, and the scent of her shampoo. He wanted to protect her and make her smile. No girl had ever left him this confused.

He looked down at the cup of punch, and suddenly he was full of remorse, and his hand trembled hard. I'll have to play it straight, he thought and turned towards the kitchen to dump out the doctored punch.

But before Alex reached the kitchen, Vivian's laughter rang out clearly against the background of party chatter. "You're so bad! I'm shocked and scandalized." She giggled. Alex turned back and watched. She tossed her hair and dropped her eyes provocatively. Alex knew the gestures. He'd memorized them from their conversation over coffee. He had thought himself the only one who could win that toss. Alex turned and walked towards Vivian, with the punch cup steady in his right hand.

He could hardly contain himself, watching Vivian down the cup of punch and ask for more.

As Vivian's mind became fuzzier and fuzzier, Alex's grew clearer. Finally, Vivian was sufficiently drugged, and Alex carried her to his bedrooms upstairs and closed the door.

Gingerly, he removed her clothes and then stopped. She was so helpless in his arms, more a child than a woman. He'd planned the evening like a chess game, but he hadn't counted on feelings of tenderness blocking his moves. Gently, he stroked Vivian's cheek. It wasn't too late. He could still tuck her into bed and walk away. Or he could follow through with his plan. Remembering her laugh and the toss of her hair, Alex made his decision. He pushed aside the tender feelings—feelings of weakness, as his father would say. He ran his hand over her naked body, relishing the jolts of pleasure that he experienced at each new curve. He laid her on the bed and began to undress himself.

In fact, the sex was disappointing for Alex. Vivian was all but unconscious and, although her body was beautiful, her spirit, her essence, was absent, making the whole physical encounter mechanical. Still, a beautiful woman is a beautiful woman. Alex relished the sight of her nudity, the scent of her perfume, and, along with the perfume, the animal scent of her body. He snapped a dozen photos before enjoying her body, and, finally, drunk and sexually spent, Alex fell into a deep sleep.

The next morning Vivian woke up in a strange bed without any idea of how she had gotten there. Along with morning, came a blinding headache, a sense of nausea, and a general feeling of exhaustion. She looked around and found Alex stirring beside her.

"What was that all about?" Alex asked. He shook his head looking shocked.

"What do you mean?" Vivian stared at him quizzically.

"You spent the whole evening coming on to every man in the room, then hopped up on one of the couches and did a strip tease. At least you saved the last dance for me."

Shocked awake by his words, Vivian grabbed the sheets and tucked them tightly around herself instinctively. She heard the words but couldn't believe them. "The last dance?"

"Metaphorically speaking, I mean. You passed out in this bed."

"I couldn't. I wouldn't. It couldn't have happened. But what am I doing here?" She tried to stop the barrage of feelings, but her mind spun like a pinwheel, and a sick stomach told her that something had happened the night before, and that the safe, happy future she had expected had been erased by one horrible mistake. "The evening's fuzzy. I can't remember much about it."

"Suffice to say that you had a very good time last night, and so did Joseph, Weasel, and Barney."

"I've never done anything like this before. That punch must have been really strong or something. Oh my God, what's everyone going to think of me?"

"Well, I did take a few precautionary measures. When I noticed that you were, blitzed and… you know… acting different, I made the guys all promise to keep their mouths shut. I told them they'd have me to deal with if any stories about you started floating around campus. So no one has to know about the evening. I figure the less said, the better. Then you passed out, and my bed was the only place available, so that's where I set you down and tucked you in."

For a second, she wondered about something. Had she passed out in his bed or somewhere else? But it seemed ungrateful somehow to question his story over such an insignificant detail. "You did all that for me?" She leaned her head against his naked chest. His body felt strong, safe, protective.

"Sure. Friends have to stick together, you know." Alex reached for his bathrobe, threw it across his shoulders, and slipped a pair of shorts on under the robe. "But I wouldn't bring up the subject if I were you—in front of Barney, or Weasel, or Joseph, I mean. Best if they just forget all about it, and the sooner the better. I mean, we don't want any of them inadvertently slipping up and blabbing something."

"You're pretty amazing!"

"For a friend."

She thumbed the blankets for a while, frowning. "Did... did you and I... You didn't say anything about yourself. Did you and I, you know, make love?"

"You were pretty much out of it, and it wouldn't have been fair. Don't think I didn't want to. I wanted to very much. But friends don't screw over friends—in any sense of the word."

Vivian smiled up at him. Out of the panic, he was like a rock she could hold on to. Someone she could trust—someone strong enough and smart enough to take care of her. He'd fix the mess she'd made of the previous evening, and her future would again be safe, full of promise, and under control. She lay back down on the pillows and, for just a moment, made a mental of picture of Richard. He'd never understand.

From the bed Vivian looked around the room for her clothes and found them on the floor in a corner. She considered getting up and going home, then thought better of it and closed her eyes. Just a few more minutes lying here, she thought. Just a few more minutes then she'd get up, get dressed, and go back to her own place. If only the throbbing headache would go away, everything would be wonderful.

<<<<>>>>

From the telephone book's yellow pages, Alex compiled a list of charter fishing boats and fishing fleets that were berthed in Bar Harbor, Maine. Numerous phone calls later, he found The Gully Wumper Fleet, owned by Oscar Cromwell and operated by Oscar's son, Richard. It was time to write Richard a letter.

*"Dear Mr. Cromwell,"* he wrote,

*"You don't know me, but your girlfriend Vivian goes to school at Yale, and I'm here to tell you that she's acting mighty friendly with a sizeable portion of the male student body. It's probably none of my business. I just figured if she were my girlfriend, I'd want to know about it. I've enclosed some Polaroid photos so you'll know I'm not just making this up."*

He didn't sign the letter. He addressed it to Richard Cromwell, c/o the Gully Wumper Fleet, and dropped it into the mailbox, and quickly.

Back in his room, Alex jotted down some ideas of what he'd say to Vivian after Richard dumped her. Would Richard mention the letter? If he did, Alex should just plead ignorance. "They all swore they'd keep their mouth shut! I'll see if I can find out who wrote the bloody letter. That son of a bitch will have me to deal with. I'll find out who blabbed, and, well, let's just say that'll be the last time he'll ever pull a stunt like that." He'd look concerned, purposeful. He'd use his little soldier look, eyes up to the heavens, and his brow slightly furrowed. That look had never failed him.

Alex knew he could tell Vivian anything and she'd believe him because she'd need something to believe in, and someone to believe in, especially if that someone could make it all be Richard's fault. "If your Richard ..." No, scratch that. "If this Richard is going to get off into a jealous rage because of some half-baked rumors and innuendoes, then, maybe, you're better off... No, I won't say it. Just know that I'll always be here for you no matter what." Alex practiced his speeches. He told the stories over and over to himself until he believed them to be true, and he could make a smooth and compassionate spiel. He had to look sincere. Careful planning, that was the ticket—that and actually believing the story. A little preparation, some thought for likely snags as well as likely opportunities, and, with Alex's innocent good looks and brains, all things were possible.

Alex had saved a couple of the photos as souvenirs of the evening. They showed Vivian, stark naked and kneeling in some especially subservient poses. He studied the pictures, using them for inspiration as he composed his comforting speech for the day when Richard should dump her.

Three days later, Vivian showed up at Alex's frat house. She had on a pair of jeans and a Yale sweatshirt, and her eyes were red. She tried a casual greeting, then broke into tears and stammers. "Somehow Richard found out. He found out about that, that stupid, miserable night. And, and he called me… he called me… horrible things. And he screamed at me. And… and…"

"He came down to see you?"

"No… No. Over the phone. He was yelling over the phone." Vivian sobbed and cried, and Alex tenderly pulled her close to him, letting her lean against his chest. "He just yelled and yelled. And he wouldn't even hear my side of the story. He wouldn't let me say anything. He called me a… a… he called me a whore. No one's ever called me a… a… I can't even say the word." She shuddered from the sobbing. Pain held her body captive and weeping into Alex's shirt.

"Oh, Alex, what on earth should I do?" Mostly she cried. And while the feelings cut through Vivian like a knife slicing through cheese, Alex found the sensation rather pleasant. As he comforted Vivian, he could touch, smell, and taste her pain. She was moist and trembling, and there was a faint, dank odor of tears, sweat, fear, and sadness. She cowered like a helpless animal, and, as he cradled her in his arms, Alex knew he'd won her, and he relished the feeling of power          that          it          gave          him.

# Chapter Fourteen

∞

In his senior year, Alex fell in love—wildly and completely—with petroleum and all its possibilities. Black gold, they called it, a smelly goo made up of partially decomposed dinosaur guts. But it was also exotic and all consuming; it sucked you in like a tar pit, or maybe more like cocaine. And it fed cars and fed on those who drove them. Big oil—source of power and ruler of empires—it owned the United States, and it owned the great military beast which was America's spawn.

Alex and Vivian were still going together, and on a scale of one to ten, his feelings for Vivian rated a nine and a half, while his passion for petroleum ran into the hundreds.

Stretched out on a couch in the commons room, scotch and soda in hand, Alex flipped through career magazines and brochures, puzzled, looking for a way into the industry.

"Remordia." He said the word out loud. It was the first time he had used the word in years, the first time since he'd caused the break up between Vivian and Richard. (Actually, Alex would have said that he'd only helped it along—sped up the inevitable.)

Just a silly superstition, he thought to himself. Suddenly his head roared, swimming with power plays and plots. He saw himself juggling thousands of scenarios. Alex had never been this drunk on scotch, but his mind had never been sharper or his thinking, clearer. Petroleum called for the riskiest of schemes and the skill to never get caught. Consequences were for others—for fools, weaklings, inferiors. Alex, like a cat, always landed on his feet.

Oil, or at least its future, lay in the Middle East, the Holy lands, and their unholy passions and economics. Arabia—land of insurrections, disasters, and poverty.

The roaring in his head dropped to a pleasant buzz. He had to own a fancy-boy United States president, he realized, one whom he could manipulate like a puppet. And Alex understood that his career path was to begin in the CIA.

And, for the image he needed, Alex should be married.

<<<<>>>>

Vivian's best friend Jocelyn had invited her to spend the weekend after graduation with her in Providence, but, right before they were to leave, Jocelyn called complaining of stomach cramps. "There's no way I'm leaving my bed for anything except hot soup," she said. And, no sooner had Vivian hung up the receiver, than Alex showed up at her door.

"Can you believe it, Alex, she totally stood me up! Two minutes before she was supposed to get here, she calls and tells me she's sick. She could have at least warned me. My bag's all packed, and I have no place to go." Vivian lit up a cigarette and puffed in exasperation. "And she didn't even sound all that sick."

Alex tapped his chin with his finger. "So your weekend's free?" He smiled at her and, with his hand at the small of her back, he picked up Vivian's suitcase and steered her towards his car. "I can fix that," he said. "Let's go find some fun." He stowed her bag in the trunk of his Mercedes convertible next to the ones he'd packed earlier with his own clothes. The top was already down as Vivian, still huffing, got into the passenger seat.

"Where are we going?" she asked. "Exams were brutal, and I really need some pampering."

"Trust me," he said and turned up the radio. Soon they were singing along with the Beatles as he eased onto interstate 95. They sang and laughed, and Vivian brushed the hair out of her face. "Slow down, Alex," Vivian said, but he didn't.

"Look in the back seat," he said, "inside that cowhide briefcase." She looked and found a bottle of champagne lying on a bed of crushed ice. A plastic baggie held two plastic fluted champagne glasses.

"Have I been set up or do you always carry champagne in your briefcase?" she asked, but Alex didn't say anything. "Very nice champagne, I might add." Vivian read the label while carefully dumping the crushed ice out of the briefcase and onto the road. "Dom Perignon, very nice indeed." She popped the cork, and the two drank champagne and sang along with the radio. You still haven't told me where we're going."

Alex took another sip. "You're right, I haven't." He laughed with gusto, and gunned the engine faster.

At Kennedy airport, Alex pulled up to the valet parking area. Waving a fifty-dollar bill in the air, he signaled for a skycap. "Air France," he told the young man who had swung their suitcases onto a metal cart.

"Air France! You're crazy, Alex. I can't fly to France. I don't have a passport." Alex handed her a small brown bag. Inside, she found a paperback book, a small box of Belgian chocolates, a crossword puzzle magazine, and a passport.

"Oh, Alex, it's my passport with my photo. How did you manage?"

Alex shrugged. "I have my ways."

"Where are you taking me? I have to tell my parents where I'm going," she giggled. From the pocket of his jacket, Alex pulled out a slip of paper and handed it to her. "L'Hotel Republique, Les Halles 7-9, Rue Pierre Chausson, Paris, France.

"Oh, my gosh." She put her hands up against her flushed cheeks and whooped in unadulterated delight. "I've never been to Paris. I've never been outside of the United States."

They flew first class. Midway over the Atlantic Ocean, the stewardess presented Vivian with a stuffed panda bear wearing a pair of wire-rimmed glasses and a Yale sweatshirt.

"For my sweetheart, a Yalie with plenty of class. I love you, Alex." The note was taped to the bear's paw, and Vivian cuddled the bear next to her face.

That night they ate dinner in a lovers' hideaway overlooking the Seine River. They drank champagne, and feasted on lobster, and crusty French bread, and green beans so fresh they snapped. A tapered candle cast dancing shadows on the linen tablecloth and a strolling musician played *pas sans Toi* on his violin. And at the end of it all, as a waiter spooned flaming rum sauce over steamy fruit-filled crepes, Alex handed Vivian a small box. He didn't get down on one knee and he didn't ask her to marry him. As Vivian undid the ribbon and slowly opened the box, Alex came up behind her and kissed her neck, his lips lingering on her skin, tasting her essence. "You're going to make the most beautiful bride in history," he told her, while Vivian, scarcely believing what was happening, pulled out a two-carat engagement ring and fitted it on the fourth finger of her left hand.

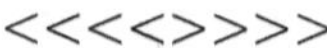

With a lopsided grin that stopped just short of an arrogant smirk, Alex breezed his way into the CIA. He was just what the agency looked for. The gift of gab, a touch of blarney, whatever you called it, Alex had it—a way of persuading people to do what he wanted. It seemed that Alex could talk anyone out of anything—a most desirable trait for a CIA operative.

His talent for persuasion worked inside the agency as well. After his first two years with the CIA, Alex managed to get whatever assignments he wanted—Geneva, Amsterdam, Florence. He'd seen so much of Europe that he may as well have been born there. And he usually managed to take an aide with him on assignment—generally a female aide with a body to stop traffic. But Alex never forgot his true love, petroleum. Most of the assignments he volunteered for focused on the Middle East.

# Chapter Fifteen

∞

As her nails dried Vivian lay back on a black leather recliner surrounded by brochures describing luxury cruises. If brochures had voices, these would be singing Calypso. Over the years their marriage had slipped into the doldrums. It seemed as if Alex was always leaving on some exotic assignment, but he and Vivian hadn't taken a vacation together in ages. She wondered if there was enough money in their savings for a two-week trip to somewhere with air conditioning and unlimited Mai Tai cocktails. Vivian had an allowance for household necessities, but Alex jealously kept track of their savings.

The jangling ring of the telephone interrupted Vivian's day dreaming. "Hey, luv, it's me. I need a favor." Alex hoped Vivian wasn't going to make a fuss. "I'm leaving for Afghanistan. Pack some clothes for me, will you?"

It was all too abrupt. Vivian felt cold and prickly. Seventeen years with the agency, and he was still getting yanked around like a yoyo. "Just like that? You want me to pack your clothing and send you out the door. It seems like you just got back, and now you're off again."

"Have to. I'm leaving Friday. For Afghanistan."

"Are you sure that's where you're going? You were just down there." She didn't mean to accuse him of anything. The words and the judgmental tone slipped out unbidden.

"Vivian, please try to understand. It's for our country, the U. S. of A. This is more than just a job, you know. It's my duty. I guess being patriotic is kind of passé these days, but I believe in this country. I have to go to Afghanistan, and that's what I'm going to do.”

“Don't I get a say in this matter? Aren't we even going to talk about this?”

“Vivian, I don't have time to argue. Just pack me up a couple of suitcases, will you. Set me up with the works.”

“How long this time?” Vivian knew she had to obey him. And she knew she could trust Alex. He was the epitome of honor. But still, she had the funniest feeling. Paranoid, that's what I am, she thought.

“Two months.”

“Will I be able to talk to you this time?”

Alex shook his head even though Vivian couldn't see him. “Probably not. I'll call you if I get a chance, but this is all top security.”

There was no sound on the other end.

“Are you sorry you married a spy?” He pouted. Of course, Vivian couldn't see it, but she might hear it in his voice.

She did, as a matter of fact, wish that he had a different job, but she couldn't tell Alex that. “Is a dangerous?”

Alex paused, and counted to three. He made his voice more intense, shooting the words out like cannon balls. “No, of course not. You don't have to worry about me.”

It worked. Vivian was worried. She began to cry. To keep Alex from hearing her crying, she held the phone away from her face. She shouldn't make him feel any worse than he probably already felt.

“And I'll have a surprise for you when I come back. Promise.”

Vivian melted. “Oh Alex, you're just amazing! Of course, you have to go. I'm just an old wimp wife. Can you forgive me for making such a fuss? And don't worry about a thing. I'll have you packed and ready with plenty of time to spare.”

He really did have to go to Afghanistan, and he'd leave right after the three-week vacation he had planned in Tuscany with Jennifer, his aide. Pleasure before business, he always said.

<<<<>>>>

Kandahar in the late 1990s was a city recovering from the ravages of war, and you had to look hard to find its charm. Abandoned buildings were common. The country was poor, the Taliban regime was oppressive, and living through coups, revolutions, and lesser military actions made the people nervous.

It was a mistake, Alex decided, a really colossal blunder, to have spent three weeks with Jennifer before his stint in Afghanistan. Better he should have spent an evening with Vivian's grandmother discussing her constipation. At least he'd have been prepared.

As Alex saw it, Kandahar was an oversized sand dune surrounded by oceans of... more sand. Like the deadly desert in some children's story. Pale yellow dirt—khaki, puce, whatever—it went on and on.

Somehow all the women had disappeared, and there were only men. That was all Alex saw. Nothing but men. The occasional swish of a burqa, a walking mountain of fabric with an eye-level slit, was a monumental female sighting, for under that fabric was a woman—maybe twenty, maybe sixty. Maybe missing teeth or sprouting a beard, but at least she was female.

Alex was sitting in the market place like a tourist—taking photos, slapping at flies, writing notes on a lined yellow pad with curled up edges, and trying not to die of boredom. The bazaar bustled with shoppers examining tempting piles of fruit. Melons, pomegranates, and apricots perched high on bright, orange splashes of cloth. And in the air, you could smell the spice —cardamom, coriander, saffron— mysterious exotic scents that conjured up adventure and romance. But Alex could see nothing worth spitting on.

The United States had planned to build pipelines across Afghanistan, but all of that was on hold because of the Jihad against the United States. Alex was hoping to uncover something—anything—that could be used to improve America's bargaining position, and he'd planted many listening devices, but, so far, he'd discovered nothing of value.

As far as Alex was concerned, the United States should get out, let the Soviets re-take Afghanistan, and then bargain with them for the pipeline. Afghanistan was as miserable a place as Alex had ever seen. The country had to hold some kind of record for coups and assassinations. And, as for entertainment, if you didn't like praying, there wasn't much to do on a Saturday night.

In the dusty air, Alex's thoughts turned to Jennifer. He began to doodle in the bottom left-hand corner of his notepad. He tried to get a mental picture of Jennifer's breasts. Ample—soft and ample, the centers dark, almost the color of chocolate pudding, with nipples that popped straight up like twin soldiers. He tried drawing her breasts, but they ended up looking like fried eggs.

A group of four turbaned figures were approaching, and Alex quickly flipped the page over on his tablet. In this country, his thoughts of Jennifer were illegal, so he pretended to examine a display of coffee. Pictures such as he had been drawing were probably punishable by a flogging in this sand pile. In fact, almost anything having to do with women was illegal in Afghanistan.

Three black-clad figures followed behind the men in turbans. They looked something like characters out of "Star Wars"—like desert spies cloned by the evil Empire. But, of course, they were women wearing the concealing garments required for Afghani women in a public place. Alex immediately raised his head to stare. The smallest of the women had huge black eyes—the largest eyes Alex had ever seen. Instead of a burqa, she wore a niqab, consisting of a black tent-like garb which enveloped her body from the shoulders down, and a scarf which concealing her hair and face. Only her eyes were exposed—huge, mysterious, black eyes. He stared intently, trying to picture the rest of the face hidden behind the folds of her black scarf.

And then he did it. He couldn't help himself. He'd simply gone too long without any fun. As the women walked by, almost as a reflex, he reached up and jerked the head scarf from the smallest woman's head. She shrieked and grabbed for the scarf, which Alex allowed to drop to the ground. Blushing, she tried to hide her face in her hands. The other two women huddled around her as she repositioned the clothing. They spoke in Arabic, their voices high pitched and angry. The words, bare-faced, muttered in the same tone as an American woman might say, bare-assed, were all that Alex could understand.

Then the women hurried along, half running, half jogging, and Alex, chuckling, followed them with his eyes. They'd disappeared from sight, and Alex was savoring the memory of the women clucking like chickens, when he felt an insistent tug at his sleeve. "Mister want girls?" The voice cracked with puberty, and Alex almost laughed aloud. This was a boy, twelve years old, fourteen at the very oldest. He stood less than five feet tall, and eight whiskers poked out from his chin. "Come with me tonight, mister. I show you some girls."

Alex turned back to the coffee, waiting until the other men had moved farther on.

"Seventy denarii, mister. You must meet me right here at eight o'clock tonight, and I take you."

Alex nodded the barest of nods. And the young boy grinned, an alarmingly wicked grin. Maybe the country had possibilities after all.

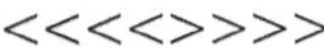

That night Alex arrived at the appointed spot full of hope. It was unusual for Afghanis to exploit their women. But the country was poor. And if a family were poor enough, if a man couldn't provide for his family in any other way, perhaps he'd be willing to sell his daughters' services.

Right on time, the boy pulled up alongside Alex in a dusty dun-colored truck. Alex got inside, and the boy engaged the clutch. His feet barely reached the pedals. He drove to the south and stopped the truck a couple of miles outside of the city where the road abruptly ended. "Come with me, mister," he said. Then he jumped from the cab and motioned for Alex to follow.

The moon was full and already visible even though the sky was still light. The boy trotted at a good pace, and Alex followed.

"What's your name?" Alex asked.

"Ahmed," the boy said. "What yours?"

Alex smiled. "Mister," he answered.

Then the boy turned and scrambled along a rocky path leading out into nowhere. "You follow me, mister," he said. After a quarter of a mile, Ahmed halted abruptly. "Seventy denarii, mister."

"Half now, and half after I see your girls," said Alex.

The boy grinned broadly. "Half now; half later," he said.

The sky grew dark, but a blazing moon lit up the landscape. They walked on for another hour, Ahmed scampering like a small goat, and Alex struggling with the rocks in the darkness, and wishing for a flashlight each time that he stumbled. The evening's adventure lost some of its charm as Alex realized that he had no idea where he was.

"We are here, mister," said Ahmed indicating a small hut, or maybe a tent, huddled in the shadows of a rocky bluff.

The air was still. There was nothing and no one around him except for the boy and the one dwelling. He listened for sounds and there were none, save for a lone insect chirping a nocturnal mating call. The stillness was comforting after the heat and jostling of the afternoon, but it was eerie to be so far away from friends and colleagues.

"Remove your shoes, mister," said Ahmed. He shouted something Alex couldn't understand, took off his sandals, and walked inside.

Alex bent to remove his sandals, then followed Ahmed. Inside was dark compared to the moonlit sands. As he opened his eyes wide trying to adjust his vision, he felt a sharp blade curve around his neck and hands grabbing his arms and searching him for weapons. Alex was thrown to the floor, and his hands and feet bound tightly with hemp.

When he could no longer move, small fingers fumbled through his pockets searching for coins. "Seventy denarii, mister," said Ahmed's voice. "Thank you, mister. I will keep the change."

Next, a turbaned figure approached Alex. He scowled menacingly, and in his right hand, he brandished a riding crop.

Fighting his panic, Alex stared at the Arab figure. "Do you know who I am?" Alex shouted. The man merely grinned. "I am Alexander Lidecker. I am an American citizen, and if you don't release me immediately, I'll report you to the United States consulate." Now the man chuckled. "And you'll spend the rest of your natural life in a filthy jail cell," Alex added defiantly.

The man finally spoke. "Do you know who I am?"

"No" Alex answered.

"Good," said the man raising his whip.

Alex had never experienced such intense pain before. He knew that he should take the beating silently, that any screaming would be considered shameful, but he didn't care. He screamed; he begged; he cried; and in his pleading, over and over, he said the word, "Remordia." And each time he said the word, a long howl broke from his throat, primitive, like the moaning of a terrified, dying animal. And Alex was terrified. With the word came a sense of foreboding that chilled him through to his soul.

Finally, the beating was over. The man spit in Alex's face. "In the market today—you thought to amuse yourself. You pulled a woman's head scarf from her face. You made her to be seen bare faced in the market. In the streets, she was bare faced. Bare faced! You brought shame on her husband, and on her father, and on her brothers. You brought shame to her whole family." He spit on Alex once more. Then, still bound tightly, Alex was loaded onto the back of a camel, taken to where Ahmed had parked the truck, and driven to a spot about a mile outside of Kandahar and dumped onto the ground.

"You should be left to die," said the man. Then he laughed, and threw a pocket knife to Alex. He gunned the engine, and the spinning wheels sprayed Alex with a stinging shower of sand as the truck pulled away in the moonlight.

'Damn the CIA and damn this fuckin' country!" Alex mumbled under his breath as he tried to work the knife with bound hands. It took Alex about an hour to cut through his ropes, and it took him most of the night to limp back to Kandahar and to find his way back to his hotel.

By morning, Alex's back and neck were stiff, and his hands and ankles were chaffed and bleeding where the rope had dug into his skin. For the first time in his adult life, Alex had gone through a whole night without thinking about women.

He'd learned all he could from the CIA. Fucking, stinking country; fucking, stinking job, thought Alex. He needed to talk to the Weasel. It was time for a career change.

# Chapter Sixteen

∞

Alex arrived at Kennedy Airport at 8:46 in the morning, and Vivian met him at the gate. She wore a pink silk sheath that clung to her curves. The neckline was cut low and plunging, revealing a little bit of her breasts. Alex had always been a sucker for cleavage. She flung her arms around his shoulders. "Did you miss me?" she whispered brushing her lips against his neck.

"More than you know," he said, "but I'm tired right now. I just want to sleep for about three hours, and then I'll show you just how much I missed you." Most of the wounds from his beating had healed, but Alex was still sore, and some scars and bruising remained on his arms and back.

Vivian swallowed and smiled. "Of course, dear. I wasn't thinking."

Alex slept until noon. Vivian brought him coffee, eggs, and bacon in bed, and afterwards they made love. She was eager, and she smelled of damp skin and lavender. After the long absence, she was almost as exciting as Jennifer.

"Did you say you have a surprise for me?" Vivian wrapped her arms around Alex and nuzzled his neck playfully. She had been quite bored for the past two months and was ready for some excitement.

"I did mention something about a surprise." Alex smiled. "How would you like to stay in a genuine mansion? A friend of mine just bought it, and we're invited over there any time I can get away. And the agency owes me the time. So how would you like to be wined, and dined, and pampered, and spend about a week or two being just plain spoiled rotten?"

"Oh, Alex, it sounds wonderful. Who's the friend?"

"Jeremy Scoggins."

She remembered—that horrible day back in college! All the shame from years ago returned, and punched her, and made her feel small, helpless, like a bug in a spider's web. She stared at Alex, mute, defeated.

Alex didn't understand. "Say something. Don't you like my surprise?"

Vivian summoned up all her strength. She had a way of wrinkling her eyes when she didn't like what she was hearing. "You mean the Weasel?"

"He and I go way back," said Alex.

"And he's one of the guys who… raped me in college."

"Hey, Viv, he's grown up a lot since then. He's really matured."

"But, Alex, remember, he… he… slept with me," she whispered. That whole awful memory hadn't gone away. It all but suffocated her—the night that she couldn't remember, the shame and dread when Alex had told Vivian how she had slept with three of his friends. And then, just when it looked like the night was going to bury itself, the horrible phone call from Richard. The sense of hopelessness came back as if it had all happened yesterday instead of years and years ago. Alex had been so sensitive back then, so thoughtful, and now he expected her to go and spend a week with probably her worst enemy. What was he thinking?

Oh, Christ, thought Alex. He should be taking Jennifer to Weasel's pad, not Vivian. It wasn't like him to screw up like that. But he really wanted to see Weasel. Somehow, Weasel had found a way to make a lot of money, and Alex needed to find out how he did it. Vivian was just going to have to live with it.

Remordia. The word danced in his throat. And then the words came out smooth as butter on a corn cob. "And just whose fault is that? After the way you were waving your butt around that night it's a wonder that only three men slept with you. God, Viv, after two months in Afghanistan, I need a little R & R. That country's brutal. You don't know the half of it."

His words caught Vivian short. "Please, Alex, I don't want to go. Can't you just go by yourself, or something?"

Alex considered the idea. Go by himself and have Jennifer meet him at the Weasel's. But she'd used up all her vacation on the trip to

Tuscany and wouldn't be able to get away. A vacation at Weasel's pleasure palace just wasn't going to be the same without a woman. "Oh, that's going to look great! Like we're planning to split up or something." Under his breath, Alex whispered, "Remordia" again. "Wait a minute. Did you think the Weasel was a part of that rowdy trio the night of the fraternity party?"

"I'm talking about the night when I passed out, and three of your friends took advantage of me. You said he was one of the guys."

"You must have heard me wrong. Let's see. There was Barney, and Joseph, and, oh, that skinny redhead with pimples. We called him 'Scar Face.' What was his name? Milton? Myron?"

"I don't care what his name was. You said Weasel was one of the guys. I'm sure of it."

"Maybe you slept with him some other night? You were a pretty hot dish back at Yale."

Somehow, she was backed into a corner. "How could you even think that?" Why was she defending herself? And why, after all those years, was the shame and terror of that night still so strong?

"You're the one who keeps insisting that you slept with him."

"Well I didn't, unless he was one of the three guys who raped me that time I got drunk."

"Raped? Pretty strong words. You're sure there weren't any other wild nights in the hay?"

"Of course not." Vivian shuddered with disgust.

"Anyway, if you did sleep with him, Weasel's had so many girlfriends, he probably won't even remember the night with you."

Somehow Alex always managed to win these arguments. Vivian couldn't see how he did it. But she had no strength left to argue. "All right, I'll go, but don't leave me alone in the same room with him."

"If you didn't sleep with him, you shouldn't have anything to worry about." Alex wrapped his arms around Vivian gently, protectively. She didn't want to spoil it by complaining.

In spite of Alex's reassurances, Vivian fidgeted during the first half of the flight to Panama. Old ghosts from that horrible college frat party kept nudging her, tightening her back and twisting her stomach. For some reason, her foot kept jiggling up and down, as if it had a mind of its own.

They flew first class, and two gin and tonics later, Vivian began to relax, and, by the time they neared their destination, Vivian's fears were replaced by the excitement of the adventure. As the plane circled its approach into Panama City, she was blown away by the raw magnificence. The ocean sparkled blue below the clouds, and, as the plane descended, tiny dots of green islands poked up through the surf. The islands grew larger and larger as the plane neared the earth until Vivian could make out the rocky peaks and palm trees, and ripples of sandy beaches.

After they'd landed, she turned to Alex wide-eyed. "Let's get a cab or something and go exploring out in the rain forest. Look. We can be waist deep in jungle in about ten minutes."

Alex frowned. "They'll be waiting for us."

"But no one's here yet. We won't stay long. Just a few minutes. Please." Vivian pulled on his hand. Alex shrugged, grinned, and raised his arm to hail a waiting cab.

They bounced along in a fifteen-year-old pea-green Plymouth for no more than fifteen minutes before coming to a path angling off the main road. It was barely wide enough for a feral pig to lumber through, but Vivian squeaked with pleasure, and, while the driver waited, Vivian and Alex got out and waded through the greenery. The effect was primordial. Vines with leaves as large as Vivian's face crawled over everything—trees, rocks, bushes. Caws and chirps, unfamiliar to Vivian's ears, and perfume from exotic flowers hung in the mist. Forgetting her apprehension, Vivian drank in the sensations. The light, drizzling rain was warm, refreshing. Somehow, the air renewed her spirits, as if she were Eve entering Eden for the first time.

But all too soon, they headed back to the airport where Weasel's chauffeur was to meet them. The chauffeur turned out to be a helicopter pilot. His eyes sparkled and his face smiled. "Come with me please," he beckoned, his voice rich and lazy, as if enjoying a joke no one else understood.

They boarded Weasel's private helicopter for the final leg of their trip to the estate. It turned out that the Weasel had bought an unnamed island off the coast of Panama, and had built a 30,000 square foot mansion on the western end of it.

Weasel greeted them at the front door. Tanned and muscular, he looked as if he'd quit aging sometime in his twenties. He wore a

Speedo swimsuit, with a towel draped over one shoulder and a bikini-clad girl draped over his other one. "Meet Stephanie," he said and smiled, lightly punching Alex's arm, then embracing Vivian like a significant friend or longtime paramour.

He ushered them through the house and onto a veranda—a sumptuous expanse of cushioned rattan seats, lava rocks, and potted native trees bearing dark red orchids. Below them, a series of swimming pools lay in a semi-circle like pale-blue jewels, with waterfalls cascading from one pool to the next. To the right of the pools, an expanse of rain forest stretched across the horizon; to the left, there was only endless ocean.

"What are you two drinking?" Weasel asked. He called towards the house, and a manservant in khaki shorts and a tie-died shirt appeared as if materializing from the sound of Weasel's voice.

They settled on mimosas, and the manservant disappeared and reappeared almost instantaneously with a bar cart.

Vivian sipped and looked around herself with the wonder of a child in Disneyland.

It took Alex and the Weasel little effort to persuade Vivian to try out the pools with Stephanie. "Have fun. Take your time," Weasel said and winked. "Alex and I'll be inside when you're done swimming."

The Weasel gave Alex a quick tour through the house. "I've always wanted a mansion, and now I have one." Each room had a fireplace. A roaring fire burned in several of the rooms, and the snapping and hissing of the burning logs drowning out the sound of the air conditioner. They circled through bedroom, billiards room, dining room, theater, library, and several rooms that had no name or function. Finally, they ended up in the main living room, artfully furnished with copper-trimmed blue velvet couches and a coffee table and end tables all copper-trimmed and topped with cobalt-blue glass.

"So life's been good to you?" Alex leaned back against deep pillows.

"You have no idea." The Weasel sipped his mimosa. "I work for some of the largest businesses in the country, and their profits are through the roof. My partners are most appreciative of my creative business acumen. This little cottage…" And here he gestured at the walls around him. "All 34,978 square feet of it, sitting on 386 acres—

I bought it with my bonus, a thank you for a job well done. I set up some trusts, partnerships, and subsidiary arrangements that will make my partners even richer than they were before." Weasel set his glass down on the coffee table."

"That's actually why I invited you out here. I have a business proposition for you; it should be to our mutual advantage. I'll introduce you to my partners. They're going to need a few favors and it's going to be your job to deliver them. You know, Alex, my partners are VERY appreciative."

And Alex and the Weasel did the goalpost dance, shouting in expected triumph, but Alex just had to say it: "I don't see myself able to deliver any of the kind of favors you're implying, certainly not anything to warrant a mansion on a private island."

"Oh, you'll be able to deliver much more than a mansion's worth of favors. You'll be saving our friends many billions of dollars. In fact, Alex, old boy, if all goes according to plan, you'll eventually have yourself a job in the White House."

Weasel led Alex into his den, a chrome, glass, and rattan-furnished man-cave the size of Alex's living room. "My retreat from the hustle and bustle," he said, gesturing around the room. He laughed wickedly and handed Alex a two-foot stack of papers. "Some reading material. By the way, you have a meeting with my partners scheduled for Thursday, three weeks from tomorrow."

Vivian shrieked like a teenager at the sight of their bedroom. "This is amazing! Alex. I can't believe we're going to sleep in here."

Alex just smiled, knowing that Weasel had dubbed this his "play room." The wall opposite the door had a solid floor-to-ceiling mirror on either side of a black-marble fireplace. The wall on the right was mostly covered by cherry-wood paneling hiding a wet bar and, on the left, stood the room's crowning glory, an entertainment center with television, stereo, and two cupboards with oh, so many drawers, and cubbyholes.

"I've got to see what's inside these," said Vivian opening up one of the cupboard doors. "Oh, Alex, look at all this stuff! She pulled out magazines—Playboy, Penthouse, and a whole slew she hadn't ever heard of. And she found video tapes—everything from romantic movies to hard porn. Vivian picked out one with a harem scene on the front. "Let's play this one for laughs," she said, and tossed it to Alex. Inside another cupboard, Vivian found neatly folded lingerie. A third one held a collection of toys: feathers, handcuffs, vibrators, some creams and lotions, a couple of small whips. "You'd think there'd be condoms in here!" said Vivian. "I wonder what's in the drawers. Oh, Alex, is this cocaine? I've never tried sex with cocaine."

Alex smiled. "You're safe with me," he said. He inserted the tape into the player. Then, as Vivian snuggled up next to him, he pushed the button to begin the evening's entertainment.

Afterwards Vivian slept, but Alex lay awake for a long time, and, when he finally drifted off, the dream overcame him immediately.


*It began in slow motion with Alex, dizzy and disoriented, standing next to a Weasel-man on the top of Harkness Tower back at Yale. "You," said the Weasel-man to Alex. "Look down!" The voice commanded, and Alex, obeyed. The Yale campus stretched out before him. The Weasel-man now stood by the main gate, hawking test answers, lecture notes, and other folders. "Friendships, loyalties, influence, and connections," he cried, "Accolades, awards, and gold-embossed parchments. All yours, yours for a price!"*

*Alex's body rose, supported on air, and his field of vision broadened revealing the entire city of New Haven, then the whole Eastern seaboard. "Yours," the voice sang. "All yours." Elation replaced the sense of vertigo as the scene below Alex stretched out farther and farther. Wall Street, Mt. Rushmore, Hollywood—even the White House—they all fit inside the boundary of his great, grand shadow. And all the while, dollar bills—drab green snowflakes—fell from the sky onto the earth below. People danced like puppets. "Yours," said the Weasel—man, "all yours." And he threw back his head and laughed. Starlets, reporters, and robot senators whirled and bowed. As bombs exploded above like Fourth of July fireworks, a miniature army goose-stepped before him—an army complete with airplanes, ships, and tanks.*

*"Will… you… pay… my… price?" Weasel-man's voice echoed up the stone walls of the tower.*

*Like a Colossus, Alex looked down upon the earth beneath him, his legs wide apart spanning the better part of the northern hemisphere. Mountains, oceans, and cities stretched out under his crotch, and billions of people darted about, living out their lives under him like wind-up toys, all part of a giant machine. Oil poured up from the earth. "Yours," the voice repeated, "All yours."*

*And Alex understood in a flash of feelings that went beyond words—it wasn't the luxuries he could buy that were important. Oh, they were nice and made life sweet. But it went far beyond that. Riches meant power, the ultimate thrill—higher, deeper, stronger than any drug. Power, to make him the most important man on earth. Everyone would look at him and bow. Even his father would be forced to humble himself to Alex. "Yes," said Alex. "Yes, oh, yes, yes, yes!"*

*The weasel's pointed finger poked through Alex's abdomen burning him as if with heartburn, but throughout his body. "Will... you... pay... my... price?"*

*"Yes, oh yes, yes, yes!"*

Alex woke himself with his own screaming. The thrill of the vision buzzed through and through him as though his blood were made of champagne.

"What is it, Alex!" Vivian was alarmed. "You were screaming in your sleep. Is something wrong? Were you dreaming?"

"You have no idea!"

<<<<>>>>

The next morning, Vivian woke thinking that she'd never slept like that in her whole life. "Will we ever be able to afford a place like this?" Vivian asked Alex. They were lying between satin sheets in a very large bed—larger than king size. She held his arm, and her fingernails dug slightly into his flesh. "Oh, will we, Alex? It would show the world that you've made something of yourself, that you're someone to take seriously."

That'll be the day, thought Alex. For some reason a vision of his father jumped into his head, a vision of his father nodding in approval. Yes, he thought, the day WILL come, and that WILL be the day.

"Four years, baby," he said out loud. "We'll have our own mansion in four years, and five years from now, we'll have the whole world.

# Chapter Seventeen

∞

At home, Alex began digging through a two-foot stack of magazines, scientific treatises, economic projections, and miscellaneous writings related to climate change. Weasel had given them to Alex in preparation for Alex's interview with the Weasel's new friends.

Junk, thought Alex. He sat in front of his J.C. Penney's desk at home and wished for better things. Idly, He flipped through the pile, throwing the papers without pictures onto the floor. Pathetic junk! Five more years, he promised himself. Just five more years, and this will all be worth it. He looked down at the dwindling pile of reading material still on his desk.

Drunken trees! Now that was more like it. He'd found a forest photo where the trees looked like wasted bar patrons five minutes before closing time. Melting permafrost, warming climates, methane emissions, blah, blah, blah. The point was that the icy ground had becoming a soupy marsh, and the trees flopped over at crazy angles. We can turn a forest into giant pile of tinker toys, thought Alex. Impressive!

Shishmaref, Alaska provided photos even more entertaining than the inebriated trees. Higher storm surges and melting permafrost cracked and tipped Shishmaref homes. Residents were about to become the first climate change refugees. There were fascinating pictures of houses tumbling off their foundations, looking as drunk and busted up as the drunken trees.

But those people are only Inuit, thought Alex. They're poor, they're not white, they don't count, and anyway, no one knows about them.

Graphs of rising ocean temperatures and rising carbon dioxide concentrations got tossed on the floor immediately. The Kyoto Protocol, a pledge to reduce so-called greenhouse gas emissions, was for loser countries. The Protocol hit the floor so hard that it almost bounced.

Photos of warming glaciers, bleached corals, pathetic polar bears, and shrinking islands were interesting but not as funny as Shishmaref.

So this is global warming, thought Alex. Curious, but expensive. What to do about it? Good question. Weasel had told Alex to, "just make it all go away." And he'd told Alex, "These folks are used to winning. So act like you're rich, and talk like you can deliver anything."

Alex frowned. Other pollution problems could be fixed by outwitting the EPA, or by hiring good lawyers, or, as a last resort, with scrubbers, and engineering designs, and hazardous waste haulers, but global warming was different. Supposedly, gases like carbon dioxide trap heat the way a greenhouse does. But carbon dioxide is the natural product of burning. The only solution to global warming is to burn less fuel. The remedies are solar, wind power, hydroelectric, mass transit, and curbing population growth. And these remedies all translate into less profit from petroleum.

Fortunately, all that science is boring, thought Alex. Most people won't put in the effort to read it. "Remordia," he said.

Suddenly, the solution became obvious.

<<<<>>>>

The Thursday meeting began with introductions, since Alex didn't know any of the five men seated around an oval mahogany table.

"Dr. Pomerleau."

"Dr. Watkins."

Each man nodded as he spoke. None gave out their first names— probably to make it clear to Alex that they were not on a first-name basis.

"Dr. Boone."

"Dr. Smythe-Huntington."

Then there was silence as the fifth man surveyed the room

squinting, his head barely shifting from right to left. His features were dark—his eyes jet black, his skin a sandy brown that spoke of deserts and turbans. A sharp black goatee emphasized his pointed chin. He wore western clothes with a curious gold tie tack fashioned in the shape of a crescent and sickle. "Mr. Efendi," he finally said with a faint smile.

"And I'm Alexander Lidecker, said Alex. "Pleased to meet you all." He hoped he looked pleased.

Dr. Pomerleau stood up and pointed to Alex. "So, Mr. Lidecker," and he emphasized the word mister. "Jeremy Scoggins promised you can make this global warming nonsense go away. How do you propose to do it?"

Alex cleared his throat, and whispered, "Remordia," under his breath. "Gentlemen, you have two choices—two paths as different as candy and strychnine." He paused and grinned. "You can corner the green energy market, develop better solar, wind, and hydro power. If you jump on the sustainable energy bandwagon early, there'll be plenty of profits. You could even invest in bicycles and running shoes."

He laughed. No one else did.

Alex discretely surveyed the room. Dr. Boone was sucking at his mustache which grew down below his upper lip. Smythe-Huntington's face squeezed itself into a grimace reminding Alex of a bloodhound tracking down a scent. He probably wanted to feed Alex to some endangered species. Pomerleau scowled. Effendi, like Alex, was interpreting the others' body language.

Finally, Smythe-Huntington said what the others were thinking. "For the price of a cheap bicycle, a person can buy about thirty gallons of gasoline. Enough to keep a car running for about a week. I'd rather sell gasoline than put myself out of business. The sustainable resources market does not sustain itself."

"Besides," smiled Efendi, "we will not be the ones without air conditioning."

"Even if we wanted to," said Pomerleau, "it's already too late. America's life style depends on burning petroleum. We can't go back."

Alex shrugged. He hadn't expected the room to fall in love with the sustainable energy concept. "In that case," he said, "I have a second option."

Alex straightened his tie. "Buy out the media. All of it. Television stations, radio stations, newspapers. Then, rewrite the news. Science is boring, so entertain them; tell them what to think, and leave out the science. Make them believe that climate change is all a left-wing conspiracy."

Pomerleau, Efendi, and the rest were hooked. Pomerleau nodded. Boone stroked his mustache.

Alex nodded as well. "How much money are you willing to throw at the problem?" he asked. "Because we'll need a lot of it."

Yes, thought Alex, this is what I was born to do. "Some will die; but they won't die for a while. I trust this is acceptable to you." The men all nodded. "The big disasters are ten, twenty years away. Maybe more."

"It's all in the presentation, not the science," Alex smiled a PR smile. "The truth doesn't matter. Say it as if you mean it, say it loud enough, and often enough. Say it at least seven times and don't get bogged down with facts."

"And if we ever do need scientists," Alex went on, "we can buy them, because everyone has a price."

Efendi coughed. "We? Mr. Lidecker, what makes you believe that you are one of us?"

Alex ignored the comment. "We search for people without moral convictions, and those unfortunate enough to need a job badly. Recent graduates and laid-off, older workers. Hell, they don't even have to have degrees in science. Any PhD will do. Or just put 'Dr.' in front of their names; no one's going to worry if it's a real degree."

Dr. Smythe-Huntington scowled, annoyed by Alex's trivializing the degree.

For a price, thought Alex. Somehow the phrase felt haunting. "Everyone has a price," he said. "So we buy enough people and sneer at the global warming concept. And people believe us just because we're loud, arrogant, and angry."

"The scientific organizations will discredit our so-called experts."

"So we create our own organizations."

Pomerleau cleared his throat. "What about bad publicity?"

"Everyone has his price," Alex repeated. "That includes reporters." He winked. "While we're at it, let's see if we can convince some priests and ministers to join our cause. The Book of

Revelations will come in handy when things get… hot!"

Alex hooted. The others chuckled.

"And we can always blame it on the gays." Alex punched Efendi's shoulder. "Am I right?" he laughed.

The room went silent.

Mr. Efendi stood up and stroked his goatee. "Mr. Lidecker," he said. "You are… not… one of us. Remember that."

"Lidecker, do you go to church?" asked Dr. Boone.

"No." Alex wondered if he should have lied.

"Then you'd better start."

For the image, of course. It only made sense.

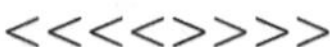

At first, the idea of church felt uncomfortable to Alex. He put it off for as long as he could, but, eventually, he began looking for the right church to be seen in. He shopped for his church the way he would shop for a car—looking for power, style, luxury, and comfort in his residence of worship. He settled on "The Holy Final Words Church of Washington D.C."

He wouldn't have to show up at church every Sunday—just often enough to say that he and his wife attended regularly. And he could always send Vivian by herself to represent the Lideckers

The church was an impressive three-story building, and the worship space rose the entire three stories, with pews circling the altar in tiers. Modernistic stained-glass windows ran from the floor at the bottom to the ceiling. Greens and blues dominated the windows, imparting a calm, mysterious aura.

Alex liked the psalms the best, especially the ones that read like adventure movies. "Let burning coals fall upon them; may they be thrown into the fire, into miry pits never to rise." This was a God who knew how to put on a good show. "He, who seizes your infants and dashes them against the rocks."

And then there was the whole crucifixion scene!

# Chapter Eighteen

∞

Johanna had a lot of freedom at the *Upstart Gazette*. She read the news and listened to conversations in coffee shops searching for topics, and came up with columns that were like no other.

## Earth ♫ Songs

The Bible vs science. You don't have to choose between them. As I see it...

In the beginning God created the heavens and the earth. And God said, "Let there be light."

Earth woke and felt a spirit forging, creating, dividing the light from darkness.

A "big bang," is what they'd call it later. They'd study the relics and clues. Some would be awed and amazed, while others, in arrogance, boasted of their scientific discoveries, as if their discoveries lessened the wonder of the creation.

Earth's rhythm was God's rhythm. The seas lapped at the dry lands, frothy edges ebbing and flowing. And Earth waited, a mixture of rocks and chemical soup, until God breathed life into her, and she brought forth microorganisms, creatures of ooze and slime, flashes of life that glimmered and died.

Grasses and fruit trees grew. And, oh, the animals! Moving creatures stirred in the waters—claws scuttering through primordial seas; many-legged worms in chitin armor, and living stars. Nourished by the bountiful feasts born on the tides, they lived, and ate, and died, and some left traces in the mud—footprints of their passage through God's time.

And God saw that it was good. It was life, and it was very good.

A pterodactyl swooped on Earth's air currents, his first flight clumsy, and halting. Then hair and feathers, and—more wonders— mothers tending their young, the beginnings of love.

And finally, weak and naked, Adam and Eve peeped into Gods light. They found food. They hid from claws and fangs, and they were fruitful. And, more than the teeming life that had come before, they knew love, and they knew God.

Others sensed it—the mother monkey licking her young's soft fur, the seal pup slurping life from his mother's teat. But humans, with their gifts of reason and language, they could understand love, feel God's spirit coursing through them heartbeat by heartbeat.

Ages passed and the clever humans survived and thrived. They learned Earth's secrets. They studied the plants that healed diseases, and learned how to cultivate crops. The weak, squirming humans survived and flourished. Who would have believed it? In a cosmic wager, who would have believed that the puny humans would have done so well!

They discovered, built, invented, and became powerful. Fire, tools, elaborate houses, roads, lamps to light the dark nights, and vessels to carry water. Then gunpowder, and with it the ability to protect or to destroy. What will the humans do with it, Earth wondered. So much power, wonderful and terrible all at the same time!

Uranium, penicillin, genetic engineering, and psychology—what tools! So great! But were the humans ready?

And that's when Earth first felt the sickness.

"My God," said Earth, "In the beginning, I'd planned to live forever. Human beings are your finest work, and my death. Each is precious, each is special, and there are too many for me to hold in my arms.

"I'm dying, God. It's only spring. And already I can feel the fever start. My snows melt. My crust dries into cracked clods. Hate rises too in the swirling dust devils."

Can we say that we love God and, at the same time, destroy his greatest work?

By Johanna Jacobson

"Look at all my mail," Johanna was leaning on Ivan's desk and working on a nine-inch stack of letters. "I love getting mail. It's the best part of this job." She opened the one on the top of the pile.

"Crackpot bitch." She looked up at Ivan. "Someone called me a crackpot bitch." She opened another letter and read it. "Okay. Here's a person with brains who gets what I'm saying." She read a few more letters, then stopped short. "Ivan, this one's telling me I'm going to hell. And the one before it called me a religious fanatic." She turned away so Ivan couldn't see here start to cry.

Ivan mumbled something under his breath.

Johanna turned back. "What?"

"They won't always agree with you, you know. Get used to it. It's called free speech. That's how you know people are alive. It's how you know democracy is alive." Ivan flicked his finger at the pile of        letters.        "Goddam        rookie,"        he        said.

# Chapter Nineteen

∞

Alex was almost asleep, when a loud hammering on the front door woke him. "It's after eleven," Vivian yawned. "Who the hell could that be?"

"I'll go find out." Alex poured out of bed and fumbled for his robe.

The Weasel stood at the front door, looking as bad off as Alex had ever seen him. Apparently, Weasel had been drinking, throwing up, and crying, and he fell into Alex's arms the moment the door opened wide enough. "It's finished! All over! Kaphhh." He tried to say "kaput" but ended up spitting into Alex's shoulder instead.

"Steady, man. I'll get coffee."  He pulled Weasel inside and sat him down on the living room couch.

"What's going on?" Vivian asked from the hallway.

"It's nothing, Viv, just a small emergency. Go back to sleep. I'm taking care of it."

Weasel, meanwhile, was trying to sit up. "I don't need coffee. I need more scotch." And he began to cry again.

It wasn't easy getting Weasel to drink the coffee, but after two cups and several spills, he was able to speak.

"It's the money, man...  The creative financing...  It's not there. We're going under. I don't want to be broke...  Hell, once my partners find out, I may be dead. Help me, Alex. I don't want to be dead."

Alex stared at the sobbing figure in front of him. "You're right, man. You do need scotch. So do I." Alex's money was also tied up in Weasel's ventures.

Two hours later, Alex and Weasel were naked in the Jacuzzi with Weasel singing his own version of opera. "My toes are numb numb,
fuckin', something', dum, dum." Weasel burped. "That's Carmen … the Tornado song."

"Tor-e-ador," said Alex in a slightly slurred voice. They'd been downing vodka shots mixed into lemon-Jell-O mini-cups which Alex had found in his refrigerator—leftovers from a party. Weasel stood up, saluted, lost his balance, and fell face down into the water. He came up sputtering and weeping. "All lost. All gone. What… am I gonna do?" He brushed foam from his face.

"It's not your fault, man." Alex licked some Jell-O off of his fingers. "You know whose fault this really is? You know why this is happening? It's because of… all the liberals. In California. That's why." "He patted Weasel's shoulder. "It's not your fault."

"Right," Weasel shouted. "Fuck California." He raised his third finger. "And San Francisco." He tried to stand up. "And Berkeley." He slipped and tumbled back into the hot tub and grabbed onto Alex for support. "I've always loved you like a son. Did you know that?"

Weasel reached for another Jell-O mini-cup. "You know what we ought to do? We ought to do… Did I tell you I love you like a mother, brother?"

He saluted Alex with his mini-cup and downed it. "I love you like the son I never had. We ought to take Berkeley out. Hell, we ought to take out California and all their pansy-ass demonstrators. If we declared war on California we'd win. If… we ran a troop of tanks from Monterey to Sacramento and just blasted 'em to hell… We should blow up a string of nu…cu…lar bombs from Monterey to Sacratomato. That'd do it. Especially Berkeley and San Fran… Hell… a man's gotta do what we gotta… We just blow 'em up and be done with 'em. We gotta do it."

They made a map of California on the living room carpet with duct tape, and drove toy trucks up and down the duct tape and farted. Every fart counted as a nuclear detonation.

By the next morning, Alex and the Weasel had sobered up. In spite of his hangover, Alex was thinking hard. "You know, we could do it. We could really do it. Not with a bunch of fucking bombs, but with money. What if California had to pay ten times as much for its energy? Hell, what if it had to pay a hundred times as much for its power? Their power's deregulated. We could fuckin' do it."

Where the duct tape map had been, Alex drew a map of California on a ten-foot long roll of butcher paper, and they used salami slices to indicate power plants. "What if," Weasel wondered, "something happened to one of the power plants?" He ate a salami slice.

On a separate sheet of butcher paper, Alex was drawing a rough approximation of California's power grid. "We gotta work this right. We funnel California's energy money into your investments. We'll have to figure a way to shelter it, and make it look legit. Like this, see." Alex scribbled along the left edge of the drawing.

"And we'll make their fuckin' governor look like an idiot. The White House boys will be pleased as champagne. They won't investigate."

By noon, Alex and Weasel had the core of their plan figured out. By three thirty, they were considering embellishments.

"And we hit the illegal immigrants. Right about harvest time. If that doesn't destroy California's central valley, I don't know what will. Make illegal immigration a felony. That'd get 'em," said Alex. "Ditto for the homos. Put all the queer sons of bitches back in the closet."

"We could fucking do it," said Weasel.

"We got to get oil goin' off shore. Hell, Texas, and Mississippi, and Louisiana have oilrigs off shore. What's wrong with California?"

"It's the fucking envirocreeps. Let 'em crawl into a clamshell and get 'et by a wolf pack."

"Send 'em all to France."

"Why settle for one power plant? What if a whole string of them went down, say during the summer?"

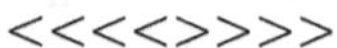

<<<<>>>>

And by the morning after that weekend, the war on California had begun in earnest. Reporters called it an energy crisis. Alex chuckled watching the evening news and knowing that he created it. He started a scrapbook with newspaper articles documenting the high points of his career:

## Energy Crisis Worsens
Californians asked to limit electricity use during peak hours.

## Blackouts Roll Through San Francisco

Governor struggles to keep California plugged in as power plants go off line, and energy prices skyrocket.

"I don't buy it," said Ivan. He slapped the paper against his desk, causing Johanna to jump back. "This energy crisis is as phony as Tammy Faye Baker's eyelashes."

"So why don't you do something about it?" Johanna asked.

"Like what?"

"I don't know. Investigate. Follow the money. Someone's making a killing."

"I'm a newspaper editor, for crying out loud, not the FBI."

"So send out some investigative reporters. Send me?" Johanna looked at him hopefully, but Ivan shook his head.

"It's too late to make today's press anyway," he said.

"Well," said Johanna, "when you hired me, you told me I had to do research." She ran to her office and began making phone calls.

"They're going to try to recall the governor!" she told Ivan the next day. "It's not just about money. It's politics, and it's huge. And the president is just letting it happen." When Johanna was excited, her hands flopped around like startled pigeons.

Ivan chuckled. "I figured as much."

"So can I have a crack at a front-page article? Unfortunately, most of this is from anonymous sources, but…"

Ivan snatched her notes from her hand and leafed through them. "Anonymous." He started to bellow. "Undisclosed source, Jerry S. says… What the hell, Johanna! You've worked at the paper for fifteen years now, and this is the best you can do!"

"But…"

"For crying out loud, this is news, not 'Spy Versus Spy.'"

"Okay then, I'm going to write a little poem."

Back at her own desk, Johanna was about to get creative. People aren't stupid, she thought. They just need a little push. Well, I'm pushy.

# Earth  Songs
## Rolling Blackouts

Beware the bureaucrat, my son,
The smarmy smile, the toothy grin.
His jabber slings a slimy song.
It hides the pilfering paws within.

The smarmy smile, the toothy grin,
When billionaires and oil wells gush,
It hides the pilfering paws within,
While power stations turn to mush.

When billionaires and oil wells gush,
You feel his talons and his roar,
While power stations turn to mush,
And free elections are no more.

You feel his talons and his roar,
His jabber slings a slimy song,
And free elections are no more.
Beware the bureaucrat, my son.

Please, readers, ask the question: Who's profiting from the energy crisis? And what is his next move?

By Johanna Jacobson

The power crisis made for lead stories and front-page news. It diverted billions out of California and into the pockets of Alex's benefactors. Once again, the Weasel had managed to wriggle out of a tight corner, and rich and influential people were appreciating Weasel's maneuvering and taking note of Alex's unique talents. Alex decided to take the next step forward in his career.

# Chapter Twenty

Weasel had set up the interview, and now Alex was waiting to meet some of the most influential people in Washington. Alex had flown to Italy a week earlier for something special to wear, and the tailor had come through with what Alex called his major-general suit—charcoal gray, but with khaki-green highlights in the material. Something about the cut of the pockets and lapels hinted of the military.

He had dressed carefully that morning; it wasn't a day for wrinkles. He'd chose a blazing-red, silk tie and pocket handkerchief, the tie held in place by a solid gold tie tack depicting the American bald eagle in flight. A second gold eagle flew just below the lock of Alex's attaché case.

An intern ushered Alex into one of the White House's conference rooms, where he found four of the president's advisors already seated around a six-foot, oval, cherrywood table. The silver-backed males, thought Alex—and one silver-backed female, Jean Grigsby. My God, but she looks like a man!

These were grizzled veterans who'd fought in political wars instead of on the battlefield, but their scars and scabs ran just as deep as those of other veterans.

John Ambrose was sixty-five, a thin prune of a man, with a frown to rival a New York subway strike. On his right sat Owen Jessup—rotund, bald, and red-faced, with a huge handle-bar mustache sprouting from below his nose. Next to him was Jean Grigsby (she should never have worn a solid black pantsuit, thought

Alex.) Carter Roosevelt completed the panel. Tanned and muscular, at forty-seven Carter looked almost boyish compared to the others.

John Ambrose spoke first. His upper lip barely moved as he talked. "Mr. Scoggins thinks that you could be of service to us, and that you have a … a certain… gift for persuasion." He looked Alex square in the face as if staring him down.

Alex pounced on the opportunity presented by the silence. "I want to advise the president." He felt control in his words. It tasted hot like whiskey, and he swallowed it and owned it. "I want to dictate policy, and morals. I want to move America in the right direction and redefine the essence of the American spirit."

Owen Jessup was not impressed. He leaned back, apparently annoyed that he'd wasted his time with this interview. "Your accomplishments may be impressive, but they don't warrant a White House appointment." He picked at his front tooth. "You're being a mite presumptuous; don't you think?"

"I want to work behind the scenes," Alex answered. "I have a unique ability to influence, and I can deliver your peoples' minds and hearts."

Owen rapped the table impatiently. "In other words, you want to be a spin doctor, a propaganda writer, a professional liar. You're wasting your time and ours. We have experts smarter than you in all these areas."

Alex smiled at the blustering words. "You're wrong. You do need me. At this time, President Bush's ratings are disgusting."

"No one believes in public opinion polls. They're too easily swayed," Carter Roosevelt answered dryly.

Alex continued as if no one had spoken. "People are gullible if you know how to work them. I can make them all fall in love with your precious president. They'll hang onto his every word."

Jean Grigsby licked her flakey lips and spoke. "We are politicians, Mr. Lidecker, familiar with the concept of putting spin on the information. So far you offer nothing new."

Alex went on. "I can do for politics what George Lucas did for the movies. I can talk Americans into anything—tax cuts for the rich, legalized wiretapping without accountability. I'll bug every phone and every computer of every senator, congressman, and candidate in the nation. We'll never lose an election again."

Alex glanced around the room. Carter Roosevelt was doodling

on a pad of White House paper. Own Jessup was fidgeting. The fools! They don't think I can do it, thought Alex. Well, I can do anything. Remordia! Jean Grigsby and John Ambrose were observing Alex with sideways glances, their expressions inscrutable.

Out loud, Alex said, "I'll legalize discrimination, repeal free speech and freedom of the press, and guarantee you and your friends immunity from any crime including murder. You name it—I can do it. All of this and more."

"Cocky words," said John Ambrose, but he nodded slightly. "Just how do you propose to accomplish all this?"

Here Alex cringed like a lion guarding his prey from scavengers, and he thumbed the latch on his attaché case.

"My plan has three points. First, Americans are used to living in safety. I say we make them afraid—even terrified. Then we provide a strong, confident leader, and they'll follow him anywhere. Right now, America is ruled by democracy. I propose that we rule with terror instead.

"Secondly, Americans don't want to think too much. Give them the illusion of wholesomeness—they won't look beyond it. As for any idiots who oppose us, we smear them with scandal. Pick anyone you like; I can find dirt on them. Next, we need the media's cooperation, and, gentlemen, I have connections with the media that you've only dreamed of. Once you own the press—and I do own the press—you own the world."

Alex looked around himself, taking stock. So far it seemed hopeful. "Consider Hitler. He was a master at it. The swastika was originally a symbol of good luck. He used it to muster an army and conquer half of Europe. We can do this with the American flag. We can subjugate the nation in the name of freedom; go to war in the name of peace."

"You want to go to war, Mr. Lidecker?" Carter Roosevelt slapped the table. "Tell me you're not considering starting a war!"

"It's an age-old magic trick. Distract with war, and the home front is yours to plunder. War has served many a dictator—why not us!"

Owen Jessup stood up. "I've seen some shady deals go down in the name of politics, but I'm with Carter on this one. You've crossed a line. You've gone too far."

John Ambrose cleared his throat. He stared off as if looking for the right words. "Still, under the right set of circumstances … It's only in this century that a ruler needs permission to go to war. When Caesar or King Richard, or Saddam Hussein, for that matter, declared war, they just up and did it, and armies gathered and men stabbed, and shot arrows, and died—with no questions asked."

And Jean Grigsby added, "You can't make pancakes without breaking some eggs."

And then there was silence thick as swamp water.

Finally, Carter Roosevelt spoke. "That's only two—two points. What's the third point of your plan?"

Alex opened up his attaché case a crack and fumbled among four manila envelopes. He passed one to Owen Jessup and one to Carter Roosevelt. Owen opened his, and his ruddy face paled. "How the fuck did you get these?" He snarled the words. Inside the envelope was Owen Junior's rap sheet—an impressive list of drug-related charges and an instance of date rape that had been hushed up by sizeable contributions to a prominent judge's retirement fund. Instinctively, Owen hunched his shoulder over the papers, protecting them from view. And there was more. His hand trembled, in spite of his efforts to remain calm, as he pulled out photos of his daughter dancing nude at a "Girls Gone Wild" party.

Carter Roosevelt's envelope was fatter. It contained construction project plans, including all the details—legal, marginal, and downright criminal—for six shopping malls, two hotels, and three planned bedroom communities in Texas, Oklahoma, and Louisiana. Carter pulled up the envelope flap, and pulled out two inches of the plans, and then shoved them all back. There was no point in looking further. He dropped his head into his hands and sighed.

"My third point is merely this," said Alex "I always do my homework."

John Ambrose was curious. "Just how many envelopes did you bring?"

# Chapter Twenty-One

∞

Alex had an office in the White House and behind his desk hung a three-foot tall picture of Winston Churchill. The frame was gilded and so thick as to border on gaudy. Me and Winnie, thought Alex, we were cut from the same cloth.

Suddenly he was in with the really big boys, and the stakes—they were astronomical—so high they would cause a veteran gambler to tremble. This game allowed for no errors. The consequences of a bad move made death seem easy by comparison. Before now, he'd been playing only for himself. Not that he ever considered the possibility of failure or defeat. Such horrible words! Before this, if he had missed something, he had only himself and his father's image to deal with. Now, if something went wrong, he'd have unhappy partners in Washington, and a second set of unhappy partners in corporate America and the corporate Middle East—unhappy and very powerful partners.

Blackmail was a funny game—something like holding a scorpion by its stinger." On the one hand, Alex held all the strings and all the power. On the other hand, an unhappy partner, should he ever get loose, could have him killed. Of course, he'd taken precautions. "In the event of my death, the following documents will be made public…"

No, he made sure that it was in his new partners' best interests to keep him alive and happy. But his victims had resources and power of their own. And he had to make himself an indispensable asset to these victims before any one of them figured out how to destroy the evidence he had against them.

This was life, not a chess game. Possibilities were infinite, and he, Alex, had to foresee all of them and plan. Contingencies, parries, thrusts, and counter-thrusts, just as in a fencing match—victory depended on balance and timing. Alex knew that his strength lay in offense. He had to keep the upper hand, and be several moves ahead of everyone else. Always on the offense. Be bold. Hit first. Hit hard. Keep hitting. Never let up.

The California campaign had been a huge success. The energy crisis had yielded over $8 billion for his corporate clientele, and more importantly, it had left the state near bankruptcy and ripe for political takeover. Plans for a recall election were already underway.

But just when it looked like the Weasel's problems had been whitewashed clean away, they began surfacing in the newspapers.

## Enron Execs Charged with Insider Trading
The once-prized commodities are now classified as "junk bonds."

## Bush Administration Tied to Enron
President Bush fought against placing caps on the price of energy in California.

They were dark days, and Alex was groping for something, anything, to make the scandals go away and to make the president look good. The tabloids were digging up stories about the twins. The newspapers criticized everything—his tax cuts for the rich, his weak environmental policy, and, finally, like a rotting carcass, the Enron scandal stunk up the air around the White House and their friends. Watkins, Pomerleau, and Weasel, were safe enough, but some of their friends' heads were on the chopping block. It seemed that Alex spent most of his days doing damage control. What he needed was a huge diversion. Alex had great friends in the news media who transferred much of the heat from the president to the Clintons, but, face it, they needed new material.

"We're counting on you, Lidecker. This is where you earn your keep." John Ambrose had barked a laugh when he said it, as if it were all a joke, but both men knew he had meant it.

The diversion had to be something completely new, completely unexpected and it had to be huge—the greatest piece of showmanship of all time. He'd been meeting with seven close friends from the CIA and FBI. So far, they hadn't come up with any new scandal items because wiretap laws were too restrictive, so Alex was considering a new angle. Cloak-and-dagger was fascinating, and it had never been exploited before—at least not in the United States.

The Seven Musketeers, they called themselves, and this was their fifth meeting—their fifth attempt to find a suitable diversion article for the news. "This may just do it," said Ernie Martinez, switching on his recorder. Ernie and Alex's friendship went way back—through the CIA days with their all-night stake outs, the close calls, and the night-clubbing until both of them were falling asleep in their whiskey.

"They're planning to hijack planes," said Ernie. He switched on the recorder. Someone was raving in Saudi, most of it swearing with allusions to dogs and pigs and Americans.

"It's Al-Qaeda, of course." Ernie stopped the tape. "They don't have all the details pinned down yet from what I've put together, but they're planning something immense."

"Ideas, gentlemen. How can we make the most out of this information?" Alex asked.

"Instead of alerting airport security, what if we use undercover FBI—hundreds of them in each of the airports!" Eddie gave the tape recorder a "good job" pat. "We could make it look like a miniature scale war, a real-life cops and robbers show. We play up the good versus evil aspect."

Marty Stillman puffed on his cigarette. "Could work," he said. "We pick an agent to be the hero and do him up in all the papers. That'd take the heat off of Enron for weeks."

Scott Holmes was the newest and youngest Musketeer. "And we do follow-up stories on the FBI and the CIA. We could pick a couple of agents with interesting stories in their lives—a handicapped kid, a battle with cancer. And we do clips of their wives and mothers talking passionately about their heroes. Later, any time Enron starts to surface, we do feature articles about out FBI heroes, and relegate Enron to page twenty-five where hardly anyone sees it."

But Alex was deep in thought. They'd use it and they'd spin it all right, but there had to be something more. While the others chattered, the word "Remordia" played in his head, dancing like a hand-tied fly bobbing over a trout's head. Thoughts formed in his mind, at first just murky impressions, and then a clear plan.

"Here's why you'll never get top billing" said Alex. "If we stop the hijackings, the departments get a little glory and the story runs for five paragraphs on page eleven." He stopped and scratched his head. "Maybe six paragraphs if we're really lucky. No, what we need is for the president to take the credit. Instead, we let the hijackings proceed. The nation is thrown into panic. And in the midst of it all, the president steps forward calm, prepared, sure of himself. He takes the reins of leadership." Alex paused. "He declares war."

Marty almost swallowed his cigarette. Ernie nodded. The others stared and were stunned.

Alex went on. "Americans must all stick together. United we stand! And as a wartime president, he has broad emergency powers. We can use them. And we have great news coverage for months, and maybe years."

Scott looked puzzled.

"This is better than sex," said Marty.

# Chapter Twenty-Two

## ∞

Alex made it a point to be by himself on the morning of September 11th. He turned off his pager and took the phone off the hook. Then he turned on the TV and, along with millions of Americans, heard the news that American Airlines Flight 11 had crashed into the World Trade Center. Almost every channel was reporting news, their cameras trained on the black plume rising from the World Trade Center's north tower. As Alex stared at the smoky wisps disappearing into the air, a second plane appeared on the horizon, and moments later, America watched in horror as United Airlines Flight 175 hit the south tower with a devastating explosion.

Witnessing it all, Alex felt like a kid at a Godzilla movie, or a four-year-old playing with his trucks and action figures, watching, fascinated, as tiny people poured from the building.

Now, rescue workers were arriving in fire trucks, ambulances, and squad cars. The cranes, axes, and hoses seemed more like toys than real tools.

Alex watched all the destruction, a director reviewing his play on opening night. No, more like a god or a screenwriter creating the greatest movie of all time. *This is only the beginning,* he thought, *only the beginning,* a house of dominoes about to topple over, one brick at a time. Old beliefs and values would make way for Alex's new America. *I can do anything,* he thought. *Anything is possible. I created reality and it came true. I always believed I could do it, but now it's actually here.* The tiniest of smirks escaped his lips. It couldn't have gone better if he'd flown the planes himself.

In a steamy cloud of smoke and dust, one of the towers

crumbled and fell. Best Godzilla movie ever, thought Alex.

But then the cameras moved in closer. On the screen, people were running, and Alex could see screams etched on their faces, could see their eyes, wide with fright, more animal-like than human. Inside Alex's head, a light switched on. Suddenly, it all became real. He could almost hear bones snapping, almost feel flesh scraping along concrete. What was happening to him? The sensation was so strong! Alex shuddered and his chest ached. It was all too much! It wasn't supposed to be this way! Only a small diversion, he thought. Sweat formed. His throat dried up.

On the screen a body jumped from a window, and Alex could feel the desperation in the decision to jump. Alex looked away. "Not my fault," he said to himself. "I didn't tell him to jump. He chose to jump. It was his decision." Alex said the words out loud, willing his pounding heart to settle.

Quickly he flipped off the television and put the phone back in its cradle. "Remordia," he screamed, "It's too much. Make it go away." He stared at the TV set as if it were a zombie.

"Remordia. Make it go away. Make it go away." When he said those words, he made a choice.

Moments later, the phone rang with an unfamiliar page's voice from the president's office requesting his presence for a strategy meeting.

Alex gathered together all his notes and speeches. More ideas buzzed in his head, and, as he planned American's reaction, his own panic subsided. "Heroes, their lives sacrificed for freedom," the headlines would read. Heroes are good—Americans love heroes.

<<<<>>>>

Johanna read the accounts of 9/11 in the newspaper and watched the burning towers over and over on her television set. The mood at the paper was somber. People spoke in hushed whispers. Jokes and pranks were put on hold.

For Johanna the stark truth of the attacks set in slowly as she scrolled through the Internet and searched through her mail for some way to address the tragedy in her column.

# Earth ♫ Songs

Dear Readers,

Like you, I watched the news clips of the plane flying into the World Trade Center, and I searched for ideas on how to address it in my column. And I realized that a cute story about furry animals wouldn't cut it. Then I received a letter from La Chandra Jones, who worked at the World Trade Center. She wrote down the events of September 11th as she experienced them, and, for my column this week, I'd like to share her letter with you:

September 11, 2001

First there was a loud "whoosh" sound, stronger than wind in a storm. Then a blast and crashing, not really like gunshot, but that was the first thing I thought of. You could see the glass bend! The windows bulged, then straightened. Harlem all over again, I thought. Up on the seventy-first floor of the World Trade Center's south tower, our office rocked like tree branches in a hurricane.

Part of me wanted to hide under a desk, and part of me wanted to get out.

No one else seemed scared. Then my boss said, "I don't know what that was, but we're evacuating now," and so we did.

The elevators weren't working, so we had to walk down in the stairwells—seventy-one flights. A hell of a long way. But at least we were going down instead of up. After about eight flights, I took off my heels. I carried them for a bit, then dropped them to the side of the steps, thinking I'd pick them up later.

They yelled a message on the overhead page—an isolated fire in the north tower. Nothing to worry about. No need to evacuate. Bullshit! Twenty-three years in Harlem made me suspicious of anyone who says there's nothing to worry about!

Kept going down. None of us really knew what was happening, or we'd have been a lot more freaked.

About halfway down, another blast. Blam! Like something exploded. The whole building rocked. Worse than the subway, I thought.

Later I figured it out. That blast was the second plane hitting our tower, but back then I didn't know what it was.

Now the air was getting all smoky. You could see the dust sort of hanging in the air. I put my sleeve over my nose and tried to breathe through the cloth, but it didn't work, and I kept coughing and choking.

Only about five flights to go. Legs hurt. Lungs hurt. But I didn't want to stop. Now people were running and crying and saying things like "Let me out." and "We got to get out of here." They were more scared than the people on the upper floors were, and suddenly, so was I. Stuff was falling and my throat was dry, crackly sort of.

Then I saw the front door, and I remember thinking, almost there, almost over. Excited to be so close, and afraid something dreadful would happen before I could get there.

Firemen were running into the building. I was so scared getting out, and I wondered if they were scared going in. And one of the guys reminded me of my baby brother. His turnouts said "Washington" on the back, and I was hoping that Washington would be all right.

Then I was out, and the air smelled so much better.
We kept running, and another rumbling blasted exploded behind us. The ground shook, and I turned around.

Then, the south tower collapsed. It just fell apart, and crumbled, and wasn't there anymore. More smoke and dust. My legs really hurt, but I ran some more anyway. I wondered if Washington had gotten killed. I hoped not, but he probably did.

And I'm thinking this was way worse than Harlem.

By<br>La Chandra Jones

Our hearts and prayers go out to the men and women who lost their lives, and to the families and friends who grieve their passing.

Johanna                                              Jacobson

# Chapter Twenty-Three

## ∞

As the weeks wore on, Johanna got more and more disheartened watching the news and reading the papers. The president's agenda was clearly to wage war. He was strong and decisive—a perfect leader and hero. It was as if he had known that the attacks were going to happen, as if he had been preparing for them. And, strangely, there was almost no opposition to his war. One lone congresswoman from Berkeley spoke out; that was it.

Each day's news brought more grim statistics. And in the aftermath of the hijackings, war seemed more and more likely."

## Suspects to Be Held at Guantanamo Bay

More than two hundred terrorists detained. "I want to learn to fly. I don't want to learn to land," says one suspect.

## A Call to War

Afghanistan is harboring Osama bin Laden, thought to have masterminded the attacks of September 11. President Bush vows retaliation. "Any country offering asylum to terrorists is an enemy of the United States," says the President.

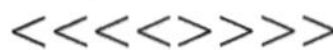

Johanna finished her column with time to spare. She'd written the article with more passion that usual, and she didn't want to spoil it with too much proofing:

# Earth ♫ Songs

This story's an oldie, but it never goes out of style:

Once upon a time in a galaxy nearby, the emperor came out of his man-cave to wave at his subjects. (It was a very luxurious man-cave, with plenty glitz and women in skimpy bikinis.) A rotten rutabaga hit him square in the rotunda. Remembering his image, the emperor looked up and smiled, waving with his left hand, while brushing away slimy vegetable matter with his right one. Pumpkin pulp pummeled his pate, followed by moldy melons and soggy succotash.

"I thought that they loved me," he cried out.

"Flying vegetables don't lie," said his advisor.

"But why?" asked the emperor. "How could anyone not love me?

"You and your nobles are stealing from the coffers. None of you pay taxes."

"No one likes taxes."

"But without taxes, we have no schools, no roads, no firefighters, nothing to serve the people."

"Rubbish. The rich can't afford to pay taxes."

"The longer you rule, the poorer the people become. In seven years, the country will be bankrupt."

"So? We get six and a half years of luxury, and seven years from now, I blame some honest shmuck for all the trouble."

A torrent of tomatoes hit the emperor's torso.

"Hell, this was my last clean robe. Now, I need new clothes," said the emperor. "And a war to take people's minds off my, er, creative finances. I want a war."

A week later, the image-maker returned with two peasants staggering under the weight of the large trunk they were carrying. The image-maker reached inside. "My finest work," he said.

"But I don't see anything…"

"A stunning creation, Your Majesty, stunning and special. Only the wise can see it." The image-maker looked directly into the emperor's eyes. "Of course, YOU can see it."

"Oh, yes, right, of course I see it. Where is it?"

"Right here on this hanger."

"I want to wear it tonight," said the emperor.

The words spread quickly. "Only the wise can see the emperor's clothes."

"But he's naked," said the newscaster.

"You're fired," said his producer. For foolish newscasters can get into all sorts of trouble. They sent the newscaster to jail on a pokey island nearby.

"The emperor is so wise," said his replacement.

"But he's also so naked," said the politician.

They sent the politician to the pokey island jail along with the newscaster. One who could see the emperor's clothes replaced him.

Some folks protested the war. "All traitors and terrorists," the emperor bellowed. The pokey island jail got pretty crowded.

And though the clothes were imaginary, the war was real. So were poverty, oppression, and injustice.

Then one day, a small boy stood up in the crowd. "The emperor is butt-naked," he said.

"Hush," said his mother.

"But, Mom, he is. His pee pee is waving in the wind, and his butt cheeks are flapping where everyone can see." He said it loudly.

"News flash!" said the news reporter. "Naked emperor fools entire country."

And the empire began to heal.

By Johanna Jacobson


Minutes later Ivan called her into his office and his face looked troubled. "You can't print that, Johanna. This is a time of war, and the nation has to stand united. This is no time to criticize the president."

"But he wants to wage war."

"You can't print that article. It shows revolting taste. End of discussion."

"And, if our government knew nothing about the attack, how come they now have enough evidence to send hundreds of men to Guantanamo Bay? And why Guantanamo, and not somewhere in the U.S., unless they plan to torture them? And how do we know that they're all terrorists? Maybe some of them are in there by mistake. Or, even worse, maybe some are activists, in prison for exercising their right to free speech. Or maybe they know something that might embarrass the president. This is the United States. We don't have a Gestapo or a KGB. We have to stand up for freedom and truth."

"Johanna, stop right now."

"What if…"

"No, you may not print the article. I don't care if the president takes a gun and goes on a shooting spree in the parking lot. He's second to God. Got it?"

"This blows, and you know it." Johanna slammed the door behind                                                          her.

# Chapter Twenty-Four

∞

"You're amazing Alex." Vivian said it so often he was starting to get tired of the phrase. "So much sadness and anger, and you just do what you have to and even manage to smile. How do you keep up your spirits?"

And Alex took to shrugging modestly because he had run out of modest answers.

"Darling," said Vivian, "Weasel called. Something about arranging a meeting tomorrow. I wrote it all down for you."

The following morning, Alex shaved with care, and, after he'd finished, he ran his fingers over his cheeks and chin feeling for any missed stubble. But no, his shaved face was flawless, as was everything else he'd done—smooth and slick. Appearance is everything, and Alex knew how to put on a good appearance. And, to make sure he wowed the partners, Alex wore the same suit he'd used to interview for the White House job. Why meddle with success?

The meeting was held in a twenty-sixth-floor conference room in Houston. Alex was the first person there, and he walked into the room ready to be congratulated.

Weasel's partners had picked an ultra-modern suite in one of Houston's finest hotels. It was a room of sharp edges ("cutting edge," thought Alex) with glass and chrome furniture. And it made Alex want to salute. There was a sense of urgency in the angles. Enormous floor-to-ceiling windows overlooked the entire city, and, looking out through those windows, Alex understood a great truth: Houston, Texas, the United States, the world—it all belong to him now.

"For a price." The words sneaked into his head startling Alex. Then he smiled. His price had been hard work, and it had all been worth the effort.

Alex turned from the windows. There, on the opposite wall, in stark contrast to the clean, modern lines, hung an enormous oil painting of an eagle flying over snowcapped mountains with a jackrabbit in its claws.

The eagle's details fascinated Alex—the massive wings drawn halfway through the down stroke, his head stretched up and forward, and the long, curved talons—so sure of their grasp—reflecting sunlight. Fantastic, exquisite, thought Alex, predation, survival, life and death.

Then Weasel's friends filed into the room, and Alex imagined himself the eagle, carrying prey in his powerful claws, and he shuffled his papers, impatient to begin.

As Alex looked from man to man, he noticed the suits they were wearing. Alex knew Italian suits, and realized that he was badly outclassed.

"Mr. Lidecker." Adam Watkins emphasized "mister." He peered over his glasses at Alex as a principal would stare down at a student facing detention. "Is this the best you could do? Are you aware of how seriously you've botched up the whole situation?"

Stunned, Alex dropped his gaze. He was about to start a war. Enron was history, and the president looked great. Surely these people weren't going to quibble about a few Arabs or soldiers when so much else was at stake.

"Sir, it wasn't my fault. I wanted to negotiate, but the president…"

Vernon Pomerleau slapped his hand on the table. The sound of his ring striking glass rang out like gunshot. "Negotiate!" He laughed and shouted in one breath. "You wanted to negotiate! What were you going to say? Please don't hurt us mister terrorist. We're sorry our towers got in the way of your planes."

The room rang with laughter. Alex looked up at the painting for reassurance, but this time he noticed the rabbit trapped in the eagle's claws. The gashes were long and deep, showing pieces of exposed meat hanging from the rabbit's thigh, and its eyes were glazed from shock, or pain, or death. Beaten, defeated, it hung in the eagle's talons, helpless.

Alex had never known defeat or failure (ugh, such unpleasant words!) He'd never considered himself the rabbit—not since the time he was four years old when his brother had stuck his head in the toilet. But now Alex stared at the men seated around him, knowing that he was playing a game of high stakes and was ignorant of the rules.

Dr. Smythe-Huntington stood up. "War is both acceptable and inevitable. The United States depends on Middle East oil, and can't be held victim to the whim of some medal-toting hot-head who decides he doesn't want to sell it, or wants to barter for higher prices. War is necessary, but you're about to wage it against the wrong nation. Iraq should be the target, you dunderhead. Get Saddam and give us oil rights to the unexplored western desert, not a bunch of friggin' barren mountains and some religious maniacs."

Shit, thought Alex. He didn't like playing defensive politics. "But what about the terrorists? Surely, we have to stop them. And the way they treat their women. What about that?"

"We need the oil right now. Terrorists are a pain in the ass, but they're not worth waging a war over. Petroleum is worth waging war over. You should know that, Lidecker."

"And they treat their women the way women should be treated," said Vernon Pomerleau.

"There was no connection between the planes and Iraq. How are we supposed to sell bombing Iraq to the American people?"

"You lie, Lidecker. You tell them that Saddam sent the planes. That's what we're paying you for, Lidecker. To lie, and to do it effectively. I believe that was the unique talent you boasted of when we took you on board."

Shit, thought Alex. He was trembling. Sweat drenched his Italian shirt. He thought now that his suit hinted of the uniform Saddam Hussein typically wore. He needed a miracle and thought the word, Remordia.

"We're waiting, Lidecker."

Alex stood up, and slowly looked around the room using the silence as his introduction. "Weapons of Mass Destruction," he said and again there was silence. So obvious! He would have thought of it earlier if the men hadn't rattled him. "WMDs! Banned by the Geneva Convention. These are Saddam's trademark weapons and his Achilles' heel. You'll have your war. First Afghanistan, next Iraq, and then Iran and anyone else who dares defy us. We're training Americans to respond to fear. And we're training them to accept war. Once they back one war, they'll back as many as we tell them to."

As Alex talked, power swelled his lungs and his voice filled the room. "Americans have never been under attack. They're used to freeway accidents and heart attacks, but they've never known terror. I can supply terror. Arab terror organizations like Al-Qaida will be my greatest weapon. Those who despise us the most will be our greatest ally. They will supply the instruments of terror. And with every suicide bomb they detonate, our position becomes stronger. Gentlemen, I'll have every man, woman, and child in the nation quivering from their breakfast cereal to their evening news. I'll pitch an ad campaign the likes of which this country had never seen—first against Afghanistan, next Iraq, and finally against any nation that dares to defy us. And WMDs will be the link to Saddam Hussein and the ultimate source of terror by which Americans will stand behind us."

The room was quiet, the air charged, and Alex knew that, once again, he'd won. Like the eagle, soaring over the mountaintops, he was anxious to get back to Washington, anxious to build his plans and set them into action.

"Saddam Hussein had weapons of mass destruction—WMDs. Soon the whole country would know the initials. Bubonic plague, small pox, anthrax, nerve agents, sarin, ricin, nuclear weapons, chlorine gas. We can scare the hell out of the country."

Following the meeting, Alex and Ernie got to work, searching the computer's database of military personnel, looking for someone with access to WMDs. Then, they began their search for blackmail material.

Alex nudged Ernie. "Holy shit! Check this one out. Sebastian Shelmore, Biological Weapons Center in Alameda. He's working with anthrax. And, oh, my, look at these photos! It looks like the good doctor's been a naughty boy!" Ernie leaned over to peer at Alex's computer screen.

Apparently, Dr. Shelmore had financed his college education as a prostitute. His clients included both men and women. The doctor had supplemented his income by selling narcotics, and he'd been arrested twice, once for pandering, once for selling drugs. Both times the charges had been dropped. An impressive assortment of naked photos followed.

"Holy, holy shit," Ernie agreed. "That's our man." He grabbed the mouse from Alex's hand and scrolled down the page staring at the photos. "Why the hell was she paying for sex?" he asked, pointing to a long-legged blond with surgically-enhanced breasts. "She could have made it into *Playboy* magazine, easy."

Alex gave Ernie a high five. They laughed, enjoyed the naked bodies, then broke out a bottle of champagne and celebrated.

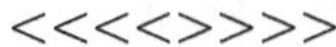
<<<<>>>>

Alex hadn't expected it to be so easy.  He had Shelmore put anthrax into envelopes and address them to Senator Thomas Daschel and Senator Pat Leahy, both troublemakers, both crusty and outspoken. And both men were likely to vote against his legislation and likely to stall passage of his bills. Assassination was so much easier than the democratic process! And with two spots on the Supreme Court likely to be vacant within the next few years, Pat Leahy had to go. Finally, as a step towards controlling the news, he added Tom Brokaw and The National Enquirer to his list of victims.

Compared to 9/11 this was a snap.

<<<<>>>>

Ten days after the infamous flights of the hijacked planes, Johanna read about anthrax in the morning paper.

## Mysterious Deaths Caused by Anthrax

Five victims dead from exposure. FBI identifies mysterious white powder as anthrax.

Johanna remembered the WMD workshop she had gone to years ago. Five mail carriers had been killed. Just as in chess, she thought, the pawns are the ones who catch the fallout. I wonder who was supposed to get the letters.

Johanna had to look hard to find out. Four of the letters were addressed to Tom Brokaw, The National Enquirer, Tom Daschel and Pat Leahy. The writer assumed that Osama bin Laden was behind the anthrax poisonings.

Johanna was incensed. So someone tries to assassinate the president's political rivals, the president gets his war; the news media gets shushed, the tabloids leave him alone, and he scares the pants off of the American public and everyone thinks Osama bin Laden did it! Isn't anyone even going to look at the White House and its advisors? Plus, they have access to all the anthrax they want through the military.

Johanna decided to check with the only paranoid left-wing activist she knew. She called up Temple.

"Watch the news tonight, and see if Osama brags about it on Arab TV," she said. "You know, the way he bragged about destroying the World Trade Center. If he takes the credit, I'll believe he did it, but I'll bet he denies the whole thing." Temple sounded so calm.

Johanna, however, was ready to explode. "And listen to the president. He's inciting people, not calming them down. Terrorists don't want to kill people; they want to scare them into doing something—like going to war."

"You've lived in Berkeley too long, girl. You sound like my mother."

"What's your mother got to do with this?"

"She was always seeing government conspiracies."

"So, how often was she right?"

"About 50% of the time—assuming, of course, that she was wrong about the Kennedy assassinations and Senator Wellston's plane crash. She was right on with Watergate."

There was no word from Osama bin Laden on television that night, but everyone knew that he was responsible for the letters with anthrax.

<<<<>>>>

Johanna paced and went to bed, thinking about anthrax. "It's no good. I'll never get to sleep at this rate. It's not fair, God. Why can't I sleep?" She turned over onto her stomach. "You can't be expecting me to do something! What on earth can I do about this? Even if I am a journalist, I write the environmental section. I don't know enough about politics to argue any of this intelligently." A car whooshed by and then the night was still.

"And what if I'm wrong? And, besides, Ivan won't let me print anything about war or political corruption." A lone cricket chirped outside her window. And the idea of making some statement wouldn't leave her alone.

"Okay, what do you want me to do? I'll write something, but you'd better help me and not leave me dangling. You left Jesus dangling on the cross. But he was Jesus, and I'm only me. Don't do that to me. Please, just please, don't expect too much." Rubbing her eyes, Johanna threw on a bathrobe, pulled out a pen and notepad and began to write about coyotes, chickens, and anthrax.

<<<<<>>>>

The next day, Johanna waited for Ivan to approve her column, a sort-of cute, sort-of silly story featuring dancing organic vegetables. Then she ran down to the layout department. "I found a typo," she said. "Can I just get into your computer and change it?" That's when she replaced the safe story with the one about the coyotes and chickens.

But, that evening, as Johanna was preparing to leave the office, she heard bellowing, and knew that she'd been caught. Ivan appeared in her doorway. His jaw was clenched, and his face had turned pink—not a good sign. "See me in my office—now," he barked. Johanna prepared to get chewed out.

"What the hell—what the bloody hell were you thinking?" On his desk lay the article that Johanna had spent the night writing:

# Earth  Songs

When Foxy Mama got a craving for chicken pot pie, Foxy Papa stuck his gorgeous, plumed tail straight up into the air and twitched his whiskers. "No problem, babe," he said. But the wooden fence around the chickencoop was sturdily built and he couldn't get in. I'll have to use psychology, he decided.

So Foxy Papa snuck into a biological weapons facility, stole some anthrax, and mailed it to the chickens.

Actually, he poured the white powder into envelopes, tied them to chicken-egg-sized rocks, and shot them over the chickencoop's fence with a catapult. But let's not quibble over the details.

Foxy had a megaphone, which he used to communicate with the chickens. "That powder is anthrax, and it's the coyotes who mailed it to you," he said. "You can't let them get away with this," And he smacked his lips as he thought of chicken pot pie. "But, no worries, we'll protect you—my brothers and I."

Now, there's always one doubting rooster in every coop, and, in this coop, that rooster was Thomas. "How do we know we can trust the foxes?" he asked.

"Boo! Traitor!" the chickens all catcalled. "We can trust the foxes. They are decent and honorable."

"So the foxes sent the chickens off to wage war against the coyotes. Armed with rifles, grenades, and tanks, they quickly vanquished the coyotes, who had only their teeth with which to defend themselves.

"You need better security to protect you from the coyote spies," said the fox. "We'll set up wiretaps, and monitor your computers." No more white powder got into the chicken coop, so the chickens knew that the foxes were capable. The foxes controlled all the chickens' goings out and comings in, as well as their phones and computers.

"Thank you, thank you," cried the chickens, clucking in gratitude. "You've truly saved us from our enemy."

And the foxes dined at leisure on chickens and eggs for the rest of their days.

Who's mailing out the letters with anthrax—a call to send our nation to war? For Pete's sake, they were mailed to Senator Tom Daschel, an environmentalist passionate about energy conservation and Senator Pat Leahy, who gave the president grief over his Supreme Court appointments. There's no evidence that Osama bin Laden sent the poison-pen letters, and it might be someone in our administration. Please, people, don't act out of fear. And don't support a government that uses war to make the president popular.

By Johanna Jacobson

Ivan's face turned from pink to hopping-mad red. He threw down the paper, leaned on his knuckles and glared at Johanna. "What the hell were you thinking? What the shit were you thinking? That you'd just sneak this by me, and I wouldn't notice? Did you think the layout editor wouldn't tell me about this? Don't you think I read the final draft copy?"

"It's why I became a journalist, to tell the truth, not a watered-down version of it."

"Where's your proof? How do you know it's the truth? And what if the paper folds? What then? How are you going to tell the truth if there's no paper?"

Johanna shrugged. "It's what I believe. It's my truth, my story, my passion."

"And I'm killing it. Consider yourself lucky that you still have a job. And if you ever try a stunt like that again, you're fired. Is that clear?"

"Yes, sir, but…"

"I'm killing it. End of discussion. And I'm keeping an eye on what you write."

<<<<>>>>

Johanna tried talking to Ivan again a few days later. "Osama bin Laden couldn't have been responsible for the anthrax. The bacterium was a domestic strain."

"Get out!" said Ivan.

"Are you afraid of the president?" Johanna watched carefully for Ivan's reaction. "Are you afraid you'll get an anthrax package?" Ivan didn't answer. "Or that they'll black-list the paper?" Ivan looked down. "That's it. You're afraid of what the president might do to you. That you'll get a real poison-pen letter with your water bill. Or are you afraid you'll get arrested? This is still America, you know. We still have free speech. Although we won't have it for much longer unless we fight for it."

"And what if you're fired? That's real close to happening right now. I'll fire you in a heartbeat if I ever see anything in print that hasn't been approved. So you can thank God, or your lucky star, or whatever you believe in, that your little scheme failed, because, believe me, if you'd succeeded, or if you ever try anything like that again, you'll set a record for out on your ass!" Ivan paced. His red face turned a deeper red. He slammed his fist on the desk. "Understand?"

"I understand. But I used to admire your courage."

"Three strikes, Johanna. Three strikes and you're out. You've already had two." She slammed the door on her way out of Ivan's office.

The bathroom was the only private place she could think of. "Do you want me to try a third article and be fired? I could really use your help. You're God. You can do anything. But I'm just me, and this is all too hard!"

## American Troops Deployed to Afghanistan
### Soldiers prepare for overseas duty.

Everyone took the anthrax scare seriously. Alex was tickled by how little it took to send the American public into panic. Flour, crushed chalk, powdered hand soap—all of these were potential weapons of terror. Now, hazardous materials specialists routinely donned protective suits to clean up mysterious white powder— everything from sugar to talcum powder.

John Ambrose walked into Alex's office unannounced and threw a newspaper on Alex's desk. "What do you plan to do about this?" he asked.

## Anthrax Worries Slow Mail Service
### Mail carriers express concern about handling mail which might be laced with anthrax.

John's upper lip actually quivered as he talked. "You've done the job too well. Everyone's terrified of anthrax. But we can't have mail service disrupted. Do something."

Alex smiled. "I'm way ahead of you." He handed John a press release he'd just finished. "It seems that there's a plot to blow up one of the bridges on the West Coast. It's fresh news, and it'll get anthrax off of the front page. Once the media stop talking about anthrax, the posties will calm down."

Ambrose smiled.

Creating news was an adventure to Alex. Each morning he reached for a newspaper eager to see what new turn the war on terror would take. But the next set of headlines almost caught him off guard.

## FBI Had Advanced Knowledge of 911 Attacks
Evidence suggests that the 9/11 attacks could have been prevented.

The White House advisors were concerned. If word ever got out that the 911 attacks could have been prevented, they were all facing jail time.

Alex whispered his good luck word to himself. Remordia. Then he smiled at the group. "This isn't a problem, Gentlemen: it's an opportunity—an opportunity to get rid of bleeding hearts without the guts to bend a rule or two. Listen to this. The FBI is inefficient. So we reorganize it and weed out any disloyal agents, the ones who might leak this kind of information to the newspapers. We'll do this with flair. We'll set up a new agency that answers directly to the president. Homeland Security, how's that for a name?"

For once John Ambrose was smiling, or maybe it was more of a leer. "Homeland Security—a perfect name. It conjures up comfort, a cozy fire, amber waves of grain, everything good and pure that our nation stands for." They shook hands on it.

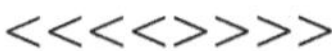

Soon Afghanistan took center stage in the news.

## Fighting in Kabul
Bin Laden's army retreats in chaos.

## Troops Reach Caves of Tora Bora
A treacherous path under the mountains will pit our soldiers' skill against the wiliest of enemies.

## Kandahar Falls
Today, the flag of the United States of America was unfurled proudly as troops marched into Kandahar.

# Chapter Twenty-Five

∞

The Afghanistan war was a huge success, and Alex was savoring the rewards of a job well done. He had never slept this well, and his dreams were so vivid, he frequently stopped to wonder if he hadn't actually lived through them:

*With a sharp, thunder-like clap and a shuddering rumble, the ground trembled, and Alex found himself at the top of a craggy mountain. Jagged rocks scraped at his legs as wind knocked Alex to his knees pushing him toward the edge of the cliff. "Now, will you pay my price... for your... life?" The voice boomed through the wind.*

*"I'm not afraid to die. I will not pay your price."*

*The wind screamed through the mountain—a banshee's wail, cold and piercing. Alex felt himself pushed towards the edge. Frantically, he grasped for a handhold, and found a pine branch, a limb growing through the tiniest of cracks in the rocks. He wrapped both arms around the branch, holding onto it for his life.*

*"Will you pay my price for your life?"*

*"No." Alex's scream sounded faint against the crashing wind that tore his clothing from his body, and he crouched, shivering and naked, clutching the pine branch next to his chest.*

*Then he saw his father's face. The mountain was gone; the wind had died down; Alex was still crouching naked, but there was only the face of his father. "I am very disappointed in you, Alexander." His words rang like an echo in Alex's head. "I am very disappointed in you." Over and over "I am very disappointed in you." Alex was aware of his shame and his nakedness.*

*The wind laughed and bellowed, and Weasel-man's image appeared,*

151

*picking his teeth with needle-sharp fingernails. "Will you pay my price?"*

*"Yes," Alex whispered. His chest burned, with the sensation of a bee sting, and his father's face took on the expression of a dried fig.*

*Again, the wind died, and the sense of terror waned, replaced by those feelings of ownership and control so familiar to Alex.*

Alex woke with a sense of urgency. Today I begin waging war against Iraq, he thought, just as I promised. Winning will be easy. We have a hundred times the weapons and military sophistication that Iraq has. They may as well use slingshots and B-B guns for all the good it's going to do them. Peacemaking won't be much worse. We'll bribe them with Yankee money and bomb the ones who don't agree. They'll come around, or be jailed, or die. They really don't have any choice.

Within a few days, his message began to hit the newspapers:

## 9/11 Linked to Saddam Hussein

New undercover evidence suggests Al-Qaeda received assistance from Saddam Hussein.

## Iraq May Have Undisclosed Cache of WMDs

White House skeptical of United Nations' arms inspection program.

## White House Hints of Nuclear Danger

The next cloud may be mushroom-shaped.

Johanna was in Ivan's office hoping to talk him into letting her print her article. "All of a sudden Iraq is to blame for 911, and we're supposed to believe it and go to war because of a rumor. Do you let your kid shoot up a school because maybe someone has a knife?"

Johanna tried to appear calm. "Ivan, you've got to let me print this. We're about to send twenty-year-olds into Iraq. They're going to risk their lives, supposedly to protect us. If they can risk their lives, we can bloody well risk our jobs."

Ivan read the story as Johanna paced back and forth. He just had to let her print it! Ivan wasn't a sellout.

When he had first hired her, he'd told her, "Write the truth; write with feeling; and I'll print it no matter what." And he'd stood by his word. But all that had happened when it was fashionable to be an activist. Ivan hadn't really had to stick his neck out. This was different. Now everyone was scared. And, as in the days of the mobs and protection money, Johanna thought, no one wanted to be the first to squeal.

Finally, Ivan spoke, slowly and deliberately, as if he were trying hard to get it right. "Johanna, I understand, and I'm killing it anyway. You think I'm a coward, and maybe I am. The whole world is watching while our country goes to war. The situation is delicate. That's a politician's expression, but it's true. Tempers are hot. Emotions are high. Everyone is afraid. And emotional, frightened people are dangerous people. I'm not going to be the one to rock the boat."

Johanna shook her head. "We used to have freedom of speech in this country. That's something you used to be passionate about. What ever happened?"

"Johanna, I'm still passionate about free speech." Ivan took out a well-worn pink and red paisley handkerchief and mopped his brow. "But I have to be practical too. All news about the war is filtered through the White House. If I want my reporters to have access to the White House, I have to print news with their slant on it. I know our leaders started a dangerous game. And they're wrong. But If I'm the whistle blower, I won't have a newspaper in which to print anything for much longer."

Then Ivan crumpled into a chair and rubbed his hands across his face as if the explanation had drained away all of his energy. "Besides, our country is set up to run on petroleum, and we don't have enough of our own. Yes, it would be nice if we had better buses and more people walked, but the hard fact is that we're just not set up for it."

"So we'll kill a few Iraqis for oil? Print that."

"There's more, Johanna Soldiers are trained to follow orders, no matter what. Even if it means their life. Even if their commander is wrong. Do you know why?"

"Why?" Johanna folded her arms across her chest.

"Because foreign enemies do exist, Johanna. And if a soldier splits up his troop, the whole troop dies. 'United we stand. Divided we fall.' 'We can all hang together, or we can all hang separately.' That's why."

Johanna stared. "But the man who said it was a revolutionary, and I think that King George III was more honest than our president. I believe that telling the truth sets us free. We're not at war yet. And it's going to take a lot of truth-telling to clear up this mess. But we have to do it now—before anyone invades Iraq and before anyone else gets hurt."

Ivan shook his head. He looked old all of a sudden. "No, Johanna. I won't let you print it." It was as if he had to muster all of his strength just to say it.

Johanna turned towards the door. "You're wrong," she said, and she held back the tears until she'd left Ivan's office.

# Chapter Twenty-Six

On her way home from work, Johanna bought a computer program on creating a web site and signed up for a community college class on web design.

As soon as she had learned enough, Johanna went to work designing her home page. She posted a picture of the earth as seen from space, and she made it turn slowly.

Below it, she wrote:

"May we respect all life—human, plant, and animal.

May joy drown the need to acquire.

May the timid find strength and courage.

May truth and justice rule our nation and the world.

She looked up from the keyboard and said to the air, "Especially me, God—may I find strength and courage."

Then she dug through her old files for all the prohibited fairy tales. Finally, freedom of the press, she thought and began typing.

<<<<>>>>

Ivan's layout editor knocked on his door. "Hey, Ivan, you asked me to keep an eye on Johanna's column. Well, she's sneaked another item into it. She referenced a website, www.fairytalesfortherestofus.com and it's not the one she uses for the newspaper."

Ivan just laughed. "Good for her! What the hell! Leave it in. If there's flack, I'll handle it."

<<<<>>>>

On her web site, Johanna posted the story of the coyotes in the chicken coop and her version of "The Emperor's New Clothes," along with everything else she'd been forbidden to write. She wondered if anyone read them and what they thought. Two weeks later, she found out when she added a chat room. Most of the comments went along the lines of:

"You're sick!"

"Watch your back. We shoot traitors for sport."

"If you'd lived in Afghanistan, you'd have been beaten and stoned by now." That's true, thought Johanna, but that doesn't mean we should stoop to their level. But she felt disheartened.

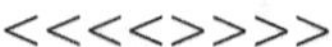

Strawberry Canyon was wet and cold and Johanna hugged her jacket close to her. "Where's the joy, Lord? The liars and bomb droppers have all the fun. What about me? Eeyore the donkey was cheerier than I am." She shivered and slipped her hands into her pockets for the warmth. "This must have been how Jesus felt at Gethsemane. Well, I'm not Jesus. And I can't drink his cup. And I can't walk his path. I'm not even a saint. And, sometimes, I'm not even very brave or very nice. I'm just me. And I can't keep working on this web site when the only feedback I get is someone wanting to stone me. So don't ask. I'm not going to do it." She nodded her head in emphasis. But she felt a tugging at her heart. She tried to ignore it—only it wouldn't go away. "Okay, I'll try. I'll keep writing. I can do that much. What's the worst that could happen? I'll go as far as I can. But I'm stopping way short of Golgotha! Just so you know."

Then she posted "The Chicken Coop, Part II."

The chickens began to get restless. The foxes were taking more and more eggs and giving the chickens less and less feed.

Meanwhile, the foxes were running low on oil, and they eyed the rabbit warren just down the way, which sat on top of a pool of oil. In fact, the rabbits had to be careful about where they dug or they'd come out all black and slick.

"I have a plan," said the King Fox. "We need something to rally the troops behind us. Let's kill two birds with one stone. (Forgive the insensitive analogy.) We need more oil, and we need to get the heat off of us vis-a-vis our egg acquisitions. So here is what I propose..."

The next day, he called the chickens to gather around him. "My fellow chickens," began the King Fox. "We have discovered that the rabbits and the coyotes are in cahoots with each other. They plan to kill us all and take over the chicken coop. They have anthrax. They have plague, smallpox, ricin and nerve agents. Such horrid, nasty chemicals! And, worst of all, they have nucular bombs!!!" The look on his face conveyed the horror of it all.

At first, the chickens were mystified. The only ones who had nuclear bombs any more were the foxes. And coyotes and rabbits had never gotten along. But the King Fox and all his advisors were so certain! "If we don't stop the rabbits, the next cloud we see may be mushroom-shaped."

Well, that scared the chickens. They chickened out, as it were. And, united against the rabbits, they forgot their quarrels with the foxes. After all, the rabbits were going to kill them in a ghastly fashion. The foxes said so, and they wouldn't lie.

Dear Readers,

You write the ending. Do we kill the rabbits? Or do we act more humane, and more human?

Peace,

Jody

There were only two comments in her chat room:

Magnum:  Kill the rabbits. And if you like Saddam so much, why don't you go live in Iraq?

Sandy Pumpkin: Thanks, Jody. It's nice to know that not everyone wants to wage war.

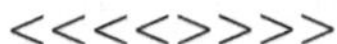

The next day, Ivan called Johanna into his office, and this time he laughed and smacked both hands on his desk. "I found your web site. Fairy tales for the rest of us. Catchy. Nice graphics, too. So you had to have the last word."

"Are you going to fire me?"

"No, I'm going to give you a raise. For your work on the paper, of course, not for the website. Way to go, shrimp! Stand up. Get counted. Watch out for rotten rutabagas!"

Ernie Martinez was quick to find Johanna's website, and he knew Alex wouldn't be pleased with it. Alex wasn't. "How could she have known all this?" Alex asked Ernie, but he just shrugged.

Alex read and reread Johanna's fairy tales. "There's no way. There aren't more than fifty people who know about Operations Quickdraw, Long Island, and Dirty Patriot, and they're all trustworthy. Unless, maybe, Hendricks got drunk and loose with his tongue. I always wondered about him."

"Wiretap her phone and bug her computer. Maybe someone'll show up on her email." Ernie said.

"We can always throw her in jail until she divulges her sources."

"But she's not putting anything into the paper. Just that wimpy blog. If we get on her case for that and it gets into the news, people who haven't seen her web site might go looking for it, and we'd end up with a really big mess."

"If she works for a newspaper, Homeland Security should already have something on her," said Alex.

A half hour later, a Homeland Security agent brought Alex a thirty-seven-page dossier on Johanna. It included her college degree, a list of credit cards, religious affiliation, favorite hobbies, stores, and restaurants, an exhaustive list of friends and acquaintances going back to college with background checks on many of them. It also contained copies of phone taps and computer taps.

Alex and Ernie spread the information out over a small maple table and poured through it. "Absolutely nothing," said Ernie.

"There has to be something. A gigantic leak somewhere. Look harder." Alex furrowed his brow. "Maybe it's nothing—or just coincidence. And there can't be that many people reading her website. Still…" He scratched his chin. "It won't hurt to keep an eye on her."

<<<<>>>>

Johanna used the name Jody in her web address, and she posted something new every Tuesday evening at seven o'clock.

Johanna's next piece was an ancient Buddhist story:

In a far-away kingdom, the holy men were fighting about the nature of God. So the king told them a story:

Once upon a time there was a certain raja who called to his

servant and said, "Come, good fellow, go and gather together in one place all the men of Savatthi who were born blind… and show them an elephant."

"Very good, sire," replied the servant, and he did as he was told. He said to the blind men assembled there, "Here is an elephant," and to one man he presented the head of the elephant, to another its ears, to another a tusk, to another the trunk, the foot, back, tail, and tuft of the tail, saying to each one that that was the elephant.

When the blind men had felt the elephant, the raja went to each of them and said to each, "Well, blind man, have you seen the elephant? Tell me, what sort of thing is an elephant?"

Thereupon, the men who were presented with the head answered, "Sire, an elephant is like a pot." And the men who had observed the ear replied, "An elephant is like a winnowing basket." Those who had been presented with a tusk said it was a ploughshare. Those who knew only the trunk said it was a plough; others said the body was a granary; the foot, a pillar; the back, a mortar; the tail, a pestle; the tuft of the tail, a brush.

Then they began to quarrel, shouting, "Yes, it is!" "No, it is not!" "An elephant is not that!" "Yes, it's like that!" And so on, till they came to blows over the matter.

> Brethren, the raja was delighted with the scene.
> O, how they cling and wrangle, some who claim
> For preacher and monk, the honored name!
> For quarreling, each to his view they cling.
> Such folk see only one side of a thing.
>
> Jainism and Buddhism. Udana 68-69
> Parable of the Blind Men and the Elephant

She got posts in her chat room almost immediately.

Sandy Pumpkin: Many gifts, many religions. I've had to straddle different cultures for most of my life.

Magnum:  They used to burn old crones like you at the stake.

Jody:  The Salem witch hunts ended years ago.

Spiderman:  You go, girl! Say what you have to say, shout to anyone who will listen, and don't stop until everyone hears you. We have to take the risk. That's what it means to have a soul. To tell everyone—friend and foe—this is what I believe, and I offer my name and my life for it. The hardest part is that it seems that we're the only ones who think this way. It's hard to be the first to weather criticism. But others will follow. We have to believe it.

Brat:  U guys R way strA-A-A-A-nge!!!!

Magnum:  Just listen to your pastor. He'll tell you what to think.

Sandy Pumpkin:  That's dangerous—not to think for yourself. You can end up with a Kool-Aid 'n cyanide cocktail.

Magnum:  Any Christian will tell you that his path is the only true one.

Shadow:  And Muslims will say the same.

Spiderman:  But it's hard to acknowledge the virtue of someone whose faith is radically different from yours.

Shadow:  Sometimes it's even harder to accept someone who's the same. Fundamental Moslems and Jews and Christians have so much in common. Guardians of their faith, they are like bloodhounds when it comes to uncovering sin, and they do not compromise. In fundamental Islam, there are bans on so many things.

Jody:  Maybe there's virtue to that, but it's the part of the elephant that I couldn't accept.

Shadow:  It is because you have never lived with death at your elbow. But when you walk through desert carrying your life in a camel's saddlebag, or when you hear rifles and soldiers, and know that only Allah can make safe your life—when you have lived this— then you understand. You dare not make a mistake; you dare not risk divine displeasure. Because your life lies in God's hands, and as you tie on your sandals, you know that it is only with God's pleasure that you do so. We believe in Allah's mercy, but we, who live with death on our shoulder, we dare not take it as already granted. We do as we are told. We pray as we are told. We love as we are told. We cannot take the same risks as the rich do. In matters concerning salvation, one cannot take chances.

Brat:  This is the stra-a-a-a-ngest chat room ever!!!!!

"Brother Walrus" was Johanna's next post.

Brother Walrus began the singing, a most unlikely leader since his voice croaked and grunted between the cracks of pianos (which were yet to be invented.) But he sang and croaked until he found the sounds that blended into music. The canary chimed in, warbling a harmonic third. Then the mice, one by one, the whales, the dolphins, Adam and Eve, of course, and the dogs, and donkeys added their spirit to the music. Giraffes beat time with their hoofs.

The chiming cradled the earth in a symphony and wafted up through the clouds to the angels. Last to join in were the peacocks, cats, and hyenas, the independent ones, the proud ones, their solitude a part of the masterpiece.


Comments appeared soon after.

Magnum:  The cat eats the mice and canaries. The dog chases the cat. Adam and Eve eat the whale, the cats, the dogs and the donkeys. The dolphins get tangled in the tuna nets. The hyenas get what's left.

Brat: Way to spoil a happy story!

Magnum:  You don't get it. The cat and the mouse aren't ever going to get along. You're chicken. Afraid of a little war. Well, listen. When your commander-in-chief tells you to shoot. You shoot. You don't ask dumb questions. You don't write stupid posts about walruses. You shoot because, if you don't, someone's going to shoot you.

Rats! That's what Ivan had told Johanna.

Jody:  What if your commander-in-chief is a shitty, two-faced, @$!$@!$ liar?

Sandy Pumpkin:  It's the extremes that get you in trouble. On the one side, there's blind obedience. It's efficient. It's clean. It's also dictatorship. It's Stalin and Hitler.

On the other side, there's free-thinking, putting kindness and love above rules. In the extreme, it's freeloading, lawlessness. Both extremes accept violence and murder.

But in the middle—when the two sides meet—it's the heavenly banquet. It's nirvana.

<<<<>>>>

After that, Magnum quit the chat room. The five of them, Spiderman, Shadow, Brat, Sandy Pumpkin, and Johanna were on the net almost every Tuesday at seven P.M. They wrote about everything, their feelings, beliefs, fears, and passions.

Funny, thought Johanna, I've never met any of these people,

and they're just about my closest friends. I wonder what they're like. Sandy's probably a cross between a theology scholar and a pumpkin farmer. And Shadow's like a wraith in robes and a turban. And Brat probably has braces—and blisters on her thumbs from typing.

Johanna saved the best for last. Spiderman. A Greenpeace warrior—strong, and young and angry—the type who'd take foolish risks for his convictions, the one in the demonstration standing up to the cops and catching the baton blows. I wonder if he's as sexy in person as he sounds on the web. And is he married?

Johanna couldn't believe she'd dared to think like this. "Oh!! Stop it!" she said to herself. "The web site isn't supposed to be a dating service. But, darn it, I can always dream."

# Chapter Twenty-Seven

∞

Her next web posting was a poem. And, although she'd never admit it, Spiderman inspired the poem.

## A Time for Heroes

This is the time that needs heroes.
We need you all on our side.
Corporate criminals, highly placed hypocrites,
It's a turnin' time.
It's time to join up
With the masses, the rest of us,
Unworthy just like you.

This is the time that needs heroes.
We need you all on our side.
Takers of money,
The great and the petty,
It's a turnin' time.
Time to give;
time to build.
Time to scatter some kindness for free.

This is the time that needs heroes.
We need you all on our side.
Politicians, and lawyers,
Twisters of truth.
It's a turnin' time.
Untwist the truth.

Make straight from the crooked.
Let honor and justice run free.

Men—strong, noble cowards
Divine, base and glorious.
It's a turnin' time.
Spin your hope, fragile spider webs,
Spin, spin and dream.
Spin your hope, strong as spider webs,
Spin, spin and dream.
For this is the time that needs heroes,
And it's a turnin' time.

She hit, "Send," and waited for her friends to answer.

Brat:  Tell my bruthers it's a turning time.

Spiderman:  Never mind Brat's brothers. Tell the whole world. We should do a turning-time project. A peace project. Imagine the impact we could make!

Jody:  A peace project. Interesting! Okay, how do you propose to do it?

Spiderman:  Is there any way we could meet? I want to see what you look like.

Johanna:  You read my mind. I'd love it. But you probably live two continents away from me. At least our time zones must be close because we're typing emails at the same time.

Spiderman:  So where do you live?

Jody:  Berkeley, California. How about you?

Spiderman:  San Jose, about an hour south of you. What are the odds! That's not too far away. How about this weekend? We could meet halfway between.

Jody:  I guess it should be somewhere with lots of people.

Spiderman:  You don't trust the Spiderman! It's a sad day when a Superhero has to show credentials.

Jody:  Hey, for all you know, I'm an ax murderer, and you need protection from me. Some place with lots of people. That's non-negotiable.

Spiderman:  Okay. Skip the halfway part. How about on the Berkeley campus—twelve noon, at Sather Gate. It's the only place in

Berkeley I'll be able to find. We can go get lunch, and then, if we can't think of anything to say to each other, at least we'll have eaten.

Jody:   Okay. What's your name, when you're not being Spiderman?

Spiderman:  Don't laugh. It's Homer Perlman. What's yours?

Jody:  I can see why you go by "Spiderman." Mine's Johanna Jacobson. Put a daisy in your lapel or somewhere, so I'll recognize you. I'll carry a daisy too. Hey, is anyone else reading this? Brat? Sandy? Shadow? Do you want to come to Berkeley this weekend?

Brat:  Mom laid down 3 rules 4 the net—non-negotiable—no addresses & phone #s, no sex talk, & no meeting anybody.

Sandy Pumpkin:  247 Elm Street. If you're ever in Vancouver, British Columbia, look me up, but California is too far.

Brat: Is Shadow around?

Sandy Pumpkin: Guess not.

Johanna:  So, Spiderman, what do you look like?

Spiderman:  Red cape, spandex body suit, classic web design—Armani collection.

Johanna: No, really.

Spiderman:  Five eleven. Dark blond hair. Not married. Not dating anyone seriously. What about you?

Johanna:  I pictured you tall and dark. I'm forty-three. My hair's almost black, and I have brown eyes. Average height and weight. Same thing with relationships. And I know this isn't a date or anything, but how old are you?

Spiderman:  Forty-four. I can imagine your face, but don't forget the daisy—just in case.

Johanna logged off, and sent a glance up into the air. "Thanks, God," she said. "I know this isn't a date, but thanks anyway."

<<<<>>>>

Spiderman was cute, not handsome. A spray of freckles covered his nose, making him look younger than forty-four. He had a daisy between his teeth, another in his lapel pocket, and a third behind his right ear, and he held up his Chinos with a Spiderman belt and belt buckle.

"Hi," he said.

The smile was really something, thought Johanna, the shy smile of a small boy. Johanna warmed up to him immediately. And, by way of greeting, she ran up to him and wrapped his chest in a hug, as if they'd known each other all their lives.

"I was afraid this would be awkward," said Johanna. "But I feel as if we've always been friends."

"It's because of the web site. I already know so much about you, Johanna. I know you're passionate about truth and freedom. And I know you're a prophet."

"A prophet?"

"Someone compelled to shout truth to the world. You're very lucky."

"A prophet! No one in his or her right mind wants to be a prophet. They all die ghoulish deaths, like getting stoned or fed to wild beasts." She flushed. There was something exciting about him, something almost magical that made her feel powerful. "And you," she said. "You don't look at all like what I expected, but you talk the way you write on the web."

"Let's get to know each other," he said, taking her hand in his. "There's a place a couple of blocks up the street where they serve really good coffee, and sandwiches too if you're hungry. How does that sound?"

"Fabulous," said Johanna. "I'm starving."

First, Homer opened her door. Then he escorted Johanna to a table, and waved his arm towards the bench behind it. "After you," he said.

"Thanks," said Johanna. "Formal manners, I love it." And she scooted onto the bench.

There was a breathy catch in his voice. "You really are a beautiful woman." He looked intently into her face, tapping his finger against his chin.

She giggled. "And you need new glasses."

"No, I need a ham sandwich and coffee," he said as the waitress came by to take their order.

"Me, too," Johanna said, "and chili cheese fries to share."

"Where did you get the idea to do the web site?" asked Homer.

"I felt I had to do something," she said. "And when my boss wouldn't let me print what I wanted, well, I decided that the web site was the best I could do. I just wish I could get more people to read it. Or understand what I'm trying to say. I'll bet most people think I'm a crackpot."

"You'd have more credibility if you'd let your readers know where you get your ideas. Do you have a source in the FBI or something?"

"No, nothing like that. It's just common sense. But the truth is so ugly! It's too hard to take in. Especially for someone who's already backed the president or the war."

"But the details… How do you get access to the details? Do you have a bug in one if the White House computers?"

"I'm no hacker. I only learned how to set up the web site a few months ago. But I do know journalism, and I can recognize censorship. When an article appears on page seventeen that should have made the front page, I know we're not getting the truth. And I know enough about oil and energy policy and politics and weapons of mass destruction to know that we're being lied to."

Once the conversation turned to politics, Johanna was set on fire. "I just get so angry and so… so… I just want to hang a sign over the freeway telling people, 'Listen! Use the brains you were born with. Hear what they're saying in Washington. The spin sounds good, and it's warm and it's comforting. But it's not logical.'"

"You have mustard on your chin," said Homer.

"And then they play the God card. God says you're holy if you bomb Baghdad. Allah says you're holy if you crash the twin towers. Christians don't annihilate people because they might have some bombs that no one was able find in the last ten years. And every time I see another American flag waving off of a freeway… well I just want to scream. All those flags really get to me."

Homer put down his sandwich. "So let's do it," he said. "A beginning to our peace project. Let's start hanging our signs over the freeways. They have enough flag material waving around to wrap up a small country. Let's show everyone what we think."

"What would we do?" Johanna was just a little apprehensive.

"Signs. We'll hang them where commuters can see them, right under the American flags that seem to be proliferating on their own." Homer's face suddenly became serious. He gave Johanna a piercing look deep into her eyes. "Are you with me?"

"I guess so."

"It's not illegal. No one can do anything to you for hanging a sign. It's an act of patriotism—exercising your freedom of speech."

"Do you think they'll leave the signs up?"

"It's still a free country. Last I heard. They'd better leave them up, or they're interfering with our First Amendment Rights."

"Okay. I'll do it. I'll hang signs at all the overpasses on highway four."

"Good girl." He leaned forward. "And I know this isn't supposed to be a date, but…"

It wasn't a great kiss, but Johanna savored the taste and the sensation.

"Do you want to go somewhere more private?" he asked. He smiled a crooked, little-boy grin. "You're very sexy when you talk about weapons of mass destruction." He put his hand on her waist— just below her breast.

"Yes, but no. But maybe we could meet again like this."

"No reason not to," Homer promised. His hand lingered at her waist. "You have Spidey's word on it." He dabbed his lips with his napkin, then picked up the bill and stood up. "We have a deal now, about the signs. You won't back out on this, will you?"

"I'll do it. Promise."

Johanna drove home feeling complete and contented. Inside her apartment, she pulled out some bedsheets and began to block out the letters of her messages, making sure that everything fit. In the background, a radio played songs from the seventies. Johanna sang and hummed along as the felt-tipped pen made shushing noises on the old cotton.

<<<<>>>>

And while Johanna was writing her sign, Alex was busy with phone calls to his FBI contacts. "I want a 24-hour surveillance at the Highway Four overpasses—priority one. A woman—Johanna Jacobson: Caucasian, height—approximately 5' 2", weight 110 lbs., dark hair and eyes, no obvious scars or other marks. She's a suspected terrorist. She'll be hanging signs at the overpasses. Arrest her and hold her. I'll make arrangements to have her transported for interrogation."

Then he called his old-time partner Ernie. "Have her flown out to McLenco Texas. There's a doctor there who's done some research with mind drugs."

"You mean like sodium pentothal?"

"What he works with is better. You don't get the babbling and gibberish you do with sodium pentothal. This guy is a genius. Here's the address. I'll get a hold of Nelson and tell him to expect Johanna."

Johanna turned off Interstate 80 and onto Highway Four, fighting the steering wheel to keep the car steady. The wind whistled and howled. I should take it as a warning, thought Johanna, and she turned up the radio in the car to drown out the sound of the wind outside. Even as an adult, Johanna was spooked by storms, relating them to the horrible night some forty years ago when her daddy had flown to London.

Johanna had hung all of her signs except for one. She took the Morello St. exit and parked a block away from the overpass. Then, carrying scissors, twine, and her last bedsheet, she walked over to where the American flag was displayed. "Make me a channel of your peace." Those were the words on her sign—the prayer of St. Francis. She examined the wire fence for the best way to anchor her sign to it. A car pulled up, but Johanna paid no attention to it, concentrating instead on the sign and the protective fencing. Something struck her at the back of her knees, and she crumpled to the concrete. She looked up to see dark shapes, maybe four or five men with nightsticks. Instinctively, she curled up into a ball, ducking her head behind her arms. The blows came so fast, Johanna had no time to think or to understand what was happening. She felt the nightsticks glance off of her legs and shoulders and back. She felt arms pulling at her hair and her legs. She heard screams and dimly knew they were her own. "FBI. Stop struggling," a voice from the dark commanded her. At the same time a burning shooting sensation bit into her hip— a hypodermic syringe. And then there was nothing... nothing until she woke up strapped to a bed in a darkened room.

# Chapter Twenty-Eight

∞

www.fairytalesfortherestofus.com The chat room.

Brat:  So what happened? It's Tuesday; 7 o'clock has come & gone. Where's Jody? Did she elope with Spiderman or something?

Spiderman:  No such luck! And she's gorgeous. And sweet and passionate, and, with a little more time, I could have fallen for her. But I think she loves a cause, especially a dying cause, more than she could ever love a man.

Shadow:  But Jody is on the computer every Tuesday like a clock working. She would not let some small thing like preventing war stop her from writing her weekly message. In fact, her weekly message *is* her way of preventing war.

Spiderman: We started talking about the impending invasion. Then we got really depressed thinking that it was inevitable, and suddenly she got agitated. "I've got to act," she kept saying. And finally, her eyes got real big and she looked at me. "I'm going to Iraq," she said. "That's crazy," I told her. "What good can you possibly do over there?" "I don't know," she said. "I don't understand it, but I've got to get over there. Call me obsessed or crazy, but… this is going to sound really dumb… it's like God is calling me. I'll get the next flight into Baghdad's airport."

Shadow:  But you cannot fly into Baghdad any more.

Spiderman:  I told her, "You can't fly into Baghdad anymore." And she said, "Then I'll fly into Iran—into Tehran or wherever, and I'll figure out how to get to Iraq from there." She just went on and on like that.

I thought of calling the cops but what could they do? So I just kept talking to her for as long as I could, hoping that she'd come to her senses. We talked until way late into the evening. And in the end, I told her to give it some time and to think about it, and then I just let her go and hoped for the best.

Brat:  Let's keep the chat room going anyway. Maybe Jody'll come back on some day. They do have Internet in Iran, U know.

Sandy Pumpkin:  And you should check the American newspapers in case Jody—or her dead body—is mentioned in one of them.

Spiderman:  You keep the chat room going if you want to, but I'm not logging on anymore. To tell the truth, Jody was always the main attraction for me.

<<<<>>>>

Ivan was livid when Johanna didn't show up for work. A week went by, and he began to suspect foul play. He checked hospitals, police stations, and morgues, but uncovered nothing.

Johanna's mother just cried when she found out that her daughter was missing. She filed a report at the police station and was told that, according to records, her daughter had boarded a plane to Iran. Martha took out her rosary beads. "Please keep her safe," she said out loud through tears.

Meanwhile, newspapers throughout the country blasted the news across the front page:

## We'll Go Alone—Troops Begin Invasion of Iraq

<<<<>>>>

[www.fairytalesfortherestofus.com](www.fairytalesfortherestofus.com) The chat room.

Sandy Pumpkin:  Jody hasn't posted anything in the last three weeks and it frightens me.

Brat:  Hey, Jody, R U back yet?

Shadow:  I am also concerned.

Brat:  Heck! I'll bet we're all worried about her, & meanwhile she's going hot & heavy with Spiderman. Romance is way more likely than foul play.

Ivan:  Ivan Buncheski here. I'm Johanna Jacobson's editor.

Brat:  Don't use Ur real name.

Ivan:  Okay, call me Big Bad Wolf. I'm Johanna's editor, and

I'm worried about her. She hasn't shown up for work in several weeks.

Brat:  She's Jody, not Johanna. & she had a date. I guess it was a date. With Spiderman.

Big Bad Wolf:  While I was drinking tea with the Riddler.

Brat:  No, Spiderman was his log on handle. His real name was Homer Perlman. & they wanted 2 meet. &, according 2 Spiderman, Jody decided 2 fly 2 Iran right after they talked.

Big Bad Wolf:  Johanna's dingy, but she's not that dingy.

Brat:  It's Jody, not Johanna.

Big Bad Wolf:  But people don't just fly to Iran on a whim. The story seems fishy. I'll have some of my staff check it out.

Shadow:  I will pray for our friend Jody. And for all the others who are in danger.

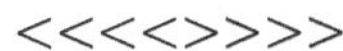

<<<<>>>

After they'd all logged off, Brat sat staring at her computer for a long time, rocking back and forth and absent-mindedly poking her mouse with a half-eaten Snickers bar. It sunk in slowly—Jody could be in serious trouble. Prayers, nirvana, the heavenly banquet, the human soul—these thoughts scurried in her head the way the white arrow zipped around her screen. If all this goodness existed, how could Jody have disappeared? She typed in United Religions, and found that such a website existed, and without a conscious thought, she clicked on "contact us."

She began typing: This sucks, sucks, sucks. Jody's dead or kidnapped or God knows what, & no one's doing 1 damn thing about it.

Brat stared at the screen with tears running down her cheeks as she typed:  This sucks; this sucks; this sucks; this sucks. So what R U doing about this????  They're doing all this in God's name, U know. Great words, great ideas, so what are U doing about all this?

I'll contact you all right, she thought as her fingers kept on typing.  So what the heck R U religious geeks doing? My friend Jody may B dead or kidnapped or in some freaky prison, & all she was trying 2 do was save some lives & make a difference, & she's probably lying in a ditch somewhere, & no one in the whole freaking world cares about her. & it's not just Jody. She's my friend, & that hurts me. But there's zillions of people like her in trouble & no one is doing squat for them. & if U think Ur so hot & religious, do something. Fix it. Make it right.

# Chapter Twenty-Nine

∞

So grateful! It was nothing short of a miracle that Maria had gotten the job at the McLenco Institute. She was quiet and shy, way too shy, and probably too young and inexperienced as well. She'd only graduated from nursing school a month before. And Maria had lived all but the last six years of her life in the Philippines. What did she know about American ways compared to someone who was born here? But she would work hard, follow orders to the letter, and provide her patients with the best care she knew how to give. She'd live up to their trust in her.

McLenco was located twelve miles outside of Waco Texas. Then it was set back from the main road about five miles down Farm Bureau Road Twenty-Three, and then three miles off of FB Twenty-Three down an unnamed dirt road with deep ruts, a road just barely wide enough for a car to drive over it. You had to really want to find the institute.

But once you rounded the last turn, the ghost town impression ended, making way for metal and concrete. The institute gave the impression of a bomb shelter approximately the size of a shopping mall. Slabs of concrete ran the length of the building, their gray monotonous plane uninterrupted except by a small door, a handful of narrow windows, and some Joshua trees and saguaro cacti stuck in the ground as landscaping. Inside, however, the institute was cutting edge, Maria learned later, with a security system second only to the Pentagon.

Dr. Nelson welcomed Maria personally on her first day. Satisfied with her credentials, he leaned forward across his desk, and looked directly into her face.

"This institute has the most up-to-date psychiatric techniques of any hospital in the world. We can provide basic medical procedures as well, but the main focus of our work is psychiatric. Much of our research deals with terrorism, and is, therefore, top secret. You'll be required to follow orders without question. National security depends on this." Maria merely nodded.

"You are not to receive visitors here at the institute. Personal phone calls should be limited to emergencies. No cameras, cell phones, or other recording devices are allowed on the premises."

"Yes, sir," she said.

"You will start immediately," he said. "Your first patient is Johanna Jacobson. She's under heavy sedation at the moment. You're to assist our other nurses with her care, and, as soon as she's able to walk, bring her to my office."

"Yes, sir. Thank you."

And with that, Maria began her work at McLenco Institute. There were few patients—they barely outnumbered the staff. Most were obviously Arab, and all were heavily sedated. Most of Maria's day consisted of tending to these patients: bathing and dressing them, providing food and medication, as well as taking vital signs— temperature, blood pressure, pulse, and such—and escorting them to and from Dr. Nelson's office.

For four weeks, she walked Johanna down to Dr. Nelson's office and back. And, each day, walking down the hallways with Johanna stumbling along beside her, Maria wondered about Johanna. Why was she here? What was her story? What had she done? And, as she had promised Dr. Nelson, she never wondered the questions out loud.

<<<<>>>>

Dr. Nelson worked with Johanna daily, and, as the weeks wore on, his smile grew rigid, and his voice tightened with unexpressed frustration. The questions were always the same. "Who are your sources? Do you have friends in the White House? The FBI? In the CIA? Where did you learn about Iraq?" And always, Johanna's answers were disappointing.

"I can't get any names from her, and she doesn't seem to be hiding anything." Dr. Nelson was on the phone to the White House.

"It's pointless to continue. We should release her."

But Alex wasn't buying any of it. He couldn't let Johanna go free and risk her talking. And her writing was too dangerous. Somehow, he had to plug the leak before his whole empire crumbled. She was a major flaw in a close-to-perfect plan. "There has to be some connection. She's got to know someone who has access to sensitive information. Did you ask her about bugs or computer hacking?"

"I did. She's been given every truth serum cocktail we have, and I've asked every question I could think of. I don't think she's sophisticated enough on the computer to do what you're suggesting."

"How about someone else at the paper?" Alex was frustrated and desperate for information.

"Not that I can tell."

Alex wasn't surprised. They'd bugged most of the computers at the *Upstart Gazette*, and hadn't come up with anything useful. "I need to know where she's getting her information." His voice trailed off.

"Well, what do you want me to do about it?"

"Keep working on her. Up the dosage. Do something, anything. I've got to find out who she's talking to. Everything depends on this. I don't care what you do, or how you do it. Just find out how she's getting her information."

"It may kill her."

"Just          as          long          as          she          talks          first."

# Chapter Thirty

∞

Alex came home from the White House to find Vivian on their couch watching the television and sobbing. A commercial was on, and Vivian had the sound turned down. He had to sound sincere. "What is it, honey?" he asked.

"Oh, Alex, it's so awful. My friend Denise just called. Her kid was stationed in Baghdad, and…" Vivian cradled her head in her hands. "God, I can't believe it. None of this stuff seems real."

"It's okay." He leaned her head against his shoulder. "It's okay. Now take a couple of deep breaths. You'll be fine."

"Of course, I'll be fine, but Harry won't." Vivian couldn't keep still. She pulled away from him, then stood up and paced. "Oh my gosh! A car exploded, and he… God… he made it to the hospital, and then… they thought he was going to make it. And then he just… he just died." Her breath came in gasps, and she couldn't do anything but cry. "See, he'd lost a lot of blood, and they thought they'd stopped all the bleeding, but then something opened back up and … Oh, God, I don't know. I don't know how it could have happened." She wiped at the tears with the back of her hand. "It seems like a bad dream … and I keep expecting to wake up and have it all go away, and… instead it just goes on and on."

Vivian turned back towards Alex and sobbed into his shoulder, and, for a long while, she couldn't stop. "Denise said he was badly cut up. I wonder what it was like. You know… How much pain… The medics said his chest had shrapnel—so much that he couldn't take a breath without tearing flesh."

"Calm down, honey. It's all okay. You'll be okay. I'm here now."

"Oh, Alex of course I'll be fine. But what about Denise? She lost a son, and his death was brutal. What about Harry's wife, Chris? She idolized Harry. And what about their kids? Todd's just a baby, too young to remember any of this, but Ashley's five and Harry had promised her that he'd be back. What on earth is Chris going to tell her? They're the ones who aren't going to be fine."

Vivian pulled herself back from Alex's arms and looked into his eyes. "The funeral will be held next weekend in Bar Harbor. We can stay at my parents' house."

She said it with certainty in her voice. Always the supportive wife, Vivian had never made plans for Alex before, especially plans that she knew Alex wasn't going to like.

"We can?" he asked. A weekend at Vivian's folks' house and a funeral sounded uncomfortably dull.

"Oh, Alex, we have to go to the funeral. She was my best friend in high school. We only stayed in touch by Christmas cards and a few emails, but I have to go to the funeral. Alex, you'll come with me, won't you? I'm so much stronger when you're beside me."

"Of course, honey. We'll do whatever you want. Don't worry. It'll all be fine."

And holding her closely, he kissed her forehead as a father would a young child, and she clung to the soothing warmth of his chest against her, drawing strength and comfort from him.

But as Alex comforted Vivian, a funny, prickling, uneasy sensation nagged at the back of his mind. A warning maybe? He pushed Vivian away on the pretext of turning off the television. Why did he suddenly feel so jumpy? He tried to use logic, but nothing fit, and, as the warning sensation wasn't all that strong or uncomfortable, Alex shrugged and dismissed it.

<<<<>>>>

The plane landed in Bar Harbor Airport, and Alex and Vivian picked up a rented Ferrari for their trip into Bar Harbor. He hadn't allowed any spare time for visiting. They'd attend the funeral and pay their respects; then Vivian would drive Alex back to the airport, and she'd stay on at Bar Harbor for a week and spend time with her family.

As they drove along the highway, songs from the seventies chimed through the speakers. Alex looked at Vivian and a sudden tenderness settled around him like a knitted blanket, and he wished that they could start over without the lying and infidelity. In some ways they'd shared so much. But then there was that stone wall protecting those things that Alex could never share—the secrets that could destroy everything.

The prickling sensation came back much stronger now, and he knew for certain that it had been a mistake to come to Bar Harbor. His neck and shoulders ached. But how could he turn back now? Maybe he could fake a car accident, or claim sudden illness. No. Any of those ploys would have him staying at Vivian's folks' house. It wasn't like Alex to be out of excuses.

Now, they were fifteen minutes out of Bar Harbor, with the funeral due to start in less than an hour. Alex had scheduled the day tightly on purpose. No, he'd just have to suck it up, make it through the next few hours and hightail it back to the comforts of Washington as soon as he could. Just a couple more hours and he'd be on a plane—with a highball in his hand, and a good movie on the screen.

Entering the mortuary, Alex felt transported into a world of old people. Walls, ceiling, carpet, furniture —everything was done in some shade of beige. Two columns, also beige, marked the entrance to each of the chapels.

"Here it is, Alex," Vivian whispered. "Harry Donovan. It's so sad, and yet it feels so good to be home. I can't explain it, but it's as if a part of me got left behind in Bar Harbor, and, all that time in Washington, I didn't even know there was anything missing."

Inside, the chapel was packed with white and beige flowers. Who ever heard of beige flowers, thought Alex. An organ groaned softly, the melody old and inadequate by Alex's standards.

"Let's visit with my folks sometime soon—just for fun when there's no holiday or anything else going on." Suddenly Vivian was animated, passionate. She hadn't felt this alive in years. "I can't believe it's been so long since I've been back home."

Vivian didn't wait for Alex to answer her. She found some old friends, and soon she was hugging and talking, and they were catching up on each other's lives. Meanwhile, Alex battled a strong and unreasonable urge to turn around and bolt out of the funeral home. The organ music was burning a hole into his brain.

He tried making small talk with some of the people there, but they were simple and boring. Alex had nothing in common with any of them. He glanced at his watch. Time dragged. He walked over to Vivian and was introduced to Sharon and Oliver, and he nodded and smiled mechanically as Oliver talked about their dog Peggy's agility trial performances.

"Cole is a sophomore," said Sharon, "and he made honor student on each of his last seven report cards. He's worked so hard, and we're so proud of him we can hardly stand it."

Alex nudged Vivian's shoulder. "We'd better sit down," he said, but she didn't notice him.

Finally the organ music died down, and a minister stepped up to a podium. "Please be seated," he said. At last, thought Alex. Another hour at the most, and then this whole thing would be over.

The organ began again with the strains of "Rock of Ages," and everyone stood up to sing. The rhythm was slow. Alex yawned and looked around the room.

In the front of the chapel stood a closed rosewood casket, polished to a handsome glow and draped with the American flag— the standard tribute for a soldier who had died in battle. Alex stared at the flag, grateful for the single spot of bright color in an otherwise drab and thoroughly depressing setting. The white stars shone crisp and clean against the blue. The stripes—alternating broad bands of red and white—reminded Alex of his life back in Washington.

Mesmerized, he stared at the flag, soaking in the brightness of the colors. Red evoked passion—the color of anger, the color of blood. Had Harry bled a lot before he died? Alex shivered knowing that a dead body lay inside the coffin—a spirit imprisoned by only a few planks of wood. What did Harry look like, sleeping inside the coffin? Alex's stomach turned; bile rose into his throat. Mechanically, he reached into his pocket for heartburn tablets.

Stop thinking like that, Alex said to himself. Instead, he tried to picture Isabella, his new intern. Isabella was so beautiful. Her large breast always made him think about sex, and her eyes were blue with an expression that was both shy and alluring.

What did Harry's face look like inside there? What expression would Harry wear throughout eternity? Peaceful? Angry? Fearful? It was a closed casket. Did they bother making his face look good? Probably not. He probably looked exactly the way he did when he died. Alex closed his eyes, pulling his attention away from the coffin. He began a mental list of the things he had to do as soon as the funeral was over. A stiff brandy on the plane was item number one.

But as soon as Alex let his guard down, the coffin drew his gaze, again reminding him of the specter inside. Without warning, Alex's conscious thoughts exploded into hallucinations, imprisoning him in a world of bizarre sensations. He smelled dank mold, as strong as if he were walking through a decaying marsh; and he remembered the mural of the eagle back in the Houston conference room, and the rabbit hanging in the eagle's grasp—its eyes frozen in final defeat. Pain and death, death and pain—chilling fingers held him around the neck, choking off his breathing. All the while, he saw the image of the rabbit. And now Alex was the rabbit, hanging in the clawed grasp, helpless, bleeding, and consumed in pain. Alex was freezing and drenched in sweat, all at the same time. Where were these thoughts coming from?

He turned to Vivian for comfort; the first time in his life that he'd sought support from his wife. He reached for her hand. She squeezed it reassuringly, and he held it like a lifeline to his sanity.

"All yours for a price." That's what the book had said. Was insanity the price that Alex had to pay? No, he was just a little spooked by the surroundings. Alex hadn't been to many funerals. No wonder he was unnerved. But he was okay, and this whole thing was just some bad dream. He squeezed Vivian's hand, drawing peace from her smooth skin and warm fingers. He'd just caught a touch of nerves. It could have happened to anyone who'd been working as hard as he had.

Then the organ music faded and died, and the minister stood up to speak. "We are gathered here to celebrate the life of Harold Donovan, a life cut short while Harry was defending our country." The minister's voice intruded into Alex's nightmares. "Harry was twenty-three years old when he died, and he leaves behind a young wife and two children. Harry died a hero, fighting for the ideals he believed in— freedom, justice, and truth."

Democracy, justice, truth—Alex recognized the drama that he scripted every day of his life. The struggle between good and evil, a life sacrificed for freedom. Americans ate this stuff up. And as Alex saw the funeral and all the hoopla for its dramatic impact, his hands steadied, and color returned to his face. The dead soldier was just a piece of this noble chapter in American history, a history that Alex was orchestrating.

"As Christians, we know that Harry is in peace, united with his Lord, and we rejoice for him. But this does not ease the sorrow that we feel for the loss of a young man who was part of our lives."

Alex imagined Harry, young and determined, with a crooked grin on his face, and a two-fingered salute. "Don't worry about me," he'd say. "I died defending my country." Then he'd drop his eyes and whisper softly, "I guess I'm a hero." Alex smiled at the mental image he'd created—a soldier in khaki standing in front of an American flag.

*"You arrogant shit head! You spawn of Satan!"* Alex jumped. It seemed so real! As if a living human voice had spoken. Alex tried to blink away the image but couldn't.

But this wasn't real. Alex tore his gaze away from the coffin, and looked at Vivian. There was a wrenching feeling as he struggled to maintain his focus on her, and he felt the imaginary soldier's eyes following him. He struggled to keep his head turned, but it was like turning away from a cougar set to pounce. Alex's essence lay in the soldier's eyes, and, defeated, he turned his head back to meet the soldier's stare. The image still stood before the flag, but now with jagged gashes along his face and neck.

Alex tried to wrench his gaze away from the apparition but couldn't.

"We take comfort in knowing that Harry died a hero," said the minister.

*"Died a hero? It wasn't time for me to die. A hero makes the choice to die. I didn't sacrifice my life for something noble. I died just because I was in the wrong place—a terrible place in a terrible time. And two days before I died, I shot at a couple of teen-age boys—who were in another wrong place. And I think I hit one of them. They weren't even as old as I was. I don't think they did anything, but they startled me, and I spooked, and I pulled the trigger without thinking. Oh, and that's what I was thinking about when I died. Otherwise, maybe I'd have been more careful. Maybe I'd have noticed something wrong with that car."*

"Are you okay, Alex? You look pale." Vivian was worried.

Alex startled at the sound of her whisper beside him. "Fine," he whispered back. And, like a madman, he turned back to the flag and the alternating stripes of white and blood. He saw the face, and with it came a bitter metallic taste filling his mouth. He began to retch and hurried out of the room grateful for the physical reason to leave the chapel.

The men's room was old fashioned. The floor had marble tile, and the stalls were painted that strange pasty green that dentists used to like. He knelt in front of the toilet and heaved until his throat was raw and his strength was spent, but the metallic taste persisted. He started to rise and felt his stomach lurching one more time. Once more he leaned into the toilet, and his stomach convulsed long after it had emptied itself.

Finally, the retching was over, and Alex stood up to rinse out his mouth and clean himself off. He'd stained his suit and ended up with wet spots where he'd sponged the vomit off with paper towels. This was Vivian's fault. She should have just sent a card with regrets. "Unfortunately, my husband's work makes it impossible for us to attend Harry's funeral…" Well, she'd pay.

Alex straightened his tie and checked his reflection in the mirror. He'd worn a red tie, and some water had splashed on it leaving a pattern of droplets on the silk. He wondered if the tie was ruined. He didn't want to go back into the chapel. He stared at the tie some more, dabbing at it with a paper towel. The wet spots were a deep burgundy color—the color of wine, not blood, he told himself. He rubbed at the spots some more, willing them to be gone. He was wearing Harry's blood. No, damn it, water, not blood. Vivian was going to pay for all of this. On his chest, Alex wore Harry's blood. No, not Harry's blood, just water, damn it! The words, "Harry's blood" filled his head along with the vision of a sucking wound. The metallic taste flooded Alex's mouth—a taste so strong that it gagged him, and Alex turned back towards the toilet, dry-heaving all the while.

When he walked back into the chapel, the organist was playing "Taps" and a young man in uniform presented a folded American flag to Harry's wife. As she took the flag, her head dropped, and the sounds of her breath echoed throughout the room.

<<<<>>>>

Following the funeral, the family held a wake at the home of Harry's Aunt Margaret. The house was a pale blue Cape Cod-style home built in the seventies up high on a hill, and it gave a good view of Bar Harbor. Through the living room window, if you looked over the rooftops and between the telephone wires, you could see the Atlantic Ocean.

The living room was set up for the wake with five folding metal tables, one of them covered with photo albums containing pictures of Harry, and the others packed with hors d'oevres. Greasy hors d'oevres, thought Alex—his stomach hadn't settled down completely—salami wrapped around gherkin pickles, chips and store-bought onion dip, some chicken wings soaked with orange stuff.

Aunt Margaret had probably made the food herself or bought it at the supermarket. You'd think she could have at least hired a caterer!

Alex tried to eat a cracker, but his mouth was dry, and he almost choked on the crumbs. He poured himself a glass of wine and sipped. What he really needed was a good brandy, but apparently Aunt Margaret was also too cheap to serve hard liquor.

Usually Alex was in the thick of any party, but this time he stood sidelined and watched stupid people hugging each other and talking about camera lenses, and soufflés, and sports fishing. The practice was obscene, thought Alex. A man had died, and his life was being celebrated with cheese balls and cabernet. It wasn't even very good cabernet, thought Alex examining the bottle, but he poured himself a glass anyway. He watched his wife hugging and giggling like a high school sophomore, acting as though these people were more important than all the influential friends they'd made in Washington. For Pete's sakes, he and Vivian had eaten dinner with senators and cabinet members, and they'd played golf with President Bush himself. Back in Washington, Alex had succeeded in ways most people don't even know to dream about. And here Vivian was acting like these little people were interesting.

Alex took a sip of the wine. His stomach was empty and the wine burned as though scratching his insides with sharp claws, but he didn't care. For distraction, he looked around the room. Harry's pictures stared at him from every wall and every corner: Harry, six years old, holding on to a string of fish and smiling like an idiot; Harry standing next to his bride Chris; Harry dressed up in a chicken suit, probably for some Halloween thing; Harry, holding baby Todd on his shoulder and the girl in a ballerina dress on his knee. What was her name? Vivian had told him, but he forgot. They had so many pictures of Harry, that they might as well have used him for wallpaper. Harry, Harry, Harry! At least this thing would be over soon, and the dead bastard could be put to rest.

Alex held up the wineglass then averted his eyes. The color made him nauseous. He tried to drink another sip, but it tasted as if blood were mixed in with the wine. His hand shook and the room swam and he staggered some as he made his way to Vivian and grabbed her by the elbow. "We have to go now. I have a plane to catch." He thought he would start retching again.

Vivian looked at her watch. "But we have plenty of time. Your plane doesn't leave for…"

"I said it's time to go now." Alex grabbed Vivian's arm hard, digging his nails into her skin, and propelled her toward the door with the strength of a football player tackling the ball carrier.

And Vivian didn't say another word. Without a parting hug for Denise or a thank you to Aunt Margaret, the two walked to the front door and down the street to where the rented Ferrari was parked. Vivian checked her arm to see if Alex's nails had left a mark.

They drove to the airport in silence. After parking the car, they proceeded to the security check area. "You don't have to wait with me if you don't want to," said Alex. He gave her a mechanical kiss on the cheek and turned away towards the window staring intently at the arriving plane.

"Fine. Good bye," Vivian said to the air between them, and walked back towards the main terminal.

Alex turned once, saw her walk away, then looked around for a lounge that served brandy.

<<<<>>>>

Back in his own home, Alex felt the strange effects from the funeral subside. He telephoned Isabella, his new intern, hoping for some diversion. He tried her landline, then her cell phone, but had to settle for leaving a voicemail message. After a quick shower he poured himself a neat Jack Daniels and flipped on the television.

Alex's mind was too keyed up to sleep, so he surfed the channels looking for some news. The troops were invading Fallujah, and Alex wanted to see what the media was doing with it. The kind of coverage they gave was extremely important. Fallujah's invasion was a great opportunity for P. R. What with war stories, explosions, heroes, and villains, Fallujah was the stuff that Americans craved, and it was Alex's job to make sure that the media made the most of it. He was in luck. The Eleven O'clock News was just starting and Fallujah was the lead story.

Flying debris filled the TV screen, as a wall crumbled leaving piles of rubble and a small pit dead as the moonscape. The scene shifted, and yet it looked almost the same. This time khaki-clad soldiers ducked behind stone walls, their rifles at the ready, then darted into the open accompanied by rapid bursts of rifle shots, explosion sounds, and shattering rocks. And suddenly Alex's hunting instinct took over and he was curious. What had they shot? Did they kill anyone, or did the Iraqis get away?

The camera moved on to a small cluster of houses, some lying in rubble. Every few seconds, a series of popping noises sounded signifying distant explosions. Then, louder than the others, an explosion blasted one of the largest walls still standing, causing the camera to shake and the picture on the screen to tremble. Behind the wall, rockets of fire burst from inside a home, shooting towards heaven. Above the fire a smoke cloud—thick, smothering, and greasy black plumed upward out of the growing flames.

Crying and screaming erupted, and three women, all thick-wasted, their heads draped in coarse brown headscarves, emerged from the remains of the house. They raised their eyes upward looking to their God to save them. One was limping; another held a bleeding hand. And they wailed, their voices high pitched, calling Allah's name, again and again till the words blurred into a single chant—Allah, Allah, Allah—over and over.

Alex shook. He reached for the whiskey, and upset the glass with his trembling fingers. It was a five-second scene at most. They shouldn't be showing this—the women hurt and crying. They looked far too vulnerable, too human.

The scene shifted. Two men carried a screaming boy on a makeshift stretcher. Alex had missed the narrative. Was it the terrorists that caused this, or was it American soldiers? They'd better not show a bleeding boy unless the enemy was responsible. He looked about eight years old. Blood drenched his clothes and covered most of his face. A thick scar cut through his right eye, and, as he wriggled and screamed, he reminded Alex of the picture of the rabbit held pierced in the eagle's claws. As Alex tried in vain to distance himself from the suffering on television, the sensation of burning and torn flesh took hold of him, and his breath turned to panting.

He tried to reach for the remote, but his fingers wouldn't work. He imagined the stink of burning flesh and tasted vomit and blood on his tongue. Once again Alex reached for the remote, but his hands were still shaking and he knocked it to the floor instead. Before this, he'd watched the fighting scenes, mesmerized, feeling strong and righteous and always wanting more. They reminded him of playing soldier as a boy, hiding behind trees shooting guns that were really sticks and making bam, bam, bam noises. But now, somehow, he felt sickened instead, and identified with the prey instead of the hunter.

Then they showed coffins, row after row, each draped by an American flag. Red, white, and blue, the colors of freedom, the colors of blood and death. Alex stared at the flags, the red and the white stripes pulsing like a strobe light. He watched the coffins roll by, still tasting blood in his mouth, and he shook and shivered, his skin goose-bumped, his soul cold as death and full of fear. "Turn it off." Alex spoke the words out loud, shouting to the ceiling. He was losing his mind. On his hands and knees, he fumbled around the floor for the remote, but couldn't see for the tears in his eyes.

Blood red, steel blue, death-pale white. Alex stared. The newscaster read on. "… one thousand two hundred and twenty-one American and allied soldiers killed in Iraq. Most died after the war was officially over."  In a panic, he flipped over magazines and newspapers. He looked under the chair. It had to be somewhere. "… the president warns that hostilities will not be over any time soon." Finally, Alex found the strength to walk over to the television set and turn it off.

# Chapter Thirty-One

∞

The next day, Alex entered the White House feeling like a sack of cement being dragged behind a truck. He'd hardly slept, but more than that, he felt as if something strong and evil held him in its grasp, choking off his air. He took a ragged breath, sighed and tried to shake off the feeling but couldn't.

Inside his office, he found Isabella waiting for him with two mugs of steaming coffee and a basket of sweet rolls on his desk.

"Where were you? I tried to call," he said, flopping into his chair below the painting of Winston Churchill. An accusing pout played across his face.

"I made a date with some friends. I didn't expect you back from Bar Harbor that soon. Would you like a cup of coffee? You don't look so good," she said.

He nodded and she brought over one of the mugs, smiling and kissing his cheek as she did so. He pointed at the basket, and Isabella brought it over as well, letting him pick out a pastry.

For a while they ate and drank, neither one breaking the comforting silence with words. But Isabella wasn't comfortable. "Alex," she asked, "how many people have died in Iraq so far?"

The words startled Alex. He didn't want to think about death today. "Only about a thousand. One thousand two hundred and twenty-one American and allied casualties according to last night's news cast. I can get a more accurate count with a phone call."

"But that's only our soldiers; it doesn't count Iraqis. And that's the only answer they'll ever give on the news. It's like we're over there shooting but no one ever gets shot. How many Iraqis were killed?"

"To quote General Tommy Franks, 'we don't do body counts.'"

"What's that supposed to mean?"

"It means we don't count dead bodies. It's cleaner that way."

"I've been surfing the net. According to the Iraq Body Count, there are between fourteen thousand and seventeen thousand civilians killed so far. That doesn't count Iraqi soldiers, and it doesn't count anyone who got buried in a mass grave or anybody buried without the authorities being notified—which happens a lot since

Moslems have to bury their dead within twenty-four hours. Also, they don't count any men of military age, because they might be soldiers."

"You've been very busy," said Alex, but his voice sounded as if researching were a shameful thing to do. "Leave the politics to the ones who've studied for years. They're trained to understand all of this." He tapped his chin with his finger and smiled a lopsided grin. It was charming and boyish, and quite disarming. "Now, what I want to know is—how do you manage to look so sexy when you bring the muffins?"

"And according to the *Lancet*, the body count is closer to a hundred thousand, and that only includes people who died from bombings and shootings. Some died because clinics and utilities were destroyed, and they couldn't get decent medical help or clean water.

Christ, thought Alex, how do you explain Arabian politics to a sexy little plaything? "Attitudes in the Middle East are different from those in America. Remember, these people are used to Saddam Hussein's rule. They understand threats and a heavy hand. Over there, killing a hundred of their people for every one of ours is the sign of a strong and efficient leader."

Brown eyes wide and fearful, Isabella's face took on the expression of a wounded animal. She didn't say anything.

How could he make Isabella understand? Alex tried, but he knew it was futile. "They don't understand anything else. If we don't kill them, they'll kill our people. As we stand here talking, more and more Arabs are joining Al-Qaeda. We need to keep peace with a very heavy hand or they'll walk all over us. Kill them before they kill us. This is the Middle East, not downtown New York."

"It's like Harlem," said Isabella. "When in doubt, shoot—preferably with a semi-automatic. And the biggest thug gets the most respect."

"Well, yes." Alex wanted to be positive, but he was not sure if he liked the analogy.

"Like the kid who brings a gun to school for protection."

Instead of continuing the conversation, which could only get ugly, Alex took a quick peek to make sure that the door was closed; then wrapped an arm around Isabella's tiny waste. He always loved the feel of her delicate body against his arms.

"You pig," she said, wiggled out of his arms, and left the room.

Christ, thought Alex. He shrugged. She'll come around, he figured. He controlled the whole goddamn United States. Surely, he could control one dewy-eyed intern.

# Chapter Thirty-Two

∞

Alex had managed to stay away from church for three months, but on this particular Sunday, Vivian was insistent. And she was probably right. He had to make an appearance. This was a godly crew that Alex worked with, and Alex had better walk the godly walk.

The gospel reading that day was the story of the Prodigal Son. Alex's mind drifted and he wondered what Isabella was doing and if she'd be free later that evening, and how he was going to get her mind off of politics and on to sex.

But Pastor Woodrow's voice was loud, and broke in on Alex's reveries. "Not long after that, the younger son got together all he had, set off for a distant country, and squandered his wealth in wild living."

Loser, thought Alex. Like all those stupid, poor folk, squandering money, and then begging their Uncle Sam for welfare. Alex saw himself as the older son. With seven million dollars and his Halliburton stock shooting its way through the roof, he needed a full-time accountant just to invest and re-invest his capital. As the preacher talked, Alex mentally counted his assets, and included Isabella and the very nice asset she sat on.

Pastor Woodrow seemed particularly passionate about this story. He all but shouted the sermon, and his words kept interrupting Alex's daydreaming. "The prodigal is right here among us." No doubt about it—the preacher was in rare form. "It's not about squandering money. It's about sin and disrespecting God, our Father."

As Pastor Woodrow continued Alex fantasized about re-decorating his office with gilt accessories to accent his picture of Winston Churchill.

"… coming back to God. For us, it's not a matter of walking miles wearing rags, but a matter of confession and repentance."

And here the pastor paused. When he continued, his words rang out like explosions—burning with divine fire, as if God Himself were speaking, and Pastor Woodrow was merely the vessel. "… a matter of our souls, on a spiritual plane, trekking their way back to God.

"In the early church, the congregation would make public testimony, each member confessing out loud to his brethren any egregious sins that he'd committed." Silence enveloped the congregation.

I'd like to hear that, thought Alex. Reality TV in church—what a show! Public humiliation!

"I invite anyone who feels that he's transgressed to come forward, and to ask forgiveness before God and His people. God offers His peace in exchange for your sins."

Fantastic, thought Alex. This service was getting better and better. All he needed was a tent, and a holy water fountain. Would some dumb asses really come up and publicly confess to whatever? What a side show! Somebody, do it, he thought. Somebody, spill and make my day.

The congregation sat still and expectant, each person searching his soul, and the silence was charged as if it were a living creature.

From the back of the church, a man leaning over his cane began to shuffle forward. The skin on his face hung in deep pouches exposing blood-filled sacs below his eyes. The man walked slowly, and it seemed as if the whole church froze in time as he made his way up to the front.

Suddenly an unreasonable urge grabbed Alex. It was like his mother's gentle arm propelling him toward the altar. Do it now. Tell it all—the lies, the schemes, the secrets. The urge to confess pulled Alex hard. Resisting it all but ripped him in two. He needed to stand, to shout. "We're murdering thousands of Iraqi innocents, and I am responsible. I—Alex Lidecker, not the Taliban, not Saddam Hussein. I am the terrorist. I made up the nuclear weapons scare and spread the rumors of Saddam's undiscovered arsenals."

The words screamed and exploded inside of his head, demanding to be heard, and Alex had to look around. Had he actually said them out loud, or had he just imagined this mad unreasonable impulse? No, the church was quiet, all eyes turned towards the old prodigal wending his long way to the front, and now mounting the steps up to the altar.

"I spent 'bout fourteen years worshipping alcohol. Lost my job, my wife, my kids." He whispered the words, but the sound carried through the stillness, and he stared at the floor while he talked, as if unworthy to lift his face. "Always told myself that I wasn't as bad off as the other guy. Said it wasn't my fault. Told myself anyone who'd been through my life, seen what I'd seen, would've done the same. And maybe he would have. But that don't matter none. What matters is what I've done. And I'm ashamed. And I feel burdened with the sin of it. See, I know the prodigal 'cause he's me, and I'm here to ask God to forgive me and to lift the burden off of my shoulders, because it's mighty heavy, and I can't carry it no more."

Like the fires of Pentecost, God's spirit shook Holy Final Words Church. You could feel it—driving hard as a blast of sleet, but also gentle like a lover's kiss, or a baby's soft skin. Power, but so much more! God's love, and with it, healing and redemption. And as the prodigal walked back to his seat, he stood a little taller, and marched with a stronger step. And, his face, oh his face! You couldn't exactly say what it was that had changed. The features were the same; the lines were still there. But it shone with God's mercy and there wasn't a soul in the church that didn't see Christ in the man's eyes.

Alex saw it too, and was shaken. The urge to stand grew stronger now, like a flying cannonball. And he was holding it back with just his little finger. To do this thing, Alex would have to sacrifice his whole life, not just his house, and money, and friends. And Vivian. But he would have to destroy his very essence, and, woven into this essence, was pride. Without it he was nothing. Mighty, god-like, victorious, and proud, the son his father always wanted, this was Alex Lidecker. Alex slumped in his seat, unable to destroy the colossus.

Next to come up was a woman in her twenties. Her platinum-streaked hair was pulled into a French twist, and she wore a beige suit smartly trimmed with a camel's hair collar and cuffs. A topaz poodle brooch sat on her right lapel.

"I've slept with eleven different men during the last year," she said, "while Eugene was stationed in Baghdad. I tried to be faithful to him. I waited. Occupied myself with everything I could think of. But months went by, and well… I'd look at myself in the mirror, and I'd brush my hair, and do my make up… all the while asking myself just who was I trying to please. What was the use? My man should be in my bed next to me, not playing soldier some thousands of miles away. I know it's not his fault that he's over there, and I'm over here. But there wasn't anyone else to blame. And I did blame him. Sometimes I think it would be easier if I were the one over there."

She tried to go on, but the words stuck in her throat, and tears threatened just behind the long, black lashes. As if protecting herself, she wrapped her arms around her shoulders, and dropped her gaze to the floor. "I could stay busy during the day, and it was okay. But then night came, and that empty nothing just crashed all around me. It's funny how nothing sometimes seems more powerful that all the woes on earth. Anyway, I tried to ignore the quiet and the aching, but in the end, I couldn't stand it. It was going to be just a drink with an old friend, someone to talk to, to laugh with, to commiserate with. But, well, in the end, he was in my bed. And after the sun came up, I said it was over, and that I'd never do it again. But the nights after that were still too quiet, and—I don't know what it is about getting into a bed by myself, but I hate doing it. And sometimes, when it was just too quiet, I'd go down to this hang-out a few blocks away, just for a drink and someone to laugh with, and sometimes it would be just that, but also sometimes I'd end up with someone sleeping with me. Each time I told myself that this was the last time.

"So today, I have to do this. And now, after my confession, I need forgiveness, but mostly I need strength, because Eugene's not back yet, and there are going to be a lot of cold and lonely nights between now and when he comes home. And I don't know if I have the strength to make it through them, but I've got to try to be faithful. If he can go over there and risk his life, I can stay true to him. Or at least I have to try."

She began to shake and sob. "And I hope Eugene can forgive me. I hope I can forgive myself." Her sobbing grew harder. The preacher held her shoulders between his hands, then, laying both his hands on her forehead, he prayed with closed eyes. Alex couldn't hear the words, but he witnessed the power; he felt spirit in the air as the preacher whispered.

Hearing the story, Alex felt pierced as if by shards of glass. He'd slept with her once. He thought her name was Crystal. And he hadn't connected with her in her bed the way he did now, twenty feet away from her, as she spoke and cried. God stabbed him. Alex saw. Life was meant to feel like this.

Alex Lidecker, the political savant, dressed in Armani, but underneath it, the real Alex, the man, wore the tattered mantle of a penitent sinner. Without noticing it, he rose from his seat preparing to discard his riches like rotting trash. He'd risk it all—respect, wealth, power. And that wild giddiness—flying on meth-like enthusiasm, he called it—that comes from cheating and winning. And now he was about to sacrifice everything in exchange for the peace that comes from an honest relationship with God and man.

But in those moments before Alex reached the aisle, his father's image flashed in his mind. And he could feel the words inside his bones. "I'm very disappointed in you." Alex paused. Remordia, he thought. He wanted God's peace, but he needed his father's respect, that and the demi-god life he'd built. Save me from this craziness, he thought. He was Alex Lidecker. He could have anything he wanted. Well, he wanted it all.

"Great sermon, moving." But Alex said the words mechanically.

After church, Alex took Vivian out to brunch at The Captain's Table. In spite of the nautical theme—the décor was comprised mostly of driftwood and fisherman's netting—it was a posh establishment, and, more importantly, it was a place where Alex had never taken any of his mistresses. The service was particularly slow that day, and, while they waited, Alex poked at his napkin and his silverware in frustration. In fact, he all but got up and paced the floor with impatience, and several times he barked at the waiter. "Are we ever getting served?"

Vivian put a hand on his shoulder. "Is anything wrong?" Then she wished she hadn't asked. Alex had been angry and distracted for quite some time. The moods seemed to come out of nowhere, and it was getting harder and harder to coax Alex back to normal. In fact, a couple of times, he'd slapped Vivian so hard that he'd left welts on her face.

"It's frustrating to be served by a gang of idiots who can't pour water let alone produce a decent meal in under a week. I can't stand incompetence." He pushed his fork into the salt shaker, which fell over against his water glass with a clang that echoed across the room. Several other guests looked over at them. Vivian turned away and kept silent until the waiter brought their food.

# Chapter Thirty-Three

∞

The following morning, Alex walked into his office trying to think up a way to charm Isabella. Maybe he'd fly her somewhere out of the country for lunch and a romantic interlude. That usually impressed his interns. There was just something about being the only two passengers on a private jet.

But the moment he opened his office, he knew an intruder had been there. At first, it was just an impression. Frantically, he looked around the room and noticed smudges on the bookcase behind his desk. Someone had been there. A break-in! In panic, he began to search his desk, then his bookshelf. Top secret information was everywhere. He poured over all the scraps on his desk, mentally categorizing all the letters, faxes, CDs, and Post-it Notes that could have been stolen. But the theft was big and obvious. He hadn't wanted to face it, to admit to himself that something he loved had been stolen. Someone had taken his painting of Winston Churchill and replaced it with one of Adolph Hitler.

It took Alex a second to register what had happened and another to pick up the phone.

"Security here..."

Alex hesitated. The intruder was probably Isabella, and she could do so much worse than steal his picture.

"Forget it." He slammed the receiver. Damn! He loved that picture—much more than he loved Isabella.

Alex stared up at Hitler's portrait, wondering. "Your eyes are dead black," he said to the picture. "Animal droppings have more character. And with that thin, shoe-polish-black hair and that silly mustache, what did Germany ever see in you?  You were like the bubonic plague. But they loved you, and they feared you, and they sacrificed ethics and reason to follow you. And they feared the Jews so much that they could kill children without shame. How did you ever pull it off?" Alex stared at the picture as if Hitler could talk.

"Oh," said Alex finally. "You understood the secret. Remordia!"

He pulled at the picture until it tore free of the wall leaving two gashes behind where nails had been. He looked around for a place to stow it, then dropped it face down on the floor in a corner.

Turning his mind away from the portrait, he began his workday, pulling memos he'd written out of the IN basket on his desk. Most of his memos were cryptic—less chance for a dangerous slip that way. He reread the notes and transcripts concerning Johanna, and decided it was time for a call to Dr. Nelson.

"I haven't been able to get anything out of her, sir," said the doctor. "At least not any names or contacts, or even any groups other than the website where you found her. The only useful thing she's offered is that she thinks she's talking to God, and she took a WMD class years ago. But as far as her knowing anyone or anything, there's nothing."

"Damn it!" This day, sure as hell stunk. Alex looked across the room at the overturned portrait of Hitler. "Damn it, Nelson, she can't have just plucked all that information out of the nether ether. Someone's must have slipped it to her."

"Well, there's not much more I can do."

"Damn." Alex needed to hit someone—to hurt someone badly.

"In that case, put her down."

"Yes, sir."

"No, wait. Have you considered old tried and true methods?"

"Pardon?"

"Old-fashioned methods."

"You mean torture?"

"Try one more time. One more session with everything you can come up with. And, yes. including torture. Then, if you still can't get anything, put her down."

"Yes, sir."

<<<<>>>>

Every now and again, Alex would think about the day in church when all those people had made their confessions. He could remember the sense of longing. It was like seeing something out of the corner of his eye, then turning to look at it, and finding it no longer there. And his soul desired it as children long for Christmas.

In his office, pretending to listen to CIA tapes, Alex stared at the space where Churchill's portrait had hung. He tried to remember what Churchill's face looked like, but all he could see in his mind was Hitler's eyes staring at him, as if penetrating his thoughts. Where was that giddy sense of victory? He was still the king, the emperor, the god. Why wasn't it sweet anymore? And he could remember power filling him until he thought he'd burst with the joy, and it was all he could do to keep from bouncing around like a two-year-old. Where had it all gone? Why the depression? Maybe, like Alexander the Great, he cried because he had no more worlds to conquer. No. He still had work to do. Iraq was far from won. The newspapers would have to be fed. There were still dollars to be made. Gas was only $2.00 per gallon. The western fields of Iraq had not yet produced their tribute. Iran had not been invaded. Indeed, there were many more worlds to conquer, but the battle was no longer joyous. Why?

A wafting sense of peace touched him, followed by a piercing ache. He remembered that day in church. What had it felt like? He tried to reproduce the sensation, but could only feel pain.

"For a price." Where did those words come from? And why was he thinking them? "For a price." A price for what?

Suddenly Alex remembered. He closed his eyes. He was eleven years old again, and all alone sitting beside Puddin' Creek. It was dark, and he was shivering and wondering how to get out of a whipping. "For a price." That's what the book had said. He remembered squinting to read the words in the dark. And was the price indeed his soul? Well, Remordia had certainly kept its side of the bargain. Was that the devil? Had he agreed to sell his soul to the devil?

But that's ridiculous, he thought. I was just a scared little boy back then. Anyway, who believes in the devil anymore?

And all the times after that—well, that was just habit. He'd always looked to the word to get himself out of trouble. But it wasn't as if he'd consciously said he wanted to sell his soul in exchange for favors. He'd never thought of it as making a pact with the devil. It wasn't fair. But then, the devil didn't play fair.

The devil?

Remordia.

The devil!

No!

The room chilled. Alex's heart all but stopped, and his shoulders slumped, aching, crushed by an unseen burden. Alex stared at the place on the wall where Hitler's portrait had hung. Where did that word come from? In his mind, Alex had said, devil. He didn't really believe in the devil—any more than he believed in God. He, Alexander Lidecker, was god. That was what he believed. That, and the word Remordia. But it was only a good-luck thing—like a rabbit's foot or a four-leaf clover. He'd never actually done anything superhuman.

Alex began to tremble, chilled as he had been that night years ago sitting beside Puddin' Creek. He remembered hugging the book next to his body, its pages musty with age. What was that book's name? Something with a "C." Chesterville's! *Chesterville's Complete Book of Spells.* On an impulse, Alex pulled up the Internet on his computer, and typed Chesterville's Complete Book of Spells. He stared at the screen for a full minute before pressing enter. Nothing came up. He typed in antique books and bookstores. Three hours later, he located a shop in New Jersey whose owner claimed to carry a copy of *Chesterville's.* With a sinking feeling, Alex reached for his car keys, and, driving as if in a trance, he headed for the New Jersey Turnpike and Ye Olde Biblioteque, a modest antiquarian bookstore in Trenton.

Alex found the bookstore without any trouble. A small, dusty building with peeling paint, it stood between two high rises. The owner Mr. Garibaldi, was a sixtyish man wearing an old-fashioned jacket with elbow patches. As he rang up the sale, he began telling Alex the saga of how he came to own Ye Olde Biblioteque. After a ten-minute discourse, Alex was able to get away with the precious book wrapped in brown paper. He loaded it into the trunk of his car and sped home.

<<<<>>>>

That evening, Alex wolfed down his dinner without saying a word. "I'll be in my den. Don't bother me," he told Vivian. "Important work. Top secret." And he fled to his man-cave.

I'm not superstitious, just curious, Alex thought, trying to convince himself of that as he pulled out *Chesterville's Complete Book of Spells*. He tore the wrapping off of the book. The musty odor inside reminded him of attics, old trunks, and historic ghosts. Carefully, he leafed through the pages. Most were a dull tan, the color of autumn leaves gone to dead brown just before winter's blanket of snow. He handled the pages gingerly. And just like dead leaves, they crackled and flaked away in his fingers. Alex tried to remember that Halloween night. "Lying spells. The craft to convince."

Hell was supposed to be hot, but Alex was chilled throughout as if suspended in ice. He found the lying spell and skipped to the bottom of the page. "… for a price. Thy essence consumed with lye. Shackled to spiked wheels. Dragged by wild oxen through rasping rocky pits. Flesh rotting from thy writhing body." There was more. "Agony not of flesh but of mind and soul." "Chill not of body but of spirit." "For hell and damnation lie not in chasms of flames but in the human heart."

Alex saw himself as a small maggot in the center of an unidentifiable rotting carcass. And he was afraid. Icy fingers tore at his heart and choked his breathing.

"Snap out of it," he whispered to himself, but his body shook. "You don't believe in any of this. And anyway, it's too late. So schedule a massage, enjoy your empire, and stop all this shit." And like the maggot in the rotting carcass, he slunk over to a wet bar in his bookcase. He poured brandy—glass after glass—amazed that he wasn't drunk. Finally, he threw up, and that cleared his head.

In the middle of the night, Alex sat bolt upright in bed and screamed, but he didn't wake up. Vivian debated whether to wake him or not. He'd been having nightmares for quite some time now. A few times, when she'd wakened him, he had just shivered and refused to tell her anything. Then he'd been afraid to go back to sleep. Well, no wonder with all the pressure he was under. He thrashed in his sleep, and Vivian wrapped a robe around herself and, feeling a little guilty for leaving Alex, went to sleep in the guest bedroom. It seemed that neither one of them was getting much sleep lately. She wished Alex would tell her what was so wrong, but he'd fly into a rage whenever she asked.

*In Alex's dream he stood at the top of the Houston conference center watching the world crawl beneath him. But, as he watched, the building crumbled under his feet, and he plummeted, tumbling head over heels in an uncontrolled free fall.*

Then he woke up.

It took him a few seconds to realize that this was only a dream and that it was over. Indeed, sometimes he wondered what was real and what was dreaming—the nightmares or his daytime life. He reached over, but Vivian was no longer with him. And he was so tired.

Vivian heard the shouting from the other room and pretended to be asleep. Lately, Alex's behavior frightened her. He hardly slept at all. And when he did nod off, he always woke up screaming.

She'd tried talking to him, but Alex never explained anything. She just chalked it up to the weight of leadership and figured it was the sacrifice that Alex made to keep his country free.

# Chapter Thirty-Four

∞

Johanna woke up in a metal cell the size of a closet, lying face up and tied down between two stakes jutting up from a hard cement floor. The small cell was dank and drafty. Johanna craned her neck trying to see around her. The room was dark but not black.

"Please, God, somehow, someway, help me. Because I'm disheartened and terrified, and all I want is to die."

"In here, Johanna, you'll find that God is deaf." The voice, a horrific roar, came from a black-robed figure that reminded Johanna of a sixteenth century executioner. A draft blew in from under the door. But it didn't chill her. Lying as she was, it brushed past her cheek, bringing home the memory of a soft breeze that had brushed her cheek many years ago.

Dr. Nelson watched Johanna's interrogation through a one-way mirror, but he couldn't see very much since the room was almost pitch black. He could see the shape of a hooded figure, and Johanna's body strapped to the floor, but he couldn't make out details. Instead, he concentrated on the sounds.

A sharp crack. Johanna's scream. Another crack. Another scream. Then a voice, heavy with accent. "Who talked to you? Who told you secrets?"

"No one. No one." There was a note of hysteria in her voice.

The tape went on in the same vein. Not very efficient, thought Nelson. For a while the sound of rushing water rushing drowned out the words. Johanna choked, coughed, and gagged. "Please don't. No more," she said.

"The name of your friend in the government."

"I don't know." Her voice broke and stuttered. She was probably shivering.

Enough of this, thought the doctor. He gave the order; the hooded figure injected a strong sedative into Johanna's arm, and she slept.

<<<<>>>>

When Johanna woke, she was back in her bed, restrained, and the doctor was bending over her, checking her pupils, her breathing, and her heartbeat. He had strapped wires to two of her fingers, her arm, and her chest, and the wires were connected to a monitoring screen. A series of syringes was laid out on a tray on the bureau.

As her head cleared, Johanna felt a sting in her arm and saw Dr. Nelson injecting the contents of a syringe into her arm. As she squirmed and wriggled, the doctor gave her a second injection, then a third and a fourth.

At first nothing happened. She lay back, staring at the doctor, wondering what he'd do next. Then the room started to dance. The drab, gray walls glowed purple and red. They scintillated, and she could taste and smell the colors. The tastes and odors changed as the colors glowed, and pulsed, and shifted to orange and yellow.

Johanna felt free even though she was restrained. Free and lacking inhibitions. She began to sing, and the colors pulsed in time to

"Your friends, Johanna—who are they? The ones who tell you secrets."

She laughed.

"Johanna," Nelson's voice softened. "I am your father. Johanna, you're my daughter, my sweet one."

"I love you, Daddy" she answered.

"Tell me who they are, the ones who tell you secrets."

"I miss you, Daddy."

"The secrets, Johanna. The spies. The snitches."

"I don't know."

"They're not patriots. They're traitors. Who are they?"

"Read me a story."

The questions continued.

Johanna had no answers.

In a last desperate effort, Dr. Nelson untied the restrains and removed the wires. Johanna staggered to her feet still singing.

"The snitches, Johanna. Who are they?"

She tried to dance and fell onto her elbows. Nelson took her arm to help her to her feet.

She punched him.

Her fist connected with his right eye, and she laughed.

"Fuck this job," said the doctor and injected the contents of the last syringe into her hip. Seconds later, she dropped to the floor.

When Maria entered the room, Johanna was scarcely breathing. Dr. Nelson had increased Johanna's medication, a mixture of sedatives labelled simply as # 127. Maria could barely feel Johanna's pulse. Alarmed by such weak vital signs, she popped a capsule of smelling salts under Johanna's nose. Johanna reacted with a faint sputter.

While Maria put in a call to Dr. Nelson, Johanna dropped into an uneasy sleep. "She almost died," said Maria. The dosage is too high."

"I told you when I hired you, never question your orders. She looks placid enough while she's medicated, but Johanna's a serious danger to our country. She even tried to attack me. Her conversations leave no doubt that, given the opportunity, she'd blow us all up for fun. And she's an accomplished con artist. Don't let her fool you."

"But she's barely conscious. Can you at least look in on her?"

"Fine." Dr. Nelson dropped his voice to a reassuring murmur. "Keep monitoring her vitals and I'll take a look at her before I leave tonight."

Johanna felt as if she were under water. Nothing made sense. She shivered with cold and with the sensation of something sinister and slimy crawling along her back. She thrashed and muttered. Most of her words were unintelligible, but Maria could make out "God," and "Jesus" over and over. Maria couldn't help wondering—if Johanna were indeed a Muslim, why did she call on God and Jesus, and not on Allah?

With some misgiving, Maria took a final check of Johanna's pulse and breathing, said a quick prayer, and left to catch up on her other duties.

Following the conversation, Dr. Nelson pulled Johanna's chart, and, wherever his hand-written directions had ordered two hundred milligrams, he inserted a decimal point in front of the second zero. After he'd finished, Dr. Nelson walked down the hallway into

Johanna's room and checked her vitals. Instantly, he punched the button summoning Maria.

"What's going on here? How much sedative have you administered to this patient?"

"Two hundred milligrams," she answered.

"Read the orders. Does that look like two hundred milligrams?"

Maria's heart stopped then and there. "Twenty milligrams, Doctor." She looked up confused. For certain, there had been no decimal there before. She'd checked the orders a dozen times, making sure she had it right, puzzled because the dose was so high. But there it was. "I read it as two hundred milligrams," she said, not even considering the possibility of questioning a doctor's orders. The mistake had to be hers, although logic told her that she couldn't have read and reread the orders as often and as carefully as she had and still have gotten them wrong. "I thought it seemed high."

"Start a new IV with saline, and… here, give me that."  He grabbed the chart out of Maria's hands and began scribbling a long list of medications, then scratched through it. "Never mind, just give her saline and glucose tonight. I'll stay with her a while until her vitals grow stronger. And Maria…"

"Yes, Doctor?"

"If she dies, you'll be brought up on charges. Consider yourself extremely lucky that I caught this when I did."

"Yes, Doctor." Maria started the saline and glucose drip, shaken and embarrassed, but grateful that the error had been discovered in time.

"Maria,"

"Yes, Doctor?"

"Don't bother coming in tomorrow."

After Maria had gone Dr. Nelson removed a syringe from his jacket pocket and injected its contents into Johanna's IV line. Several minutes later he checked Johanna's pulse. Thirty beats per minute. He checked it again five minutes later. Twenty-nine. Then twenty-seven. Then twenty-three. He dropped Johanna's arm wishing he'd used a stronger dose.

Johanna had only the faintest sensation of her arm being dropped, but she missed the warmth of his hand on her wrist. She felt so cold—as if her body were packed in ice. She would have shivered, but she lacked the strength.

She tried moving an arm, a foot, a finger. Nothing worked. Am I dying, she wondered. When she found the strength to squint open her eyes, Johanna had the sense of peering out unfocused from inside her body, so she was probably still mortal, her soul still attached to her body. And such a heavy body it was! She tried to move her arm again, but she might as well have tried to move a boulder. Johanna remembered once, as a child, trying to pull her father out of bed. Try as she might, she had not been able to budge him. That's what her body felt like.

And then she knew it for sure. I am dying, she thought. I'll be dead by tomorrow. It seems pathetic that my life is almost over, and I accomplished so little. But I did try... And she drifted into unconsciousness.

*Then a face appeared in her mind. He was five-year-old Alex; his lower teeth protruded like a bulldog's; he towered over her like a giant; and he didn't play fair. She lived it all over again: falling into the carrot patch, the taste of the dirt, the gagging sensation, his weight on her stomach.*

*And then the shame. And the violation, and betrayal, when Alex had told his story, and the teacher had believed him. The humiliation stung. The fury in her heart burned strong.*

Her body twitched. Her mind roared.

*In her mind, she bit his finger hard, and, when she released it, his shape shifted from boy to bear, then shrank to that of a scorpion.*

*Johanna snarled. She was wearing army boots, and she stamped her foot to crush the scorpion, but he scuttered away across a patch of hot white sand.*

*Seeking safety, he ducked under a dried-up branch, but Johanna picked up the branch exposing the beast. A twig broke off and with it she poked at the scorpion, prodding its claws, and watching it fend off her thrusts like a miniature boxer, whipping its tail forward into empty air all the while.*

*Just a bully, thought Johanna.*

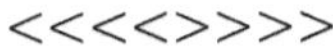

Even though Dr. Nelson had said he'd stay with Johanna, Maria worried about her. Johanna's vitals were so low! Maria had known that there was something dangerously wrong. She should have said something different to the doctor. All she'd told him was that the dose seemed too high. If she'd actually told him that she was administering two hundred milligrams, he'd have corrected her right there, and Johanna wouldn't be near death. I didn't deserve this job, she thought.

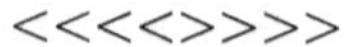

*Johanna's dream shifted; a marshy coolness replaced the sand and heat devils. Johanna followed the scorpion, her stick poised to hurt. And as she ran, Johanna shrank until she was almost as small as the scorpion.*

*Now the sun was shadowed by a canopy of mossy branches cooling the chase below—the hapless scorpion and the girl with the stick. The ground was damp and clammy. Putrid whiffs of rotting carcasses filled the air: to the left a crushed snake, his fangs shooting forward in final defiance, and to the right a bloated boar's carcass, stuck in a pond of oozing mud.*

*Ignoring the death stench, Johanna prodded the scorpion with her boot, pushing him ever closer to the muddy pond. And then she backed the scorpion into the ooze. His motion slowed and his legs kicked helplessly as thick mud coated his armored limbs. Johanna followed, plodding through the goo, pushing the scorpion farther into the middle of the pool, ignoring the slime creeping up around her ankles.*

*The five-year-old boy replaced the scorpion in her dream. In a cry of rage, Johanna pushed him deeper and deeper into the muddy pool until his body broke the plane of liquid and he sank beneath the ooze. Johanna backed away stepping high as the mud came up to her hips, and it sucked at her legs with each step pulling her off balance.*

*Had he died? He must have. Johanna had finally defeated the playground bully, the bossy five-year-old with the freckles and the grimace. But she didn't feel victorious, only small and vindictive. He was just a kid, she thought, doing the kind of dumb thing kids do.*

*With a sigh, she turned back towards the center of the pool where she'd seen his body go down. It was probably too late. She should give up. And even if she could fish him back out, how was she going to clean the mud off to let him breathe? She took another step forward. There was nothing solid beneath her feet. She sank to her armpits, then took a breath as mud and death closed over her head.*

Doctor Nelson checked Johanna's pulse. Twenty beats per minute. He'd hoped that it would drop faster. He didn't want to be anywhere near Johanna's room when she actually died. A few minutes later, he checked it again. Eighteen. Then seventeen. He entered Maria's code into the monitoring equipment, increased the speed of the drip, and disconnected the audible alarm. Then he left the room, planning to wait another few minutes before calling the orderlies to remove the body.

*Underneath the suffocating blanket of mud, Johanna flailed her arms around. She drew a breath, inhaling slime. She tried to cough, and her lungs shut down. Her hand, thrashing in panic, found a finger, and then a shoulder, and then a little boy's body. She was dying. Johanna knew that. Her last act would be one of kindness. She pushed his wriggling body upward toward air and life. I wonder if he made it, she thought. And then, there was only blackness.*

# Chapter Thirty-Five

∞

Maria finished her chores as quickly as possible, then ran back to Johanna's room to peek in through the doorway. She didn't dare actually walk in—in case Dr. Nelson was there. She'd been told to stay away. Disobeying orders, thought Maria. Guilt came easily to her. She slowed to a walk while practicing what she'd say to the doctor. "I'm so sorry, Doctor. I think I might have left an earring in here." She wasn't good at fibbing. She pushed open the door.

But Dr. Nelson was no longer in the room. Maria looked at Johanna's monitor. So little movement! Only a few shallow blips to show that any life remained. Why wasn't someone here? Where was the doctor? He said he was going to stay with Johanna. Terrified, she reached for the button to call code blue—a patient in crisis, but she held back. She wasn't supposed to be in the room.

Just then, two men in smocks opened the door startling Maria. She wheeled around. The larger man spoke. "We understood that the patient in this room has passed." And they entered with a stretcher to take the remains.

"But…" Maria wasn't sure what to do. "But she's not dead."

The man grabbed Johanna's wrist and felt for a pulse. "Close enough for government work," he said, and he elbowed Maria out of the way and unhooked the I.V. drip and monitors.

Maria felt so very small and inadequate. She whispered the Hail Mary prayer. Then she watched the men roll Johanna's body onto a stretcher. "What will you do with her?" Maria asked softly.

"The institute will dispose of the body. There's a small crematorium about thirty miles away from here." He nodded towards his partner. "We'll take the body as far as our morgue. As soon as someone has to drive into town, they'll take the body the rest of the way."

"May I come with you?" she asked. "Johanna was my first patient here."

"Suit yourself," he said. "I'm Stanley. My partner here is Vince."

They wheeled Johanna's body into a waiting van, and drove a mile down an overgrown path to a metal Quonset hut about thirty feet in length. The men had to pull hard to get the door to open, and, when it opened, the creaking groan made Maria jump. Inside, dust and mouse droppings littered the floor; spiderwebs covered the walls and ceiling. Maria's eyes adjusted slowly. The only light came from two windows on the right wall. Here and there a Styrofoam cup or a candy wrapper gave evidence that humans had also used the shed. Then she blinked as Vince flipped a switch to turn on a naked light bulb that dangled in the center of the shed.

The building seemed to be a back-of-the-lot storage area. Row upon row of shelves lined the walls, holding medical and mechanical odds and ends—plastic and metal tubing, switches, old smocks and blankets, and various strange metallic gadgets unknown to Maria. A stack of cardboard boxes, each about three feet wide, seven feet in length and two feet tall were stacked against the far wall, and Maria shivered realizing that the boxes were coffin-sized. A metal closet resembling a meat locker stood in one corner of the room. Without ceremony or deference, the men dumped Johanna's body into one of the boxes, lugged the box inside the metal closet and, slammed the heavy door shut.

Outside, Maria paused. Vince locked the shed, and checked the lock. While the two men waited for Maria to get into the van, Vince stamping his foot impatiently. "I'd rather walk back," she said, turning her steps toward the institute.

"Suit yourself," Stanley huffed.

"We really shouldn't let her…" Vince started to say.

"What's she going to do? Steal the body? Just get in the van." A minute later, Stanley gunned the engine, and the Maria watched the van passing her on the dusty road.

Johanna's mind burst out of its oblivion as hallucination after hallucination followed:

*The house was old with many rooms, and Johanna wandered through them unafraid, opening doors and peering into cupboards.*

*The boards on the steps creaked under her feet as she climbed. In the attic a canopy of oak branches formed the ceiling, and shaggy, moss-covered rock hugged the wall. Johanna sat on a rock, not wanting to get up ever. But she had to. She had to see what was below, and so she descended, dreading the rooms in the basement.*

*There was only one door, and Johanna felt revulsion touching the knob, but she turned it anyway and went inside. It was the doctor's office. A two-foot stack of papers littered the doctor's desk. And she stared at Dr. Nelson but couldn't see his face—only shadow.*

*His words blurred like runny Jell-O "In here, Johanna, you'll find that God is dead." And as he spoke, Johanna's mind exploded with impressions of pain. The floor melted into oily pools. She stared. One of the pools caught fire. A hose lay just outside the door. And she stared as the paper jumped alive with orange flame, and now she saw the doctor's face clearly. The blaze caught at the edge of his white coat, and still she sat watching. The sound of running water jingled just outside the door.*

*Flames caught her. She felt the heat and the burn, and still she sat not moving. Fire burned around the two of them, consuming both, the doctor and Johanna, and she couldn't make a move towards the water.*

*And God said, "Johanna, get the water."*

*And she heard and sat, stubborn, wallowing in the pain that was now more her own creation than his.*

<<<<>>>>

Maria kept walking towards the institute until the two orderlies were out of sight, then turned back towards the shed at a brisk trot. The sun hung low on the horizon, and the sky burst into pinks, oranges, and reds. As she jogged down the path, thankful that her uniform included sensible nurses' shoes, she thought about all the things she had seen at the institute. Something was very wrong. Certainly, their methods differed from what she had been taught in nursing school. Even criminals were treated with more dignity than Johanna had been.

And why, if Johanna were Muslim, did she talk about God and not Allah? That didn't make sense. Of course, she could have been hiding her religion, but, as drugged as she was, she couldn't have kept up the pretext of Christianity for long.

Maria was scared. She didn't know everything.

And who had called the orderlies? Maria was the only one who could have known that Johanna had died.

The door to the building was padlocked. She examined the lock and checked the door for gaps or weak spots. She examined the windows. Maria was reluctant to break the glass, but she finally managed to pry one of the windows open, squeeze herself inside, and get the light turned on. Fearfully, she opened the door to the metal closet. A blast of cold made her shiver. Slabs of beef and pork, speared on thick hooks hung in a row. So it was a meat locker.

*Inside the burning room Johanna sat, stubborn and unforgiving, with both her body and the doctor's twisted in pain. And the hose lay just outside the door.*

*"You let me down, God. You asked me to hang the signs, then You dropped me in the middle of hell and left me. And I was scared and hurting, and I called you and asked you to help me, and you didn't. And I never did anything to deserve all the pain."*

*"Johanna."*

*"And now you expect me to forgive."*

*"Johanna!"*

*Reluctantly she rose and quenched the flames with water, water that laughed as children running through lawn sprinklers in August. And, through black, oily smoke, she caught a glimpse of the doctor's face.*

<<<<>>>>

Maria knelt next to the box on the dirty floor of the shack and removed the lid. It was mostly an act of respect—a wish to commend Johanna's soul to God with some final act of reverence.

The jostling motion nudged Johanna as she dreamt.

*"Puppy Face," said a voice in Johanna's dream. Two arms reached out to her.*

*"Daddy."*

Her breath stilled.

*She held out her arms, and they were sailing across oceans in a pirate ship made from a cardboard box.*

Maria looked down into the coffin. It seemed such a pathetic end, but, oddly, Johanna's face looked peaceful, almost happy. Shivering, Maria sat down on the floor of the meat locker and made the sign of the cross. Then, Maria was weeping, strangely caring about this person whom she barely knew, whom she'd never seen except in a deeply drugged state.

She reached into the box to hold Johanna's hand one last time. The hand quivered. It was just a reflex and meant nothing. Maria knew this from her training. But she felt for a pulse nevertheless, and she found it beating stronger than it had back at the hospital room. She touched Johanna's nose and felt a slow steady stream of air. She shook Johanna, but Johanna remained unresponsive.

"Get up. Wake up. If you want to live, get up." Maria prodded and jostled and screamed at Johanna, but Johanna remained still. "I need your help. I can't get you out of here by myself." She dragged the box out of the locker and scooted it towards the padlocked door. She examined the walls looking for sheets of metal that could be peeled back. She looked up at the window through which she had crawled. It was so high off the ground! Maria tugged at the box, sliding it toward the window, all the time doubting she'd be able to get Johanna out. And she propped up the box containing Johanna's limp body and pushed it towards the window's opening, grateful that Johanna couldn't feel what Maria was doing to her. She got Johanna's body halfway out the window, then realized that what she was planning was impossible. She might be able to get Johanna out through the window, hopefully without major injury, but she could never carry Johanna the mile or so back to her car. Johanna's body only weighed about a hundred pounds, but it was still more than Maria could manage by herself, even if Johanna came to and could stumble. And if anyone caught her walking with Johanna… Maria didn't even want to think of the consequences. She needed a way to get Johanna out through the window. She needed to think.

So Maria dragged the box back towards the shelves where the other crematory boxes were stored, and pushed it against the wall below the bottom shelf. Then she chose another box, moved it to the spot in the locker where Johanna had originally been placed, and loaded it with four pork roasts, hoping that their weight was close enough to that of Johanna's body. Then she climbed out the window and jogged back to the parking lot at the institute where she'd left her car. Had it only been that morning? It seemed like an entire lifetime had passed in the course of that day.

Jasper and Dakota were tired. Delivering the body for cremation and picking up a package for Dr. Nelson were their last tasks for the day. After that it was beer, pool, and, if they were lucky, company for the night. Jasper pulled a fat ring of keys from his pocket, and jingled them looking for the one belonging to the lock on the shed's door. Meanwhile, Dakota rolled a dolly from the truck bed onto a hydraulic lift gate, then lowered it to the uneven crushed-rock path. "Come on already. It's way past quitting time, and I'm starving."

"Don't stroke out," Jasper answered. "I've just about got it."

From inside the box, Johanna heard the door creak open. The squeaking was loud, like a peacock's cry, and Johanna startled from the sound. "Help! Help! I'm in here." She thought she was screaming, but no sound came out. She thought the words, but could not make the sounds. A noise, she thought. Any noise. Her left hand rested on the bottom of the casket, and she scratched the cardboard with her nails. Her hands were weak, as weak as her voice. She scratched again.

"Do you hear anything?" Dakota shivered. He didn't like being around cadavers.

"Probably mice."

"Let's just get out of here."

"No," Johanna's mind yelled, but her mouth stayed quiet. It was too hard, too foggy. She tried to move her arm, but it stayed limp. She heard the men shuffling about the shed, and she heard the locker door click open. With all the strength in her body, she willed her hand to scratch the cardboard. She opened her mouth to scream. A groan, almost silent, finally escaped her throat.

Dakota jumped. "We're out of here—right now."

Without bothering to load up the dolly, they picked up the coffin that Maria had left in the meat locker and hauled it out to the waiting truck. Johanna heard the sound of the door pushed shut, and the noise of the lock clicking into place. "Please, help me. Help me." She mumbled, but it was too late. She heard the motor grumble to a start, then the sound of tires spraying gravel. And the sound grew smaller as the truck drove into the distance. And then there was nothing—the inside of a box and nothing else.

*At first Johanna's dream came in flashes like movie teasers. Then the impressions slowed and gelled into a dreamscape below a blood-red sky: Cauldrons reeked and smoked. Horned creatures, almost human, chanted, writhed, and screamed till Johanna thought her heart would burst.*

*Smoke snaked outwards, calling, enticing. Street gangs were the first humans to respond: Bloods, and Crips, Skinheads, and Arian nations, their tattoos and bandanas pledging allegiance. Knives flashed. Shots rang. Some shrieked and fell.*

*Others arrived. Armies gathered—some in tatters, some in business suites, and some in death-white hoods. Marching through time as well as space, some in robes and tunics, others in uniforms, their medals and sabers glowed bright. Some could barely stand; others strutted power. Some wore armor, others—priests' robes. Some wore street clothes, and some were merely naked.*

*From man to man to woman to child they passed a smoking torch that carried no earthly fire, but rather that hatred hidden in their souls. And it seemed the passing would not stop.*

*The devil, large and black, laughed with a drowning roar.*

*Anger, a smoke-brown flame, flashed in gun muzzles—mirrored in the eyes of both victim and oppressor. Fear stood on icy tendrils. Pride, steel gray, rode as a knight on stallion, and, with a mighty belch, turned noble into base.*

*The devil's laughter bellowed. He'd won the world. Some souls he torched with hate; others he drowned in fear, or poisoned by pride, or froze in despair. It didn't matter how they died. The devil had them.*

*From one to the next, they passed the torch, as furies united and winds twisted into tornadoes.*

*And hate filled Johanna also; it shook her like palm branches in a hurricane.*

*"Join us if you want to live," the voice roared. "Take the torch. I am stronger than you."*

*She wanted to roar, to take that torch and burn everyone who had held it.*

*But the humans, they were merely carriers, serving evil as his jeeps and horses, spreading hate like a virus. She couldn't destroy them; they were weak like her.*

*Instead, she stood naked, so small, so weak.*

*"I choose love," she said.*

*And waited to perish.*

*"And I choose love," said a nameless voice behind her.*

*"And I," said another.*
*"Christ's blessings."*
*"Shalom."*
*"Namaste."*
*"Salam."*
*The chorus swelled from seven to thousands, to legions upon legions—the soldiers, the street gangs, the children, the beggars, and the kings.*
*A raven snatched the torch from human hands and dropped it into a far-away pit.*

It was almost dark when Maria returned in her car. She pushed the window open and began to crawl into the warehouse, trying in vain to see inside. She clambered back out, turned on the car's engine, and pointed the headlights towards the shed, and again pushed her head through the window. Afraid of what she'd find inside, Maria hesitated on the sill, then jumped down and made her way, stumbling towards the light switch.

She found the shelves where the cardboard coffins were kept, then dragged out the one on the floor, thankful that it was heavy. At least the body was still inside. Hopefully, it was still alive.

Maria was trembling now, afraid of being alone, afraid of someone discovering her, afraid that Johanna was already dead, afraid of ghosts, afraid that Johanna would pull out a gun and shoot her, and afraid of so many other things. But she opened the lid, and gingerly reached inside and touched Johanna's cheek. Then she felt under her nose for the warm air that would indicate breathing. Johanna did not move. Her skin was cool, and there was no breath coming from her nostrils.

No, Maria thought. She began to rub Johanna's cheek, gently at first, then harder. She wanted to shove the box back under the shelf and run. "Please," she said out loud. "Johanna, you have to wake up. She pulled Johanna's arm, and found it pliable, not rigid. Again, she felt for breath under Johanna's nostrils, and was rewarded with a faint puff of air. She felt at Johanna's neck for a pulse, and found a slight thumping—weak and very slow, but also regular.

Maria cried. "You just cannot die now, Miss Johanna, not after all of this. You made it this far and against so much. Please, stay alive just a little longer."

Panicking all the while, she pulled at Johanna's arms to get her upright, but the body was limp and uncooperative. With frenzied jerks, Maria tried to boost Johanna up towards the window, but the body always ended up back on the floor, and Maria despaired of ever getting her out of the warehouse.

And finally, her nurse's training took over. If there's one thing they taught us, thought Maria, it was how to move a limp body. And she breathed slowly and deeply to calm herself. Maria rolled Johanna onto her side, and slung Johanna's upper torso across her back—the fireman's carry. Using her legs and back, Maria staggered upright, then made her way towards the window, and leaned Johanna over the sill with Johanna's head lolling outside. "I'm sorry, Miss Johanna. This will probably hurt you, but I don't know how else to do it." She climbed outside, squeezing her own body through the window past Johanna's limp form, bloodying her shins as she scrambled over the sill. I must open the car's back door first, she thought. Then she knelt on the hood of her car and, pulling on Johanna's arms, scraped her over the sill. Johanna's body thudded headfirst onto the hood where Maria caught Johanna's arms. Squatting next to the car, Maria was able to sling Johanna across her shoulders and stagger around to the open door and drop her inside. Johanna ended up flopped on the floor, and Maria gunned the engine and drove away praying that she wouldn't be stopped at the gate.

She questioned the wisdom of bringing Johanna home with her. What if Johanna awoke and became violent! Or suppose a neighbor came by and saw her, and called the police! But Maria couldn't think of any safer place to leave Johanna, and so, with much misgiving, she drove home thankful that night had fallen, and that she'd probably be able to get her into the house without attracting any attention.

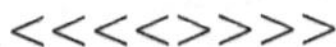

<<<<>>>>

Maria's home was a converted army barrack, which she shared with her father, mother, and two younger brothers. Her father hauled debris and did what odd jobs he could find. Her mother cleaned houses and baby-sat. They had all made sacrifices to send Maria to nursing school in the hope that she would make good—would raise herself and her family out of poverty. Well, thought Maria, that dream is over. And, she cried bitterly for losing the American dream, and for shaming and disappointing her parents. And she cried because she was so frightened of what could happen next.

Ordinarily she shouted a greeting to her parents when she entered the house. This time Maria entered silently. And she laid Johanna on her own bed, limp and unresponsive, but with a slightly stronger breath and pulse.

What have I done, Maria asked herself, staring at Johanna's limp body. What, in God's name am I doing now? Maria had never bent rules before. She'd never questioned superiors. And now, and now, she'd flagrantly disobeyed orders. She felt trapped as if walls of water were about to drown her.

Someone else had done this, someone reckless, foolish, someone in Maria's body who was not Maria, and now she, Maria, was left to deal with the consequences. For she was sure that sooner or later she would be caught, and maybe jailed as a traitor. And what if Johanna were to die in her apartment? This was more than she could deal with.

Maria bent over Johanna's body checking her pulse one more time. It seemed the only thing she was capable of doing. Why had she done it? Johanna was in all likelihood a terrorist, a cruel and dangerous person, and an enemy of the United States of America. And she, Maria, had let her loose to prey on innocents.

Maria shuddered thinking about the country she had just betrayed. She remembered swearing her allegiance to the United States. She thought about everything that this country had given her—an education, an opportunity for her family to have a comfortable life, a life that she couldn't have aspired to in the Philippines. She remembered how large and brilliant the flag had seemed the day she pledged her loyalty to the United States of America. And now, now she'd thrown it all away. And for what?

Gently she passed her hands over the welts and bruises on Johanna's body. A few places were still infected. Some scars ran deep—great ropes of reddish, thickened skin knotted over her stomach and the insides of her arms and legs, the sensitive, tender parts of her body. And Maria understood—the country to which she pledged her loyalty would not allow this to happen. The United States that she loved, that she had promised to defend, was a country that did not condone torture. Whatever Johanna did, she was not entitled to such treatment. And whoever did this, whoever condoned this, was an enemy of the United States.

Maria startled as her mother entered her room. She wiped at her tears. Her mother tipped her face quizzically. "What happened?"

"She has been hurt. Maybe killed. I didn't know what to do." Maria's mother left the room. Quietly she came back with a small bottle of antiseptic. And she kissed her daughter.

"I have been… fired," said Maria.

"We will make do." She handed the antiseptic to Maria.

Maria swabbed the weeping sores with antiseptic and covered them loosely with bandages. She gave Johanna the best of her nurses training. And tending Johanna, for the first time that day, she felt herself an American.

# Chapter Thirty-Six

∞


Big Bad Wolf:  It's true. Johanna was a passenger on Swissair flight 472 leaving San Francisco International at 2:18 on Saturday.

Brat:  Then she really left. The way U guys were talking I thought she'd been kidnapped like in some spy movie. I guess we just have 2 wait & see if she gets online from wherever.

Sandy Pumpkin:  Half a minute. This is all wrong. How could she meet Spiderman at 12:00 and board a plan at 2:18?

Sandy Pumpkin:  Spiderman said they were together until evening.

Brat:  Maybe Spiderman was lying about being with her.

Shadow:  This has the feel of body? my country at its worst. People disappear and are not heard from again. Sometimes a body is found. Sometimes they languish in prisons, and sometimes they just disappear.

Sandy Pumpkin:  It doesn't sound right to me.

Brat:  I have a bad feeling about this.

Big Bad Wolf:  I'll have my staff do some more checking.

After he'd turned off his computer, Ivan made a note to have one of his staff check for traces to corroborate the Spiderman story, but, actually, he'd already made up his mind. Johanna was either dead or in terrible danger, and he couldn't imagine a common criminal being able to fake Johanna's departure to Iran.

Feeling scared and helpless, Brat Googled "United Religions" and was surprised to find a link to a prayer chain:

Allah be praised, have mercy on your child Jody and be with her in her peril.

Comfort, and bless, and save, dear Lord, all those in peril, our soldiers, Iraqi and Afghani men and women and children, and especially our friend, Jody.

Keep watch, dear Lord, for those who work or watch or weep this night, and give your angels charge over those who sleep.

Great Jehovah, God of Israel, Isaac, and Jacob, I ask your blessing for all your children. Keep them safe this night and the next.

May the power of the Buddha protect all in danger.

The prayers and blessings continued. They numbered in the thousands.

Worlds away in Mississippi, Martha Jacobson knelt before her statue of Mary thumbing the rosary and whispering prayers.

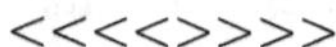


By morning, Johanna was showing the faintest signs of consciousness. The next day, she was fully awake, but her body began to twinge and shake—the first symptoms of withdrawal from the heavy medication she'd been subjected to. Maria had covered her with an electric blanket turned up to high. And now she turned it off as Johanna vacillated between cold and hot. As soon as she thought it safe, Maria began feeding fluids to Johanna, first sugar water, then a little soup.

Sometimes Johanna moaned. Sometimes she cried out.

"I wish I could help the pain," said Maria.

"I've known worse," said Johanna through chattering teeth.

Maria gently touched her shoulder and Johanna jerked back startled. "You are safe here, Johanna, for the time being," she said. "And I will give you food and shelter until you are strong enough to leave." Johanna held her arms crossed over her heart as if protecting herself, and she rocked back and forth. Her eyes had a hunted look, resembling those of a wild animal more than those of a human. And Maria winced imagining what must have happened to make Johanna behave this way.

Johanna did trust Maria. She trusted her because Maria made no demands on her. And she trusted her because she had nothing else to hang on to.

At night Johanna woke screaming from nightmares, and in the day, she screamed with panic attacks. She rocked back and forth incessantly, as if calming herself from unseen terrors, and she jumped, startled after even the simplest, most benign noises. She spoke, but in halting sentences, each thought carefully coaxed from her throat.

Towards the end of the month, the panic attacks lessened, and her behavior approached normal, although Maria could tell that Johanna was still a very troubled soul. And finally, one evening after dinner, Johanna looked at Maria, sighed, and told her, "I need to go now."

"You're still not well." Maria knitted her brows in concern. She felt as if she were losing her sister. But she also knew that Johanna was right. For everyone's safety, Johanna had to leave.

That night she put some money next to Johanna's bed. "Three hundred and twenty-five dollars—it's all I can spare," she told Johanna. "And I put a map next to the money. There is a green star next to the bus station. Take the money and buy a bus ticket anywhere. It's best if you leave the country. They think you are dead. They will not come to look for you. They say you are a terrorist, but I don't believe it. I hope I am right. I wish you well."

As the tears cascaded down her cheeks, Johanna began to rock back and forth. "Thank you for everything. When I can, I'll repay the money."

Johanna's words caught Maria by surprise. "Keep the money," she said. "And it is best if I do not know where you go. God speed."

# Chapter Thirty-Seven

∞

The dinner had begun on a promising note. Alex and Vivian were dining with the Pomerleaus and with Vernon and Sophia Smyth-Huntington. Vernon and Sophia had rented a private house on a tiny island just off of Martha's Vineyard, and Vivian was in heaven. Almost every room had a bay window, and most of the windows looked out over the water. Vernon had just purchased a twenty-nine-million-dollar apartment complex in Dallas and was hosting the party to celebrate the deal.

Ignoring the conversation behind her, Vivian watched the sunset's afterglow over the cape's waters. At least, she tried to ignore it, but every so often a barking laugh or a raucous shout disrupted the calm beauty of the Cape. Vernon was peacock-proud of the way he'd bargained. "And then I said, I said… listen to this. I said, 'If you think you can… if you think you can… SCREW with me…'" But no one was listening. Edward Pomerleau was comparing Schwarzkopf's strategies of desert warfare to those of Patten, while Alex talked politics. Vivian focused on the sunset over the gentle surf. Men with their machismo, she thought.

It was meant to be a posh, yet intimate party. A cadre of caterers had started the liquor flowing, and Alex and Edward were already slurring their speech as the waiters ushered the guests into the dining room. Vivian, Sophia, Vernon and Edward's wife Gloria, though not as inebriated as Alex and Edward, were nevertheless working on their second cocktails.

I'm the most beautiful woman here, Vivian thought to herself, and she sneaked a look at herself as she passed an antique-brass-framed mirror on the way to the table. She'd worn a floor-length, royal-blue chiffon gown paired with silver and diamonds.

Raising his highball glass, Edward sputtered out a toast. "A tribute to glory and honor."

"To glory and honor," shouted everyone at the table.

"To glory and honor," Edward continued. "To war, and to the military contracts that go with it." He gave a modest chuckle at his own joke, and Gloria, Sophia, and Vivian knew enough to laugh.

"A toast!" shouted Alex, "A toast to war!" and everyone raised their glasses and drank.

Vernon stood up. "But what have we done lately?"

Edward rose to his feet, then wobbled and leaned on the table to steady himself. "Just what are you implying?"

"I mean we look better bombing and winning than we do pissing on guerrilla warfare," said Vernon.

"More bombing, less pissing," said Edward. The men cheered.

"More bombs, less piss," Alex agreed enthusiastically.

Right then Vivian lost her appetite. While the rest of the table cheered, she put down her glass and turned her head away from the table.

Edward reached across the table and poked Vivian with a fork. "What's the matter, sweetheart? Is the scary old conversation too rough for you?" He kept on poking, aiming for her breasts with the fork as he spoke.

The rest of the party burst into unchecked laughter. Vivian just stared unsure what to say. She was used to being the center of attention, but not the butt of a joke. Even after forty, she was exceptionally beautiful with long, long legs, a tiny waste, and eyes that sparkled and danced. And she knew how to flirt. And that was usually enough to ensure her a crowd of male admirers.

The laughter died down and everyone at the table turned to watch her squirm. Normally Vivian would have ignored the rowdy conversation. Boys will be boys, and all that. But the guests were all so drunk and so loud, well, it just made the cheering too macabre, too brutal. "I can't see toasting death," she finally said.

"Your wife sweet on Muslims, Alex?" asked Edward.

"Sweetheart needs an at... an attitude adjustment." Vernon pointed at Vivian with his highball glass. The ice cubes clinked in emphasis. Alex laughed too. He'd drunk enough liquor to make everything seem funny, including Vivian's discomfort.

"You're all disgusting when you're drunk," said Vivian. She'd had drunk enough liquor to make her careless. Alex was supposed to be defending her honor, not laughing at her.

"What? Alex, can't you handle your woman?" This came from Edward, and, again, the table laughed. Alex had been sipping Wild Turkey neat. As the conversation turned on him, he downed the rest of his drink with one swallow and slammed the glass on the table.

"God damn it, Vivian, shut up and… behave yourself." He rose to his feet, swayed a bit, and, in a display of bravado, smacked her cheek with his open hand.

"You show her," said Vernon.

Egged on by Vernon, Alex had to keep going. "Shut the fuck up, you understand! Just…" Alex was drooling a bit. He wiped his mouth with the sleeve of his shirt. "Don't say anything else for the rest of the evening or you'll know what sorry means." Alex picked up his empty glass and slammed it down so hard that it shattered. "Barkeep! Another drink over here! Customers are dying of thirst." He pointed to the broken glass. "And clean up this mess while you're at it."

<<<<>>>>

From that point on, the evening deteriorated. Their conversation became more vicious, dragging itself out until two in the morning.

As Alex drove home, Vivian sat silent, willing Alex to stay on the road as if her concentration were steadying Alex's driving.

Out of the corner of his eye, he could see the tension in Vivian's face. He sensed her fear and it fed his bravado. Suddenly Alex was amused. He swerved the car, then righted it making the back wheels spin into fishtails.

Vivian gasped aloud, and Alex laughed. "When are you going to learn to trust me?" he asked.

She didn't answer, and Alex jerked the wheel one more time, chuckling as the tires squealed. "Let's just get home," Vivian said finally. "We're both tired and angry. And slightly drunk. We can talk tomorrow."

"You, self-righteous cow," said Alex. "Do you know… do you … do you have any idea who those people are? Compared to them, the president is a… a… a slimy-toad lackey. Pomerleau is the fourth richest man in the world and Smyth-Huntington owns half the senate and a third of the house. These are the men who really run the country. Hell, they just about run the whole damn world. And they can make me very rich and, and, very suc… successful or they can have my ass in a sling if my dumb-ass wife offends them, and I'll spend the rest of my life scrubbing toilets."

Vivian laughed—a nervous laugh. "I scrubbed toilets back in college." The wrong thing to say, but there were no right things, and silence wasn't working either. Alex's speech alarmed her. Usually Alex could hold his liquor, but, on this night, he was shouting and swinging his fists.

"What's that supposed to mean?" He stomped hard on the brake, enjoying the high-pitched scraping and the car's crazy jerk reaction to his foot. He turned off his headlights. The road was dark.

"I'm sorry. Please let's just get going before someone rear-ends us."

He gunned the engine in neutral, then suddenly engaged the motor, and the car lurched forwards.

"Please," said Vivian.

"What?"

"Please." He was heading in the wrong direction. Surely, he knew it. Vivian realized that he was doing it on purpose to scare her. Well, it was working. "Please take me back home."

He raced the engine driving as fast as he dared in the direction of the inky darkness. Because he had a plan. After ten minutes he slowed the car, looking for a road that was little more than a footpath. At last, he saw it and veered towards it. Vivian didn't dare say anything. The path led to the infamous Ditch Bridge on Chappaquiddick Island. Now Vivian's breath came sharply as she realized where he was taking her. After all those years of marriage, he knew how to punish her. Alex chuckled recalling the newspaper headlines about Ted Kennedy's car driving off of the road. And he swerved the car sharply causing it to skid sideways.

They were approaching the Ditch Bridge now. The night was still. The mud-brown supports—stubby post-people—cast shadows and reflections like specters on the inky waters below. Alex and Vivian were alone on the bridge, the same bridge where a very drunk Ted Kennedy had driven off of the road, and where Mary Jo

Kopechne had died on an evening much like this one.

For a moment Alex chilled, sensing the stillness, as if ghosts inhabited the waters. He remembered an evening very long ago sitting on the bank of Puddin' creek. He had been a scared eleven-year-old back then on a Halloween night, believing himself surrounded by ghosts and wicked spirits. He remembered clutching the book of spells to his body, and finding the mysterious word Remordia inside.

He looked over at Vivian and he could see how pale her face was, even with the very limited amount of light. And her fear fed his courage.

"Did you say something?" he smirked and gave the wheel a quarter turn.

"Nothing. Just forget it." She stared at the road ahead and breathed a relieved sigh as they passed the last upright, leaving the bridge and its ghost behind.

"Maybe you'd rather walk." The road was a worn-out path with black water on both sides. He swerved the car again.

"Maybe I would."

Alex leaned across Vivian and pushed open her door. The car lurched drunkenly. He pushed at the button keeping her seatbelt fastened, but his hands shook and he couldn't undo the buckle.

"I'm sorry." Vivian was reaching for the door, trying to close it. "It's been a long night. Can we please just get home?"

"All night you made me look stupid. Now you're trying to tell me how to drive."

"I'm sorry, Alex. I didn't mean any of it."

"You're damn right you didn't."

"I'm sorry."

"Not as sorry as you're going to be." At last his fingers found the button. The seat belt flew loose and he shoved Vivian out of the car. "See how well you like it walking solo." He laughed and gunned the engine. He gunned it again, and, as Vivian grabbed on to the doorframe, he started forward, slowly at first, then faster until Vivian was almost running to keep up with the car.

"Please, Alex, I'm wearing high heels; I can't see." Her foot twisted and the car jerked free of her grasp, leaving Vivian staggering, and then falling backwards.

Alex drove on for another couple of minutes letting Vivian stew in the darkness. He stopped the car, turned off the engine and listened. One cricket chirped, his song a forlorn rattle, far, far away. Had Vivian learned her lesson yet? The gloom sent shivers down Alex's back, and he restarted the engine and turned back to pick up his wife.

He drove back slowly with his lights in high beam. And he turned on the radio for company against the disturbing stillness. You ready to behave yourself? That's what he'd say. Maybe he'd forgive her for behaving foolishly, maybe not. He avoided calling Vivian's name. No sense in letting her know that he was looking for her. Let her worry a few minutes more.

But there weren't many remarkable landmarks on that dark stretch of road, and, anyway, Alex hadn't been paying much attention to the scenery. He came to the bridge and turned around. Minutes stretched by, and he still hadn't found Vivian. He had counted on spotting Vivian walking along the road but, in the gloomy blackness, she was nowhere in sight.

He drove slowly until he came to the end of the road. Then he swung the car around. Damn! He must have passed her. But why hadn't she yelled? Maybe she didn't recognize him in the dark. Or, maybe she was playing games too. He u-turned the car and backtracked one more time looking for Vivian. This time he called to her in the darkness. "Game's over. Where the hell are you?" Then "Damn it, Vivian, tell me where you are so we can go home and get this fuckin' evening over with." He honked the horn. "Fine, if that's what you want, I'm leaving you here. Go ahead. Spend the night in this muck. See if I care. Someone's sure to find you tomorrow and you can get a ride home in a tuna truck." And, finally, "Hey, Vivian… okay, I'm sorry already. Where the hell are you?"

She had to hear him. The small stretch of road just wasn't that long. Why wasn't she answering? It wasn't like Vivian to hold a grudge, to play games, to make Alex stew. No, that was his style, not hers. Besides, he held all the cards. He had the car with its warmth, a stereo, and transportation home, while she was crouching somewhere in the bushes. So why didn't she answer?

It took a while for Alex to admit the possibility that Vivian couldn't answer him. That she had hit her head or had fallen into the water. But it seemed so unlikely. No one ever passed out from a bump on the head, except in the movies. He dug through the car's glove compartment and then through the trunk looking for a flashlight, but there wasn't one. He set the headlights on high beam and pointed them at the stretch of bushes ahead. Then he climbed out of the car and began examining the road bit by bit. There had to be a simple explanation. Surely Vivian was okay. She hadn't fallen that hard.

But this was Chappaquiddick; the bridge was already home to one ghost. And Alex sensed evil in the air around him. He was cold and scared, as scared as when he'd been an eleven-year-old boy running away from home, and realizing that he didn't have the resources he needed to run away.

Disheartened, Alex sat down on a rock. Puddin' Creek all over again, he thought. Back then he had run away from a whipping. How simple that would have been compared to this! His wife was missing, he was responsible, and he was very drunk, and he had very unforgiving partners. They would forgive him for driving drunk, or for losing, or hurting, or even killing his wife. But they would never forgive him for getting caught. Suddenly he shivered violently, chilled by the misty air and the thought of his partners.

And just as on that night long ago, he was sitting by swampy water with darkness caused more by evil than by the night. He could see himself holding that book of spells. "Remordia," he said aloud and waited for the jitters to subside.

The solution was obvious. He'd go home. Tomorrow he'd call the sheriff. The alcohol would be out of his body by then. If she were alive, no harm no foul. If she were dead, he'd be distraught. Alex began practicing his story. "It's all my fault. We had a fight, and she jumped out of the car. I started to follow her, but it was dark, and she was running."

The story shaped itself in Alex's mind. Brilliant, he thought. He spoke the words out loud as he worked out more details. "She'd had a lot to drink, and she was stumbling about something terrible. 'Keep away from me,' she said. And she was taking awful chances running full tilt through the brush. I was afraid that, if I kept chasing her, she'd fall and hurt herself." No—better yet: "She told me, 'If you don't leave right now, I'll drown myself.' She kept screaming 'I'll drown myself. I'll do it. Don't think I won't!' She kept shouting it over and over. So I told her 'Okay, calm down. I'm leaving. You don't have to run anymore.' I told her, 'Call me tomorrow, and I'll pick you up.' I thought she'd be okay. There was a house just a few hundred feet down the road from where I left her. She was acting so weird, and it scared me. I left. I didn't know what else to do."

He saw it all. It was simple, really. He'd never be blamed. Maybe he'd answer a few difficult questions, but there'd be nothing more than that. And Alex sighed bitterly. "God, help me. I won't do it," he said. Instead, he pulled out his cell phone and dialed 911.

They arrived in minutes—instantly, it seemed to Alex. First a lone patrol car with two cops. When Vivian didn't answer their shouting, they called for backup. Several more cars arrived, then a search and rescue unit, and some volunteers with dogs. They set up floodlights bright enough to illuminate a football stadium, and began combing the area where Alex said he'd last seen Vivian.

One of the first two officers drew Alex aside. He's just a kid, thought Alex. Red hair, freckles, he could have been Opie.

"What happened here, sir?" the cop asked.

"We had a fight," Alex said.

Does he have a hidden microphone? Uncomfortable questions kept popping into Alex's head. Was his speech slurred? Was it obvious that he was drunk? He didn't feel drunk. Suddenly everything was clear and amazingly simple. Vivian could be hurt. She could be in danger. Or she might be dead. Nothing else mattered.

"She stormed out of the car," he said finally.

"She stormed out?"

"No." Alex stopped, shaking his head helplessly. "Wait a minute."

"Take your time," said the officer.

"We fought. I said, maybe she'd rather walk. She said, maybe she would. So, I pushed her out of the car."

"Why did she say she'd rather walk?"

"Because I was trying to scare her."

"Scare her?"

"I was… I swerved the wheel. The car fishtailed. I slammed on the brakes. I sent it skidding. It almost jumped the side of the bridge."

"Why would you do that?"

"Because I was very drunk."

The officer hesitated. He called over his partner. Then he began the words of the Miranda Rights. "You have the right to remain silent. If you give up that right, anything you say can and will be used against you in a court of law. You have the right…"

Alex knew this was coming. They cuffed his hands behind him, ducked his head under the doorframe, and sat him down in the back of the patrol car. Alex wondered if he would regret his honesty after the liquor had worn off the next morning.

They took him back to one of the police stations on Martha's Vineyard, and he found himself in a small gray room with the only door locked. Alex had the disoriented sensation of not knowing exactly where he was. He stared at his hands. It all seemed so strange. Funny, Alex thought, he should be terrified, but he wasn't. In a dazed sort of way, he felt like he'd just come home. It was probably the liquor, because Alex didn't believe in God.

Two sergeants walked in, officers Maxwell and Dugan according to their name tags.

"So how did all of this happen?" asked the one called Maxwell. He had pepper gray hair and a slightly darker mustache.

"You'll forgive me if I talk slowly," Alex said. "I'm used to lying, so it'll take some doing to come up with the truth."

Got to be the liquor, thought the officer.

"And I need a lawyer, but first, let me tell you about tonight. And, listen, can you let me know when you find my wife."

Alex told his story slowly, and the sergeant caught it all on tape. The easiest interrogation he'd had in months.

A third policeman walked in. "Your wife is in Martha's Vineyard Hospital," he said.

"Is she going to be all right?"

"There's concussion and some swelling, and she's still unconscious. That's all they know right now."

Alex's head throbbed, and his mind bounced around as if on springs. But one thought kept surfacing, and he said it out loud. "If she dies, I'll be charged with manslaughter, won't I?" He looked at the officer.

"Not necessarily. Cooperate. Tell them everything."

Alex smiled wryly. "If I tell them everything, I'll never get out of prison."

It's got to be the liquor, thought the officer.

Alone in a jail cell, Alex thought about Vivian. Surely there were good times too. Why couldn't he remember them? She really is the best part of me, thought Alex to himself. And I really treated her like a heel.

The next day dawned amid iron and concrete for Alex. A pale yellowish light illuminated a sink and toilet in the left corner of the cell. Not even that is private, he thought.

Alex took a deep breath. His head ached, and it made his other senses more acute. Somewhere off to the right, metal clanged against metal, reverberating harshly off the hard surfaces with no rugs or curtains or pillows to soften the sound. It was so strange, having no control over himself or his surroundings. A mysterious "they" determined where Alex would be and what he would do.

Alex sat on his bunk staring at the blanket. He set about removing all the lint bumps with his fingers. There was precious little to occupy his time. He had no watch, and no way to know how long before something would happen—breakfast, lunch, exercise—any break from the monotony would be welcome.

"Visitor, Lidecker." Even the guard's voice was harsh, and the unexpected sound jerked Alex to his feet. Nothing seemed real. It was as though his mind were in some pathetic movie. Head throbbing, he stood waiting to be escorted to a visiting area by a uniformed jailer. No one appeared quite human in here.

The visitor was Abraham Franklin, "the best lawyer money could buy" if you could believe his business card. Weasel had made the arrangements. Alex had never needed a criminal lawyer before. Alex eyed the business card through a thick plate of glass. Then he eyed Mr. Franklin. Thin, balding, and immaculately dressed, he stood out from the surroundings like a Rembrandt in a five and dime shop.

His small eyes studied Alex. "What the hell was in that drink?" He finally asked. His thin lips split into a smile. Alex just shrugged, and Abraham Franklin continued. "The only words out of your mouth last night should have been 'I want my lawyer.' You're no fool. What the hell happened?"

"I can't really explain. I just felt like I wanted to make a clean breast of it. Needed to confess. So badly. Like cleaning gangrene out of a festering wound. Cleaning out the rotting muck and saving the soul. It sounds so stupid now. I don't know what else to tell you."

"Well, don't ever do anything like that again. If you want to confess, talk to your lawyer, or talk to a priest, but for Heaven's sake, don't talk to the police." Abraham Franklin threw his hands up into the air and shook his head. "We'll suppress everything you said last night. I really am the best lawyer money can buy. Your friend Mr. Scoggins, with his connections, should be able to help as well."

Abraham Franklin grimaced like a wizard with a stomachache. "Your wife is in a coma right now. If she lives, all they'll have on you is drunk driving. No problem. We can bargain that down to nothing. If she dies, that's a whole different ball game. It's manslaughter and all your boy-scout enthusiasm from last night will stir up some real shit."

"If she dies…" Alex couldn't grasp that. Surely Vivian would be fine. She couldn't die. That didn't happen to Lideckers. "She can't die," Alex said feebly.

"We'll figure something out. You were upset about your wife. The police took advantage of you."

"The funny thing is…" Alex ran his hands through his hair and grimaced from the hangover. "The funny thing is I don't want to suppress any of it. This is the first time in years that I feel… I feel like I'm real."

"As they say on TV, you're in a heap of trouble, boy. Now be a good little soldier, and shut your trap and let me do my job."

<<<<>>>>

Alex posted ten thousand dollars in bail. The Weasel had wired it. He stopped at the house just long enough to wash the grime of jail off of his body, and to put on clean clothes. From there he drove as quickly as possible to Martha's Vineyard Hospital. "Vivian Lidecker," he told the volunteer at the front desk, and was directed to intensive care.

Inside the enclosure, Vivian lay motionless, hooked up to monitors. Alex started to sit on her bed and then hesitated. He feared touching her, feared that he might break her. Vivian looked so fragile, so vulnerable. But Vivian had always seemed vulnerable. At least she did ever since he had married her. Funny, she had been so spunky in college, determined, and sure of herself. What had happened between then and now?

Alex thought back to the Vivian of his college days. That Vivian was gorgeous, and full of life, and sexy as hell. But this Vivian! Her face was swollen and splotched with purple, yellow, and blue-black. It didn't look like Vivian. It didn't look human.

He took Vivian's hand tentatively torn between two prisons, the one of steel, concrete, and stink, and the other attached to Vivian's hand—a dead body that hadn't died yet. He pulled his hand away as if he'd been holding manure. He began to wonder, could Abraham Franklin pull it off? What if he told them to pull the tubes and pumps, and let her go? Could Abraham Franklin beat the charges? No. He had to wait it out a respectable amount of time. Alex, more than anyone else on earth, knew the value of appearances. So he picked up her hand again.

# Chapter Thirty-Eight

∞

Ivan's reporters were able to find records of all the documents Johanna needed to fly to the Middle East. Curiously, none of her friends or acquaintances had known that she was planning to leave the country. And no one had received a letter, post card, email, or smoke signal from her since that day. "Bloody hell!" he said out loud. Would it have somehow made a difference if he'd let her print her columns in the Gazette?

"If they can risk their lives, we can bloody well risk our jobs." That's what Johanna had said before she created her website. Well, thought Ivan, if she can risk her life, I can bloody well risk my job. And he began to type his editorial.

Dear Readers,
One of my writers Johanna Jacobson is missing. If you know anything about her, please contact the newspaper.

Now here's the worrisome part. According to the police, she boarded a plane for the Middle East; but according to her friends, she was in Berkeley while the plane was taking off. And I know Johanna. She's done some dingy things, but I'll bet my diploma that flying off to Iran isn't one of them. So I'm worried about her.

Johanna wrote the column "Earth Songs" and she wanted to use her column to protest the Iraq war, only I wouldn't let her because it wasn't politically correct. The fables that she wanted to print are on her website www.airytalesfortherestofus.com

When you open your paper, you deserve the truth—the best product we can offer. Instead, we've been feeding you great drama.

But we left out the unpleasant parts and the controversial parts, and the parts that might be costly to powerful people. We slant the news in favor of corporations, some of whom made 1000% and greater profits in Afghanistan and Iraq.

The newspapers barely mention petroleum. Much of our crude oil is imported, and we need Iraq's petroleum to keep oil companies' profits high and to keep us driving. And most car commercials today are promoting SUVs. Few communities are improving their mass transit systems, or encouraging citizens to drive less.

Thirty percent of you believed that weapons of mass destruction had been found in Iraq, and eighteen per cent of you believed that they had been used against our troops. Not true!

Global warming has begun to melt glaciers and erode coastlines. Climate in Alaska is changing. Stronger storms and rising oceans threaten the existence of some islands and low-lying areas. But no one talks about it—at least not in this country. And no one will—until some massive hurricane devastates a large area of the United States.

Our world is overcrowded. In the sixties, we talked about it. Now it's a forbidden subject. And, as long as the world is overcrowded and people are greedy, we'll have wars.

We can't print the whole truth anymore because censorship happens, more than you realize.

American civil liberties are in danger. Freedom of speech, freedom of the press, and freedom from unlawful search and seizure have already been compromised. Saying the press is almost free makes as much sense as telling a woman she's almost pregnant.

Odds are that I'll be fired—better to go out in a blaze than a whimper.

Sincerely,<br>Ivan Buncheski, your editor

The following afternoon, they fired Ivan. He didn't have a chance to get the next day's edition to press. Gerald Vance, the owner's son-in-law, replaced him. He understood how to play the newspaper game.

First off, Gerald Vance called everyone together for a meeting. "You all know why Ivan was fired. He got creative with the newspaper, and put his own wishes against the good of the paper.

Should any of you decide you can't follow orders, you'll be fired too. What are these orders? Very simply, everything ready for press goes through me—every article, every advertisement, every obituary, every semicolon, every period. Nothing hits the paper without my approval. Any questions? No? Good. Back to work, everyone. We have a paper to get out."

Occasionally, Gerald Vance was seen cursing under his breath and tossing a paper in the hopper to be shredded. Otherwise, it was business as usual.

<<<<>>>>

Alex went to the hospital every day. Fortunately, his schedule was busy enough that he could make the visits short.

After the first few days he'd become used to the surreal scene—catheter, IV tube, monitors. And he got used to putting on the worried face of a devoted husband. "I'm right here with you," he said picking up Vivian's hand. "I'm here baby." He crooned softly to her, and then stilled his voice allowing his mind to leave the room. Because he needed a plan in case Vivian didn't wake up.

Meanwhile, Vivian was on life support, buying Abraham Franklin precious time to plan his defense. How unfair life was!

Two weeks had passed. Vivian's face was losing its puffiness and becoming more human. Alex took her hand as he had done every day since the accident. Well, Vivian, you're getting your revenge now, he thought. You're half dead, and I'm shackled to you, and we're going down together. We may as well be on the Titanic.

At home Alex's mailbox was stuffed with cards. "We're all praying for you." "God bless you both. If we can help in any way…" "May God's peace and love surround you during this difficult time." And each night a casserole and salad arrived at his house with a hand-written note from someone in the parish.

Most evenings, the casserole went straight into the garbage disposal. Alex preferred eating out. The house had too much of Vivian's essence—paintings she had arranged in the living room, the China pattern they had picked out after they had gotten engaged, the fragrance of Vivian's perfume lingering in her side of the closet—the whole house was saturated with Vivian.

But on one evening after a tentative knock at the door, Alex decided he was too exhausted to go out. He accepted the Tupperware dish, its contents still piping hot, and he murmured some appropriate gratitude to a beaming middle-aged lady in a purple coat. He'd forgotten her name, but covered admirably.

She'd baked him a tamale pie, pungent with garlic and peppers. Suddenly Alex was ravenous. After a tentative bite, Alex poured himself a beer, shoveled a mammoth portion onto a plate and ate like a starving man. Doubtless, it was the peppers that made him dream as he did.

*Visions flashed, running towards him like ghosts in a haunted house. First, Pastor Woodrow's voice rang out. "It's not a matter of walking miles wearing rags, but a matter of confession and repentance…"*

*Then Vivian's bloated face begged, "Please, Alex."*

*Sand, and rubble, and the kind of heat that dried life out of the desert swirled above and below him. Turbaned, olive-skinned shadows shoveled bodies into ditches, and within those ditches, the bodies lay piled high like plague-killed cattle, silent but for an occasional moan or high-pitched scream.*

*Then Vivian's face appeared, scratched and bleeding. Her eyes—were they begging him, accusing him, or hating him, or were they still in love with him in spite of everything?*

"Stop," his own shouting woke him. In the darkened room, *Chesterville's Complete Book of Spells* whirled before Alex's eyes. He smelled the musty paper. And he heard the words as if spoken aloud. "For a price. For a price." The words shouted through the darkened stillness over and over.

"Dragged by wild oxen… not a chasm of flames, but in the human mind and heart."

"It's not a matter of walking miles wearing rags, but a matter of confession and repentance."

Well, Alex had written his path. He had to walk it. He staggered to the bathroom, and rummaged through the medicine cabinet for Vivian's sleeping pills. With, jittery hands, he shook out a half dozen pills and swallowed them, cupping his hand under the faucet for water with which to wash them down, then staggered back to bed.

*Vivian's bloated face wrapped around him. Her essence, a whispering ghost, lay beside him and blew through him like a chill wind.*

*"Not a matter of walking miles wearing rags, but a matter of confession and repentance."*

He sat bolt upright, crying out into the night. "Let Vivian live. Let her live. If you just give back her life, if you just let her live, I'll go to Pastor Woodrow. I'll tell him everything. Just make this thing be over."

The next morning, he called the pastor. "I need to talk to you—as soon as possible."

On the other end of the phone, Pastor Woodrow checked his appointment book. "I have time tomorrow at eleven. Can you meet me at the church?"

"Fine." Alex's terror melted. The sharpness drained from his voice. "I'll rearrange my schedule. Thank you very much."

Instead of driving to the White House, he searched out the public library—the main branch. He handed a list of literature to the clerk at the desk: the script to the opera, "Faust", "The Devil and Daniel Webster", and "Damn Yankee"—the classic stories of lost souls. He read for hours, scrutinizing the Devil's pacts, and the critics' analyses. He wrote notes on a Steno pad, but most of the notes were silly, and he scratched most of them out. At the end of seven hours, he had two sentences, two themes that kept showing up in the commentaries: "Love," and "repent and forgive."

If hell was real, it was probably like the state of mind he'd been experiencing for some time now. Finally, he wrote a third note. "It's all just superstition?" And he left the library.

Early the next morning, Alex got a surprise call from John Holcomb, one of Vivian's doctors. "We have good news, Mr. Lidecker. Vivian has regained consciousness. She opened her eyes, and she even said a few words. We're all optimistic. It's too early to be sure, but given the very encouraging signs, I expect a near-perfect recovery."

Feeling decidedly awkward, Alex entered Pastor Woodrow's office. "How's Vivian doing?" asked the pastor. "We're all praying for her."

"She woke up yesterday. She's able to talk a little. The doctors are hopeful."

Thanks be to God," said the pastor.

"The prayers really helped. It's been rough the last couple of weeks, but I think the worst is over. Thank you for being here for me. I just needed someone to talk to, but it looks like the sorrow is over and light is shining. I'll be fine. I just wanted someone to talk to." And he left the pastor's office unhealed.

From the pastor's office, Alex drove to the White House with a throbbing headache. He tried to concentrate on a pile of reports, but gave up after a few minutes. "I'm not feeling well," he told his secretary. "Cancel my appointments. I don't care who wants to see me. I'm going home."

He all but ran to his car, and, driving home, he turned up the radio's volume trying to drown out the words that played over and over in his mind. "Not a matter of walking miles wearing rags, but of the heart repenting."

On entering his house, Alex headed straight to the liquor cabinet and poured himself a Jack Daniels—neat. He drank it and poured another one. Then he searched through his dresser until he found the pistol and magazine of bullets that he'd carried with him since his CIA days. He loaded the pistol's cylinder and sat staring at the weapon as the words from the old spell book poured through his soul with a will of their own. "Agony not of the flesh but of the soul."

# Chapter Thirty-Nine

∞

They never did figure out who put together the front page of the *Upstart Gazette* that day. Lester Jenkins who ran the presses had to be involved as did Pamela Mason. She was the one who shredded documents, and she was probably the one who had rescued the letter that appeared on the front page on December 17th. Lissa Caldwell had been Ivan Buncheski's personal secretary for fourteen years. She had opened his mail, and now provided the same service for Gerald Vance. She was probably in on it too.

## *Upstart Gazette*

Evil wins when good men and women sit silent.

A hundred thousand people died to keep me rich. My country paid me millions for doing worse than nothing. But if you met me, you'd probably like me. You see, I'm a liar, and a very good one. I can make you believe anything. I can feed you vomit on a stick, and you'll swallow it and ask for more. It's a gift that I have, or maybe it's really a curse.

And I work in the White House.

America, you need to wise up. We're a country that focuses too much on PR—on appearance. We overlook substance. And meanwhile democracy in America is dying. You're giving up your freedom, your goods, and even your safety in the name of national security.

The world's best hackers work for Homeland Security. We're bugging everyone, not just terrorists or even suspected terrorists, but senators, congressmen, and anyone who questions what we do. Just watch—senators and congressmen who stick their necks out usually get caught on the wrong end of a scandal. It's what Nixon tried to do when his men were caught breaking into the Watergate hotel.

Hitler said that the memories of the masses are short. That's what I was banking on—that you wouldn't remember enough to compare yesterday's statements with today's news. And it's safer and more comfortable to forget. But please don't forget.

Dictators have used war as a diversion for centuries. And they've gotten rich by attacking weaker nations. We invaded Iraq on a lie. Remember the speeches before Iraq's invasion? Remember the threats of a mushroom cloud?

After 9/11, we rounded up hundreds of suspected terrorists, and we just held them for two years. The United States doesn't do that. Americans have rights. And if these people can be imprisoned without due process, so can all of us. Are they guilty of terrorism? Or are they political opponents? But that's not all. They're not just being interrogated—they're being tortured. Tortured!!! Since when has our country condoned torture?

I am responsible for many dirty tricks. I am responsible for the anthrax letters, and, with them, I tried to assassinate Senators Thomas Daschel and Pat Leahy.

I created phony scientific societies to convince Americans that global warming is only a myth.

I manipulated your news. I made you hate. I made you afraid. I fed you the opposite of all that's good and holy on this earth.

Remember the long fight for the rights of all minorities—the marches and the protests. Some died defending human rights. Fifty years of progress could disappear in the wag of an elephant's tail. Prejudice against one minority sets a precedent for discrimination against any minority.

When you fly the American flag, remember what it stands for: human rights, freedom of speech, freedom of worship. When you say "God Bless America," pray for our nation—for justice, for peace, for freedom.

Because of my dirty tricks, and deep tax cuts, and because of the wars, American economy has taken a huge hit. (You see a few hundred dollars from the tax cuts. We see billions. We use them to buy elections.) Our bad real estate management will have millions facing foreclosure. In a few years, the whole thing will come crashing down around us. Someone else will deal with the consequences. Don't blame him for the mess.

And don't give up on democracy. It's the best defense against the likes of me. In a dictatorship, everything I've done would be considered normal.

By Alexander Lidecker

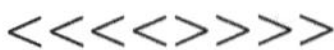

Alex put the paper down. His face flushed at the thought of thousands of people reading his confession—and the number could swell to millions or even billions when other papers around the world ran the story. Poor old Abraham Franklin would be sputtering geysers when he found out about Alex's piece. The funny thing was—Alex didn't feel scared, even though he knew he'd have to pay for what he did with years in jail and a lifetime of shame. "I'm very disappointed with you, son." His father's words. But the words had lost their power. Maybe you're disappointed, Dad, he thought, but I'm pleased and proud. For the first time in his adult life, Alex felt truly free.

He re-read the article twice more. The powers in Washington would call him a traitor; Alex knew he'd finally earned the right to call himself honest. Then he documented as much evidence against himself as he could remember. He implicated Pomerleau, Watkins, Efendi, the Weasel, and all the rest whose approval he'd courted so doggedly—was it really only a couple of years ago? And he made copies of all the evidence—two hundred and sixty-eight copies to be exact, and he sent them to two hundred and sixty-eight different law enforcement agencies, as well as to newspapers and television stations—just in case the United States attorney general failed to prosecute him and his cronies.

<<<<>>>>

The *Upstart Gazette* fired Lester Jenkins and Lissa Caldwell, figuring they were probably in on it. Most of the staff walked out the same day. The *Gazette* hired scabs and tried to put out an edition, but no one could get the presses to work. Probably Lester's doing, but they weren't sure. The following day, a few other newspapers across the country ran the *Upstart Gazette*'s infamous frontpage article. Slowly, more newspapers followed suit.

But Ivan Buncheski had put aside a sizeable nest egg. With the help of his former staff and a good credit reputation at his bank, Ivan was able to borrow enough money to launch *The New Upstart*. He hired back all his former employees.

In preparation for her trip, Johanna bought a backpack, a toothbrush, a couple of changes of clothing and underwear, and a one-way Amtrak ticket to Vancouver.

The train trip was soothing. She stared out the window at the pleasantly changing scenes. Desert, city, mountains, forest, more cities, small towns. She read and worked crossword puzzles, and sometimes just rocked back and forth with the motion of the train. She ate nutrition bars and apples. She washed them down with packets of juice. There was only one nightmare during the whole trip, and she told the passenger next to her that her skin had somehow gotten pinched in the zipper of her backpack and that was why she had screamed. Panic attacks happened as well, but she managed to stifle the urge to shout.

Johanna got off the bus in Vancouver, bought a map, and, fingers crossed, she navigated the city hoping to find Sandy Pumpkin's house.

She hesitated a moment, then knocked at the door of 247 Elm Street, a modest, beige stucco cottage, surrounded by huge terra cotta pots sporting splashes of bright red geraniums. The man who opened the door was slightly stooped with silver hair pulled behind his ears into a ponytail. His face was lined, and his skin was the shade of sawdust. First Nation, thought Johanna, maybe Cree. He was in his sixties or seventies, or maybe older. It was hard to tell. In fact, the old man reminded Johanna of a tree, gnarled and stately, someone who had stood silently and observed much of the world.

Johanna cleared her throat, not knowing how to explain. There was no guarantee that the address Sandy Pumpkin had given her was the correct one. She was too trusting, too quick to believe. But maybe he lived in this house with the old man. Johanna suddenly felt scared and foolish. "My name is Jody, and I've been exchanging emails with someone at this address." She hoped the old man wouldn't be shocked.

"Oh, my dear girl," he said. And the tears threatened to overcome him. "I am Sandy Pumpkin!" He wrapped his arms around her and brought her inside, and his touch was light and tender, as if carrying a wounded bird in his arms.

# ABOUT THE AUTHOR

Elaine Glimme began her unlikely writing career with a few unplanned explosions in the lab where she worked. In the interest of safety, she turned her hand to writing.

Elaine also wrote *Through Unfamiliar Waters,* a sequel to *Temporary Address*. If you want to find out what happens to Alex and Vivian, this is a must read.

She wrote *The Molly Chronicles* as well. Her dog Molly claims authorship for *The Molly Chronicles*, but Elaine says that Molly has always been delusional and has a swelled head.